texas pursuit

Lone Star Intrigue Books

TEXAS HEAT
TEXAS PURSUIT

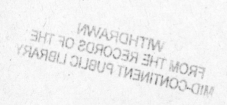

texas pursuit

LONE STAR ★ INTRIGUE
BOOK TWO

DEBRA WHITE SMITH

AVON
INSPIRE

An Imprint of HarperCollins*Publishers*

TEXAS PURSUIT. Copyright © 2010 by Debra White Smith. All rights reserved. Printed in the United States of America. No part of this book may be used or reproduced in any manner whatsoever without written permission except in the case of brief quotations embodied in critical articles and reviews. For information address HarperCollins Publishers, 10 East 53rd Street, New York, NY 10022.

HarperCollins books may be purchased for educational, business, or sales promotional use. For information please write: Special Markets Department, HarperCollins Publishers, 10 East 53rd Street, New York, NY 10022.

FIRST AVON PAPERBACK EDITION PUBLISHED 2010.

Library of Congress Cataloging-in-Publication Data

Smith, Debra White.
    Texas pursuit / by Debra White Smith.
        p. cm.—(Lone Star intrigue ; book 2)
    ISBN 978-0-06-149325-6 (pbk.)
    1. Texas-Fiction. I. Title.
    PS3569.M5178T47 2010
    813'.54-dc22
                                                        2010002632

10 11 12 13 14   OV/RRD   10 9 8 7 6 5 4 3 2 1

PROLOGUE

He gives me the creeps, Tanya thought.

She'd barely noticed the tall, distinguished man the first time he passed her plane seat. They'd just recovered from air turbulence, and her new son, Coty, had been crying. Tanya had glanced up just in time to see the man observing her on his way to the restroom. At first glance, his eyes had been as kind as his smile. Tanya had dismissed him as yet another good-hearted traveler who suspected she'd just adopted Coty.

But he'd just passed for the third time . . . and smiled again . . . and glanced toward the empty aisle seat . . . *again*. Tanya hunched her shoulders and held Coty closer. She brushed her lips against the sleeping child's forehead and focused out the window. The clouds floating beneath the plane appeared as soft as Coty's blanket. The engines' hum had nearly coaxed her into a nap before *that man* snapped her fully awake.

She directed a frown toward his back and willed him to feel her disapproval, but his forward focus indicated he sensed nothing. As a professional woman, Tanya had learned the necessity of keeping up her guard against unwanted advances. So she erected the invisible wall that protected her from predators and prayed the flight from Korea would remain uneventful.

Coty stirred in her arms and whimpered. During the last couple of weeks, she and the eighteen-month-old toddler had become a family. Tanya had fallen in love with the olive-skinned child from the moment she saw his photo a year ago. His cleft palate had only endeared him all the more. Now her dream of being a mother was a reality. The surgeries Coty faced were but one of many blessings Tanya planned to bestow upon him. She nuzzled his hair, relished the smell of baby shampoo, and wondered yet again if God would one day bring a wonderful man into their life who would be a gallant husband and phenomenal father.

"Excuse me," a woman's voice interrupted her longing thoughts, and Tanya glanced up to see the flight attendant accompanied by *that man.*

She stiffened. "Yes?" Tanya questioned and focused solely on the attendant, whose badge indicated her name was Kim.

"This gentleman is claustrophobic and needs an aisle seat."

Tanya's gaze shifted toward the man. The cut of his suit, the gold ring on his pinky, bespoke success in business; but his panicked eyes revealed less confidence while flying.

The attendant continued, "We were wondering if—"

"I'm so sorry to intrude," the man injected, his smooth voice distressed. "It's just that I don't do well sitting at the window. I requested an aisle seat, but they said this flight was fully booked and now here's this seat open."

"Probably someone who missed the flight," the attendant explained.

Tanya focused on the empty space and wondered if she might have misjudged the man. His anxious expression and the perspiration trickling down his temple validated his claims of needing some space. As a physician's assistant, Tanya certainly understood the physical limitations of the claustrophobic. Her mother couldn't even tolerate elevators.

"Well . . ." she hedged and wondered just how hard-hearted she'd appear if she turned him down.

"Please . . ." he begged.

What's it going to hurt? she thought.

"Okay," she agreed.

"Thanks so much," he said, his dark eyes pools of liquid relief. He rubbed his forehead and eased into the seat.

Tanya shifted Coty until his head rested on her shoulder. Patting his back, she stared at the clouds and purposed not to offer the man another glance.

Maurice Salazar settled into the seat, pulled the monogrammed handkerchief from his suit pocket, and dabbed at the water on his temples. He then wiped his clammy palms and tucked the handkerchief back into his pocket. He'd splashed his temples with water from the lavatory to give the appearance of sweat. The clammy palms were the result of a genuine assault of nerves.

He cut a glance toward the thirty-something woman he'd just manipulated. She looked so much like Eva he'd nearly called her by name when he saw her get on the flight. But her red hair, caught in a ponytail, was a shade lighter than Eva's. Her eyes were blue; Eva's, green. This lady dressed casually in slacks and a simple T-shirt while Eva's taste ran toward skirts and jackets. Furthermore, Eva was now about fifteen years older than this lovely image of femininity. She'd been twenty when she broke Maurice's heart.

He swallowed a sigh and wrapped his fingers around the armrests to stop himself from stroking her hair. There'd be plenty of opportunities for that in the future. But for now, Maurice would savor the old memories and plan to make new ones.

Even after all these years, he couldn't remove the memories any more than he could discard Eva's yellowed photo, still in his billfold. No matter his successes, Maurice never felt whole without her. He'd promised to marry Eva . . . to give her the best. But once she discovered his family's profitable business was less-than-legal, she'd chosen God over him.

He hated God then.

He hated him now,

Maurice clenched his fist and released it just as swiftly. Swallowing, he cut a glance toward his new companion and wondered if perhaps fate was giving him another chance at happiness. In his twenties, he'd dreamed that Eva would return. By his thirtieth birthday, Maurice had stopped such romantic nonsense and turned to women for what they could give him. But now, sitting next to this Eva replica, Maurice revisited his youthful fantasies and relished the future.

This time, he wouldn't let her get away . . . *no matter what.*

CHAPTER ONE

Shoot!" Sonny Mansfield glared at his crooked bow tie in the dresser mirror. The only thing he hated worse than a tuxedo was a bow tie. Being forced to wear both was too much to ask—even if it was for his brother's wedding. Jack and Charli had taken a year to finally tie the knot. Although tonight's wedding was small and private, they were doing it to the max, replete with formalwear and an upscale dinner in Tyler.

After fumbling the tie into a lopsided failure, Sonny ripped it off. "This should be illegal!" he growled and glared at his flushed face, only heightened by his blond hair. Sonny glanced at his watch. Jack had insisted that he be there by six sharp. It was only five after, so he wasn't doing *too* badly.

As if his stress weren't high enough, his stomach emitted a furious growl, and Sonny debated whether to grab a sandwich before he left. "No time," he admonished himself and stuffed the rebellious tie into his coat pocket.

He raced up the short hall and through the living room cluttered with photography paraphernalia. Dodging a camera tripod, Sonny banged the door shut and double-checked to make sure it was locked. Only when he was halfway to his pickup did Sonny notice the black Cadillac parked at the curb . . . and a tall, lean man crawling from the driver's seat. Smiling, the man offered a wave, and Sonny slowed to a stop.

"Are you Sonny Mansfield?" he called.

"Yes." Sonny discreetly checked his watch and could nearly feel Jack tapping him on the shoulder.

"Got a minute?" the guy questioned.

"Uh . . ." Sonny hedged.

"I'm looking for a private eye." The man paused within a few feet. When he offered his hand, a diamond sparkled from his ring finger. "My name's Kelvin Stuart."

Torn between the smell of a new case and the obligations to Jack, Sonny pumped Kelvin's hand and prepared to set up a meeting later.

"My ex-wife has disappeared with our son, and I'm looking for her. Do you take those kinds of cases?"

Sonny noted the fine cut of the man's business suit and recognized a good-paying client when he saw one. More than anything else, Sonny needed a good-paying client this week. Even with the freelance photographs he was selling, the economic slowdown had taken its toll on his budget; and Sonny was on the verge of having to dig into his savings to make this month's house payment. If Kelvin was as loaded as he appeared, Sonny might very easily come away with enough to complete two house payments.

"I take any case that's legal," Sonny replied. "But . . . I'm already late to my brother's wedding." He glanced at his watch. Five more minutes had lapsed. "Can we set up a time to meet . . . maybe tomorrow morning?"

"What about this evening?" Kelvin's eye twitched. "I haven't seen my son in three months."

"Well . . . okay," Sonny agreed. "But it might be after ten."

"No problem. I don't mind." The man's measured smile revealed even, white teeth. "I've been told you're the best." The worried glint in his eyes mixed with a tinge of hope, and Sonny recognized the symptoms.

Yet another man was being done dirty by an elusive female who didn't have the heart to at least let the poor guy see his own son. Women knew how to get to a man when they wanted revenge—at least one in his life certainly had. No telling what this guy had done wrong.

Probably left his socks on the floor, Sonny scoffed. *A crime punishable by death!*

He swiped at the beads of sweat along his forehead while the smell of the neighbor's grill sent a new rumble through his gut. Trying to ignore both the hunger and the heat, Sonny neared the tree that shaded his yard and jerked his cell phone from his pocket.

"Give me your number, and I'll call you when I'm free." Once the man's number was stored in his address book, Sonny added, "We can meet at a restaurant in Tyler. Does that work?"

"Absolutely!" Kelvin's tense face relaxed into a smile, and a trickle of perspiration slid down his temple. "Thank you so much! And I'm willing to pay a bonus to get quick service."

Sonny grinned and thought, *Ca-ching, ca-ching.* "I can do quick," he said.

"Good." Kelvin gave him a thumbs-up and motioned toward Sonny's truck. "I won't keep you now. We can talk more tonight."

"Great," Sonny agreed and strode to his Chevy with a farewell wave toward his new client. He laid the phone on the dashboard and had just slammed the door when the old theme song from the *Dukes of Hazzard* TV show filled the cab. He didn't have to even look at the screen to know the caller was Jack. Sonny had saved that distinctive ring especially for Jack, simply because it annoyed him.

He flipped open the phone and said, "What?" into the receiver.

"What!" Jack retorted. "Where *are* you?"

"I'm leaving home now," Sonny replied and cranked the truck.

"I promise, you're going to be late to your own funeral!"

"I'll try," Sonny agreed through a grin. A glance over his shoulder validated that the Cadillac was pulling away from his small, brick home. "But if you're a pallbearer I seriously doubt I'll make it late," he added. "You'll probably have me there the night before!"

"Hardee-har-har," Jack drawled. "Just get here, will ya!"

"I'll see your mug in five minutes flat." He put the truck in reverse and zoomed from the driveway, onto the road. "And I need help with my bow tie, man. The thing is *possessed*."

"I'll help you with your bow tie," Jack threatened through a chuckle.

"Yikes!" Sonny laughed and put the truck in drive. "Maybe I'll get Ryan to help me."

"Yeah. And take some lessons from your older brother. He was here thirty minutes ago. Nice and *early*."

"Hey! I'm early!" Sonny quipped and hung a hard right while ignoring the neighborhood stop sign. "I'll be there forty-five minutes before it starts."

"And that's about as good as it's ever going to get with you. Right?" Jack's teasing took on an anxious edge.

"That's *very* good for me," Sonny retorted and then sobered as he considered how he'd feel in Jack's shoes. His brother's stress level had to be skyrocketing.

"Ya doin' okay, man?" Sonny prompted as he neared downtown Bullard.

"I'm so nervous I'm about to collapse," Jack admitted, a tremor in his voice.

"You're not backing out on us, are you?"

"Are you kidding? Not in a million years. It's just—" He stopped. "I don't know. I've never gotten married before, and it's as nerve-racking as all-get-out. On top of that, Bonnie's been running around like a chicken with her head cut off and our nephew's in the big middle of it. The only person who could get Bonnie to behave was me. She's on a tear because she knows her mom and I are going to be in Colorado for a week. No matter how many times I tell her I'm taking her to Six Flags for my honeymoon with *her*, she can't understand why she can't go on *this* honeymoon. And I promise, I've already seen Charli three times in the last hour, and only *one* time is supposed to be bad luck. The last time I saw her, the heel on her shoe had broken, for cryin' out loud! If we pull this off without a major fiasco, I'll *eat* your bow tie."

"Just calm down," Sonny encouraged. "It'll all be over by eight. And then you'll have the honeymoon to look forward to," he added through a grin.

"That's easy for you to say! You probably won't ever even *get* married!"

"You got that one right," Sonny agreed. "Especially not if I have to wear a bow tie again."

Tanya O'Brien hung the last painting on her bedroom wall and sighed. After two months of living in Bullard, Texas, she finally felt safe enough to finish unpacking and hang her paintings. Tanya's watercolor bouquet hung next to a floral painting by her grandmother. The styles were so familiar the two could have been brushed by the same hand. Only the signature *M. Malone* indicated that Tanya hadn't painted the explosion of flowers spilling from an overturned wheelbarrow.

"I was taught by the best," Tanya whispered a mere second before a three-year-old's delightful squeals echoed up the hallway.

"Happy slide!" her son exclaimed.

Tanya's eyes widened as her motherly instinct kicked in. Coty was too delighted after being quiet for too long. She darted from the room, up the hallway, and entered the kitchen. By the time she'd taken her second step she knew her instincts were right. Coty had been up to mischief—if the empty vegetable oil bottle spinning near her thrashing cocker spaniel was any indicator.

And her flat sandals did nothing to stop her own slippery trip. As if she was on a sheet of ice, Tanya slid toward the microwave stand and only barely missed the crash by flailing her arms. By the time she rammed into the wall and gained her balance, Coty was laughing all the louder.

"Mamma slide!" he cheered and began standing. "Coty slide!" he declared while vegetable oil dripped from the hem of his shorts. Coty attempted a step, fell to all fours, and scooted to the middle of the room. He flopped to his side as laughter gurgled from his soul.

"Oh, Coty." Tanya sighed, and as all exasperation eased from her, she couldn't stop her own chortle. After a series of operations for his cleft palate, Coty had blossomed but was still catching up on his verbal skills. Now, nearly two years after the adoption, Coty filled her life more than she'd ever imagined—with enough laughter . . . and fiascos for triplets.

"Come on, sweet boy," she crooned. After examining her new linen shorts and T-shirt, she thanked God for Spray 'n Wash and carefully lowered herself to all fours. "Let's get you in the bathtub. We'll go from there."

"Coty slide!" he insisted and daringly lurched toward the dog.

"Nooooo!" Tanya bellowed as Coty crashed to his belly, spun toward the cabinets, and slammed into the doors. The impact flipped him to his back, and the breathless silence ushered in a terrified wail punctuated by Happy's distressed barking. Coty gazed at Tanya through teary eyes and reached for his mother.

"Oh, Coty," Tanya crooned and crawled toward her son. "You silly boy." She gathered him into her arms with no thought for the added stains to her outfit.

After only seconds of clinging to his mother, his cries abated. Tanya rested her head on his and stroked his cheek.

On the heels of a hard sniffle, the child said, "I slide again," and strained against Tanya's hold.

"Oh, no, you don't, mister," Tanya firmly asserted. "We're getting you in the tub and Mom's going to clean this mess up."

"I slide again!" he insisted and pushed Tanya's arms.

"Bath, bath, bath," she said in a singsong voice and struggled toward the edge of the kitchen.

"No!" the child demanded and arched against her hold. "Slide!"

Panting, Tanya managed to keep her hold on Coty while knee-walking out of the kitchen. Once on the edge of the hallway, she stood and kicked off her backless sandals. By that time, Coty had started a scream-fest, and Happy was hopping along the hallway, yelping in counter-rhythm.

"I slide! I slide!" Coty screamed.

"Look," Tanya encouraged, "we'll put bubble bath in the tub, and you can slide in the tub, okay?"

He stopped screaming, relaxed, and gazed into Tanya's face. With a smile, she tickled his tummy, and he gurgled out a laugh. "That's a good boy," she encouraged, and the ringing phone mingled with her words.

"Woops!" Tanya exclaimed and suspected her father was on the line with his evening check-in, since he called at six thirty every night. "That's probably Granddad," she added.

"Gran-da," Coty repeated.

"Wanta talk to Granddad?" she encouraged.

"Gran-da," the child repeated, and his face dimpled into a smile that put a spark in his eyes . . . and Tanya's heart. She'd encouraged her father to stay close to Coty in the hopes that he would be a strong, male role model. So far, the effort had produced a solid bond between the two.

"Well, come on," she encouraged. "Let's get you wrapped in a towel, and we'll grab the phone in my room."

By the time Tanya reached the phone, the sixth ring had started, and she was afraid her father had already hung up. But her breathless, "Hello," was met with his cheerful greeting.

"How's my girl tonight?"

"Fine," Tanya assured.

"No strange men lurking in the wings?" he prompted, a smile in his voice.

But Tanya knew that smile was a mask for the genuine worry that had been their companion for almost two years—at least until she escaped Dallas and moved to Bullard, ten minutes south of her parents' home in Flint.

"No strange men tonight," she assured through a laugh. "Not unless you count a three-year-old coating the kitchen floor in cooking oil and taking me and the dog for a nice slide as strange."

"I think we can safely say that is *really* strange." Ed O'Brien chuckled.

Happy's toenails clicking up the hallway reminded Tanya that the dog was as oily as the child and that he needed a bath as well. She caught sight of the dog out of the corner of her eyes. Next, her gaze slid to the thick-piled Oriental rug claiming the center of her spacious bedroom. Like the rest of the house, the rug was immaculately clean and still smelled of carpet deodorizer.

"No, Happy!" she scolded. "Scat! Get!"

Not used to Tanya's tone of voice, the dog lowered her tail and backed away from the doorway.

"Dad, I've *got* to go," Tanya rushed. "I'm oily. The dog's oily. Coty's oily. And we all need a bath."

This time, his laughter held no worries. "Do you need your mother and me to help with the cleanup? We could even keep Coty for you again tonight."

"No, not this time," Tanya asserted. "You had him two nights last week. You already do too much as it is."

"Gran-da!" Coty demanded. "I wanta talk Gran-da."

Sighing, Tanya remembered her promise and said, "Coty wants to talk to his main squeeze. Do you have time?"

"You bet," Ed agreed. "I always have time for that little guy."

As she handed her son the cordless receiver, Tanya smiled. There was nothing greater than having such supportive parents. Their love for Coty was every bit as great as their love for their only daughter. Even though Tanya had ignored the well-meaning people who warned her against adopting as a single parent, she was growing more aware of just how valuable a father was in a child's life. She held no regrets in choosing to adopt yet couldn't squelch the latent hope that she and Coty might find a man of God to complete their little family.

Once Coty had control of the receiver and was telling his grandfather about the sliding puppy, Tanya darted toward the hallway where Happy lurked near the doorway.

"Come on, Happy," she encouraged. "Let's get you outside."

She set Coty in the empty bathtub, towel and all, and left him babbling at his favorite man while scooping up the dog. The cocker spaniel licked at her face and whined for approval. "You're a good puppy, yes you are," Tanya encouraged and scratched the dog's ears. "I'm sorry I scolded you, Happy-Happy. You're just a little too oily to stay inside right now. After I wash Coty and change into some grubbies, I'll come outside and give you a bath."

Instead of using the back-door exit in the slick kitchen, Tanya detoured through the utility room on the other end of the house and released Happy into the fenced yard. As she'd done for two months now, Tanya scanned the classic neighborhood for any signs of a lean, dark man with a suave smile and desperate eyes. The row of middle-income brick houses met the backyards of similar houses on the next street over. As a physician's assistant, Tanya was blessed to be able to lease an upscale home in one of Bullard's older neighborhoods.

But even her accomplished career and good income hadn't protected her from Maurice Salazar. According to the Dallas police, he'd have to do more than buy gifts, ask for dates, and watch her to get them to take action. So far, he'd done nothing illegal. Nevertheless, Tanya couldn't shake the feeling that her life had been in danger . . . and might still be.

She closed the door and hurried through the house. When she passed the bathroom, she glanced inside to see Coty still telling "Gran-da" about his day. On her way to the front door, logic insisted she had no reason for compulsively checking the street. Nevertheless, Tanya couldn't stop herself. Keeping her ear tuned to Coty's distant chatter, she opened the front door, stepped onto the fern-decked porch, and scanned one length of the street and then the other. The tall oaks lining the road bespoke peace and safety.

Yet her mind confronted the peace with the memory of the hours she'd spent on the plane with Maurice Salazar. After a season of silence, he'd finally begun talking. *What a delightful flight companion you are,* he'd purred with the sophistication of a gentleman's gentleman.

Tanya's initial fear of him had subsided the longer she considered his immaculate grooming, excellent manners, and kind demeanor. *You're such a good mother,* he'd continued, and the compliment was so subtle she'd missed his intent until they were a couple hours from landing. When he mentioned that she reminded him of someone named Eva, Tanya suspected his interest was much more than passing politeness . . . and perhaps his claustrophobia had been feigned. Tanya had tried to communicate her lack of interest, but that hadn't stopped Maurice on the plane . . . or after the landing.

He waited at the gate and had the audacity to capture her hand and kiss it. Struggling to manage Coty, Tanya couldn't extract her fingers from his, no matter how hard she tried. Even now, she smelled the stale cigars on his breath. After she left the airport, she glimpsed him following her. Little did she know the nightmare had only begun.

Shivering, she sighed, stepped back into the house, and whispered, "Oh God, please don't let that man find me."

CHAPTER TWO

Sonny Mansfield stepped into Spring Creek Barbeque. He'd suggested the restaurant because they stayed open until eleven o'clock and offered more privacy than the strip of fast-food joints lining South Broadway.

He ignored the tray sitting on the edge of the buffet and went straight for the glasses. Not even the smell of smoked ribs could entice him after the feast he'd enjoyed at the wedding dinner. That party had gone as smoothly as the wedding; and now the couple was off to Colorado. Sonny could only hope they'd always be as happy as they seemed when they drove away. After filling a cup with ice and following with tea, he offered them a silent toast, wished them the best, and gulped the cold liquid. Once he paid the cashier, Sonny merged into the dining room.

A brief scan of the sparsely occupied room reminded Sonny they were closing in an hour. He spotted Kelvin Stuart at a corner table. Their gazes met. Kelvin nodded.

Striding toward him, Sonny was stricken with how refined Kelvin appeared—almost like some high-dollar executive, polished to perfection. He'd been so distracted over making Jack's wedding on time that he'd missed some of Kelvin's finesse.

When he arrived at the table, Kelvin stood, offered his hand with a polite bow of his head, and said, "Good to see you," his cultured voice turning the words into a rhythmic meter.

"Likewise." Sonny placed his tea on the table and shook the man's hand. Before releasing the grip, Sonny noticed his nails were perfectly manicured.

Kelvin's eyes wrinkled with a kind smile. He still wore the dark suit, and it looked as fresh as it had hours ago.

Conversely, Sonny had ripped off the bow tie and tuxedo jacket the second he left the wedding party. Once in his truck, he'd plunked the cuff links in his cup holder and rolled up his shirtsleeves. Now he couldn't wait to get home and strip down to his boxer shorts and T-shirt.

But first, I need to earn some money, he thought and settled across from Mr. Stuart.

Kelvin pointed to a mammoth piece of cherry pie sitting near his coffee and said, "All you want is tea?"

"Absolutely," Sonny said and patted his gut. "I stuffed myself on everything from baby back ribs to shrimp to cheese cake."

"Ah yes, the wedding," Kelvin said with a hint of anguish in his dark eyes. "Our wedding was in Las Vegas . . ." His gaze slid beyond Sonny to some far-off memory beyond the here and now. "Let's just hope your brother's marriage turns out better than mine."

Sonny glanced toward the man's left hand—no signs of a wedding band. "So you said you're divorced now?"

"Right." Kelvin's tight smile bordered on painful.

Sonny stopped a wince. He'd once have been glad to get married if Karen had at least given him a chance, but she never even called.

"We agreed that I'd have equal time with our son," Kelvin continued, "but she changed her mind. I had to go out of the country for a business trip. When I came back, she'd disappeared."

"Didn't you get a court order?" Sonny prodded.

He shook his head. "She insisted on a do-it-yourself divorce, and we had an out-of-court agreement. I took her word that if I paid child support—"

Sonny groaned. "You took her *word*?"

"Yeah." Kelvin's shoulders slumped. "We'd adopted Coty from Korea nearly two years ago," he explained. "I paid all costs. She'd already begun adoption proceedings when I met her. Looking back now, I think maybe she just used me to get the child." He glanced down and pricked his cherry pie with his fork.

"She said she'd always dreamed of adopting from Asia. So had I, actually. Not long after we returned, she dumped me and demanded a divorce. Next thing I knew, the divorce was over and she'd vanished. I think she may be in Texas, but I'm not sure. I'm starting with Texas and have hired private eyes all over the state to see if they can find her. I want to hire you to cover northeast Texas. If she doesn't surface in Texas, then I'll take it state by state." His fist curled on the table. "I refuse to give up."

"Do you know any of her relative's names? Her parents maybe?" Sonny asked.

"No." Kelvin shook his head. "She was always really vague about them. I think it was on purpose." He shook his head. "No—I *know* it was on purpose. Anyway, all I have is her name—Tanya O'Brien." He pushed a piece of lined paper toward Sonny. Kelvin pointed to the woman's name on the second line and grimaced as he laid a snapshot next to the name.

Sonny lifted his brows. While the redhead holding the Asian toddler appeared tired, even the dark circles under her eyes didn't hide the fact that she was attractive. With her hair in a ponytail and only trace makeup, she appeared about fifteen years younger than her ex-husband. Even though she didn't look like she had one malicious cell, Sonny dashed aside all doubts. Lots of women looked as harmless as grass snakes while they had the venom of a cobra.

She probably blinded this poor cat from day one, Sonny thought and then dismissed any more speculations. Wherever the blame lay, Sonny needed the money. It wasn't up to him to decide who was at fault. *Only problem is,* he thought, *trying to find Tanya O'Brien might be a waste of time. Forget the needle in a haystack. She could be a microscopic ameba in a haystack.*

"She never took my last name," Kelvin continued. "At the time, I was too blinded by love to suspect a thing. I was naïve enough to chalk it up to her being a modern woman." His eye twitched, and he toyed with his silver cuff link.

"I've learned the hard way that you have to pay attention to every tiny thing a woman does and keep your eyes open," Sonny growled, "especially when it comes to kids. I've had my share of hard knocks."

"Exactly," Kelvin agreed. "I hope you're as quick as you are understanding." His encouraging smile was filled with hope. "Like I said, I'll roll in an extra thousand to whatever you ask if you can find her quickly. I've been on her trail for months now. I'm tired of the chase and ready to see my son."

Sonny stopped with his tea glass halfway to his mouth. Then he set down the glass, swallowed his impulsive smile, and stated, "My usual fee for a quick turnaround like this is two thousand dollars plus expenses—whether I find her or not," he dared to add.

"I understand your fees. I never ask anyone to work for free. But if you give me her location within two weeks, I'll fork over three thousand in cash."

"Count me in," Sonny said through a grin. *With that fee, I can make three house payments,* he thought. "Is the number you gave me the best one to reach you on?"

"Yes. That's my cell. I have it with me all the time."

Sonny grabbed his tea glass. By the time he'd downed half of it, he decided this was one case he would enjoy as no other. Even though he hadn't seen or heard from Karen in eleven years, he didn't think he'd ever get over the shock of discovering she'd given birth to his son and never even told him about the child . . . or about placing him for adoption.

Maybe finding this guy's son will help me finally put my ghost to rest, he thought . . . a twelve-year-old ghost with curly blond hair and gray eyes . . . a ghost he'd named Sonny Jr.

Two weeks later, Sonny trolled a classic neighborhood in Flint, Texas, only a few miles from his home in Bullard. After the meeting with Kelvin Stuart, Sonny had systematically taken one town at a time, starting with the bigger ones like Tyler and Longview. After tirelessly combing several large towns, he'd followed a whim and decided to look closer to home. Even though there were no O'Brien's in the Bullard phone directory, he'd discovered only six in the Flint directory. He'd spent all day yesterday checking out four of the families. Sonny drove to each of their houses and simply observed at a distance. After discovering two of the couples were too young to have a grown daughter, he'd also eliminated two more families simply because they were the wrong race.

This morning, he woke at seven. By nine, he'd eliminated the next O'Brien from his list when a man and woman who appeared to be near ninety emerged in Sunday best and were helped into a waiting vehicle. Sonny assumed they were being picked up for church. Whatever the case, they were too old to be Tanya O'Brien's parents—grandparents, maybe.

Now Sonny cruised the final neighborhood, eyeing all the houses in the four-hundred block of Sycamore Street. The frame homes reminded him of the house he was raised in—nothing fancy, but solid as Noah's ark. Two houses away from 410 Sycamore, he pulled his Chevy pickup to a stop, rammed it into park, and turned off the engine.

A shiny black cat darted across the road with a swooping blue jay on its trail. He chuckled. *That cat doesn't have a chance*, he thought. Sonny narrowed his eyes and gazed toward the home two doors down. *Neither does Tanya O'Brien*, he thought. *I'm on your trail, sistah. You might not be Karen, but for now, you're close enough.*

"Now, if only this is the right house," he mumbled and began to sense the deadline pressure. If this home wasn't Tanya's parents' then Sonny had hit a dead end on his first campaign. Kelvin said the bonus would happen only if Sonny presented the information tonight.

He unlatched his seat belt, tilted his chair back, and crossed his arms. Despite the pressure, Sonny covered a yawn and reached for his coffee cup. It was as empty as it had been the last time he tried to pump his body with more caffeine.

"Shoot!" He turned his key in the ignition only halfway, lowered the automatic windows, and clicked the key back. The tepid summer breeze oozed into the pickup, replacing the air-conditioned coolness; and soon even his shorts and tank top began to feel too heavy. He settled his head against the rest and wondered how long he'd sit here before spotting the people who lived at 410 Sycamore. Sonny kept one eye on the O'Brien's place while the other eye took a break.

He'd barely slept since he started this job. With Jack's wedding two weeks ago and the stress of Kelvin Stuart's job, Sonny had felt as if he were trapped between dramas. Both of them brought back too many memories. The memories always ushered in the resentment. He'd have been glad to marry Karen, and make their family complete. He couldn't lie to himself and say he was ever madly in love with her. But getting married would have been the right thing to do for the baby—at least, in his mind; not in Karen's, obviously.

Sonny's gut hardened. He gritted his teeth. He could go a year or more without thinking of Karen and his child—or rather, he could go a year or more suppressing the memories. And then they'd come at him like ravenous beasts, devouring what trace of peace he'd managed to carve out.

Jack had always assumed Sonny's drinking had been the result of his repeated failures to make the cut for the NBA. Little did his big brother know the NBA had precious little to do with the drinking. Trying to blot out the memory of a child he never saw was way harder to handle than missing the cut on the NBA.

And the hardest part of all was admitting that he'd done to his child what his father had done to him—something he'd vowed to never let happen. While his dad and mom were still married and they did the family holiday thing, Sonny rarely saw his dad. Not as a child. Not now. His father had been too busy building his trucking empire to take time for his kids. So his mom's brother, Uncle Abe, had filled the fatherly gap in their lives.

Sonny brushed his index finger across the star tattoo on the inside of his right forearm. After his uncle's death, Sonny had taken the World War II medal to a tattoo parlor and came out with the imprint on his arm. The medal ranked higher than even a purple heart and gave Sonny a level of honor to aspire to.

But Sonny couldn't find anything honorable about the business with Karen. "At least she didn't abort the baby," he groused. He'd never considered himself the conservative sort. But despite himself there were still a few dregs left over from all those years his mom dragged him to Sunday school. Even though Jack seemed convinced Sonny was a pure heathen, he did have a few traditional bones.

He lifted his head and pointed a bleary-eyed gaze toward the O'Brien's place. Still no action. His eyes were closed again before he leaned against the headrest. Another yawn followed.

"You can't go to sleep you moron," he chided himself. "There's a hefty payment on the other side of this." *I should go buy another round of coffee*, he thought and glanced toward the newspaper he'd bought at the same convenience store the coffee came from.

The headlines were what had grabbed him: "Highway Patrolman Acclaimed as Hero." The highway patrolman pictured was none other than Sonny's brother Ryan. The guy hadn't mentioned a word about being a cover boy. Sonny had barely skimmed the article, which hailed Ryan's skill in chasing down a car with a kidnapped teen inside. When the car crashed, he'd dug in and pulled out the girl. The car's explosion killed the jerk who'd nabbed her. The girl who'd only been abducted an hour before had come out unscathed.

As much as Sonny wanted more details, he couldn't force himself to reach for the paper . . . or resist closing his eyes amid a cloud of sleep.

The jolt came when distant laughter pierced the haze in his mind. A vehicle's door slammed. Sonny's eyes popped open. He sat straight up and checked his watch. An hour and a half had lapsed since he checked the time.

With a groan, he peered toward the O'Brien's place and spotted the source of noise. A seventy-something couple was walking across the yard while a young woman chased a laughing, Asian toddler from behind. Since they were dressed in their finest, Sonny assumed they'd been to church . . . and that the Honda sitting at the curb must belong to the woman—a woman who looked just like the photo of Tanya O'Brien.

Sonny sat straight up, gripped the steering wheel. "Bingo!" he breathed through a smile.

The dark-haired child darted from the sidewalk in pursuit of that black cat Sonny had seen earlier. The feline dashed toward the road, and the mother lurched for her son. Never had Sonny been so glad to spot an attractive redhead—and not for the usual reasons.

Rubbing his face, he eased back in the seat and grabbed the morning paper from the passenger seat. Using it as a shield, he focused on Ryan's photo. But the whole story diminished in the noise of the O'Brien's activities.

"Come back here, you little tiger," Tanya teased while the child's laughter filled the neighborhood.

"Let's go in the house, Coty!" Grandpa cheered. "We've got a new puppy!"

"Puppy!" Coty echoed.

"You just said the magic word . . ." Tanya's voice blurred into lower-toned conversation that drifted to silence.

Sonny gradually lowered the paper. No sign of them. He grabbed a pen from the clutter on his dashboard and jotted down the Honda's license plate number. If all went as planned, he'd wait until Tanya left and simply follow her home. But it never hurt to have the license number to help his search should Plan A fail.

"I'll just wait," he muttered and glanced toward the empty coffee cup, but wished for a cold bottle of water. His mouth felt like it was full of whatever that goo was in the bottom of his refrigerator. Sonny refocused on the newspaper article and tried to get his mind off his discomfort . . . and his rumbling stomach. If Tanya was here for a Sunday family lunch, it might be two hours before she left.

CHAPTER THREE

Sonny whipped his Chevy truck into the mall parking spot near Kelvin's black Cadillac. He switched off the hard-core country music, killed the engine, and grabbed the envelope from the dashboard while his client crawled from his car. After he slid from the truck, Sonny's high-topped sneakers met the concrete that radiated enough heat to blister his soles were he barefooted. He still wore his tank top and shorts and was glad of it.

"So you found where she's living?" Kelvin asked as soon as Sonny slammed his truck's door.

"Yes." Sonny stepped forward and extended an envelope. When Kelvin reached for it, Sonny thought better and held the information out of reach. "My payment first," he said with a measured smile.

Kelvin narrowed his eyes. A hot breeze wafted out of nowhere. The evening traffic whizzing up and down the nearby street only intensified the moment. A flitter of disgust marred Kelvin's features. He gritted his teeth. And Sonny sensed this client could get nasty if angered too severely. Nevertheless, he didn't flinch. Kelvin's eye twitched before he pressed his lips together and then rounded his car. He whipped open the door and removed a small manila envelope from the glove box. After slamming the door, he marched back to Sonny and slapped the envelope against his palm.

Sonny opened it, fingered the contents, and then nodded. "Three thousand cash. Thanks!"

"That's what we agreed on," Kelvin snapped. "Now give me the info."

Sonny's gaze shifted to Kelvin's. After slowly lifting one brow, he delivered the information. Kelvin ripped into the envelope and pulled out one sheet of paper. The top line read, "Tanya O'Brien Profile." Sonny knew one glance would give Kelvin her address, the make of her new car, and her license plate number. Not much information, but all he needed to find Tanya. Sonny had never been more shocked than when he learned the woman was only minutes from his home.

Kelvin's eyes took on a hungry gleam that was matched by the tenor of his chuckle. Squinting, Sonny scrutinized the man and wondered if his classy clothing and suave demeanor might be hiding a dark disposition. After shooting Sonny a smile that was as insincere as it was stiff, Kelvin turned for his car, slipped inside, and never bothered with a goodbye.

Shoving the envelope into his short's pocket, Sonny watched Kelvin's departing Cadillac gleaming in the evening sun. The job had been profitable, and he'd been proud of his thorough, swift job . . . until he encountered Kelvin again. An instinct he didn't question insisted Sonny get Kelvin's license plate number before he turned the corner. Sonny crawled into the truck, grabbed the pen from his dashboard, retrieved the newspaper, and wrote the number across the top.

Maybe Kelvin Stuart wasn't telling me the truth, he thought. He closed the truck's door, cranked the engine, and turned the AC on high. The cool air blasted him with as much impact as the Alabama CD. Frowning, he switched off the music and went back to his thinking.

Kelvin had told Sonny he'd been victimized by a scheming woman, and Sonny hadn't questioned his story much because of his own past. Sonny clamped his teeth together and decided to get brutally honest. Even if Sonny's past had never happened, his need for money had stopped him from analyzing Kelvin's story very much. But now, a barrage of doubts clouded the house payment emancipation.

Kelvin had said he and Tanya were married, yet he didn't even know her parents' names. "Odd," he admitted. *Kelvin doesn't look like the sort who'd be gullible enough to be taken in on the level he claims either*, Sonny deduced. *Why would anybody with his obvious money be willing to settle any divorce outside court?* While he had known of more than one person being taken advantage of on this level or even worse, the man who devoured Tanya's information was the antithesis of the victim he'd posed as.

Sonny propped his elbow on the window ledge and fingered the thin scar he'd acquired last year when Lola Briones beat the living daylights out of him with her secret weapon—a shoulder bag that felt like it had bricks in it. Of course, when Lola saw he was bleeding, she stopped the assault and turned repentant, but it was too late. Sonny had already sustained an injury.

He shook his head. *You'd think I'd learn from my mistakes*, he brooded. Lola and her family had *not* been happy with their estranged brother when he walked onto the scene, expecting his share of his mother's money. They'd been even less happy with Sonny for taking the job.

Sonny wasn't in the mood for any more scars. If Tanya O'Brien were somehow being victimized by Kelvin Stuart, then no amount of money was worth the end-pain—his or Tanya's.

In the short time Sonny had observed Ms. O'Brien, she had stricken him as the honest sort—if you could tell anything about anybody's character by looks. *Maybe I need to go to her place and watch her again before I make my call*, Sonny thought. He leaned against the headrest and closed his eyes.

I might be overreacting, he reasoned. *Kelvin Stuart is probably just a wealthy codger who's used to paying people to take care of anything he needs done. He let a pretty face get to him, and now he's got grief to pay.*

Sonny opened his eyes. "If I let a woman get to me like he did, I'd probably look like a vulture when I found out where she lived too," he mumbled. "For cryin' out loud," Sonny exclaimed and lifted his hand. "I *did* let a woman get to me!" He slammed his fist against the steering wheel and yanked the truck into gear.

But as he left the streets of Tyler and neared Bullard, more doubts nibbled at the back of his mind . . . doubts that suggested Kelvin Stuart couldn't be completely blameless. Sonny tapped his fingertips against the steering wheel and again debated whether he should observe Tanya O'Brien one more time, just to make sure she really appeared as guileless as his first impression. If Kelvin Stuart was telling the truth, and Sonny detected anything that indicated Tanya was a cutthroat female, then no harm was done. But if Sonny's doubts increased, perhaps it was in Tanya's best interest for the two of them to meet.

He glanced toward the license plate number. *Might not hurt to get Ryan to run it for me*, he thought. Sonny pulled his cell phone out of his shirt pocket and pressed the automatic dial number that instantly rang his brother's cell.

"Yello," Ryan's mellow voice floated over the line, and Sonny chuckled.

"Blue," he replied.

"What do you want?" Ryan playfully growled.

"I've got a license plate number I'd like you to run. That is, if you can find time between interviews. From what I understand, you're the hero of the hour."

"Just doin' my job," Ryan drawled.

"Next thing you know, you'll be wearing a cape and leaping sky-scrapers in a single bound."

"Yeah, in downtown Bullard, Texas. Woo-hoo," Ryan mocked.

"So when are you going to learn?" Sonny challenged.

"Learn what?"

"If you're going to risk your neck rescuing a woman, why not make it someone your own age?"

"Or maybe *yours*?" Ryan parried.

"You know I swore off years ago," Sonny retorted. He slowed the vehicle and hung a right off Highway 69 onto Lynch Street. After passing four houses, including his own, he kept on driving. "Listen, can you get me the scoop on a license plate number as in, yesterday?"

"Okay, give me the number, and I'll see what I can find out," Ryan said. "But you owe me."

"Right. Next time you need a sitter for Sean, just send him on to Uncle Sonny."

"How about tomorrow night?"

"Tomorrow? That's quick." Sonny had maneuvered several city blocks before he slowed near James Street.

"Yeah. I've got him all week. Shelly's on vacation," he said, a wor-ried edge to his voice.

"What's the deal with that?" Sonny asked. He normally didn't press Ryan about his ex-wife, but when Ryan volunteered informa-tion Sonny usually didn't mind being nosy either.

"She's going to Oklahoma with a group of people from church. One of them is some guy I've seen her with a few times. I don't like it, but—"

"There's nothing you can do about it?" Sonny winced for his brother.

"Yeah," Ryan admitted with a sigh.

"Still no chance with you again?"

"Not yet. If not for Sean, she'd barely give me a hello," he added, his voice strained. "Can't say I blame her. I blew it to smithereens, but—anyway," he said on a huff, "there's some sort of a dinner tomorrow night sponsored by the city counsel."

"And you're the special guest?" He cruised to a stop at the curb and gazed up the cozy neighborhood street toward Tanya O'Brien's home. The movement at the lawn's edge caught his eye.

"It would appear."

Leaning forward, Sonny examined the mother and son frolicking in the water sprinkler. "Well, is there some kind of an award in the wings your dear ol' brothers should know about?" he queried.

"Not going there," Ryan replied.

Sonny rolled his eyes. "If you won the Nobel Peace Prize you'd never tell a soul."

"Look, can you keep Sean tomorrow night?"

"Sure. Bring him on. I'll take him fishing out at Jack's or something."

"He'll love that," Ryan replied. "Now, give me that number, and I'll get your info ASAP."

Sonny placed his truck in park and grabbed the newspaper. After reciting the number, he gazed toward Tanya and then posed a spontaneous question. "You wouldn't happen to know a new woman in town named Tanya O'Brien would you?"

While Ryan paused, Sonny flipped the AC blower to low and directed the vent away from his face.

"Ryan? Did I lose you?" he finally prompted.

"No, I'm here. Are you trying to set me up with someone? Because if you are—"

"No, no, no," Sonny scoffed. "Nothing like that. I've been working on a case, and I was just wondering if you'd run into her 'round town."

"Not that I recall," Ryan replied. "Not unless she's that new physician's assistant at Dr. Dan's. Sean had his checkup last week and there was this new redhead in the office. Not bad on the eyes, but all business."

"Hmmm . . ." Sonny replied as Tanya ran through the sprinkler with her son close behind. She'd been attractive that morning in her Sunday dress. But in a pair of drenched shorts with her hair in tangles, she was endearing . . . enchanting; and Coty's cherub face in full smile spoke of an adoration that went deep.

Sonny couldn't stop the ripple of attraction, despite his vow to a womanless existence.

"Are you still with me?" Ryan questioned.

"Yeah. Still here," Sonny replied. "Gotta go. Just let me know what you find out on that license plate number."

"Sure thing," Ryan replied.

She's a good mother, Sonny thought as he flipped his phone shut. When he thought of Sonny Jr., he'd prayed more often than not that his son's adoptive parents were as caring as Tanya O'Brien now appeared. In his mind, Coty's black hair became blond. His dark skin grew fair, and Sonny imagined himself on the porch, watching his child playing with his wife. If his child and wife were in danger, he'd certainly want to know someone was looking out for them.

Finally, he shook his head, rubbed at his eyes, and mumbled a reprimand, "Stop it, you moron."

When he got his focus back, he wondered what Tanya's side of the story was. He slipped the cell phone into his shirt pocket and brainstormed for a shortcut into her life. No way would he just walk up, tell her who he was and what he'd done. Sonny preferred to hover long enough to learn if Kelvin Stuart was telling the truth. Once that fact had been established, he'd better know what to do. Until then, Sonny would stay close—just in case Tanya needed a strong arm. That meant he must find an excuse to be in her life without alerting her to his true motives.

That's when Sonny's gaze trailed toward the apartment over her garage. Before he refocused on Tanya and her child, Sonny's attention snapped back to the garage. His eyes widened as the first seeds of an idea germinated. With the idea taking root, Sonny began to strategize. By the time the idea was in full bloom, he was nodding. "Perfect," he predicted through a slow grin.

CHAPTER FOUR

Mun more time, Mamma! Mun more time!" Coty screamed. With a playful squeal, Tanya darted through the water sprinkler. A glance over her shoulder proved that Coty trotted close behind. His shorts and T-shirt clung to his drenched body just as hers did. The afternoon at the park had been long and hot; she now relished the cool spray prickling her skin. When she turned on the sprinkler before going inside, it had simply been too inviting. Tanya had been the first to dart through the water while Coty squealed and clapped. He hadn't stopped cheering since.

Tanya burst from the sprinkler and paused near the steps. "Are you ready to go inside and get a bath?" she encouraged, but wasn't surprised by Coty's protest.

"No, Mamma!" Coty insisted. "We play more!"

"I'm going to sit here and watch you play for a while, okay?" Tanya lowered herself to the steps and pulled her wet hair away from her face.

Hands on hips, Coty observed her with puckered lips before giving his approving nod. "Okay," he said and whirled through the water again.

Sighing, Tanya was as thankful for the reprieve as she was surprised that Coty hadn't protested. After her mom's fried chicken lunch with all the trimmings, Tanya had fought off sleep. While Coty napped, she'd spent the afternoon working in the yard. The small pile of limbs and dead leaves she'd raked from under the bushes attested to her labor. Once Coty woke up, he'd been such a "big helper," it had taken Tanya twice as long to get half as much done. Finally, she quit trying and took him to the park.

The boy certainly liked his mommy's attention. *Just like all kids*, Tanya thought and gazed across the street at the family of four piling into their minivan. She'd barely gotten to know the Rileys, but had seen enough to know the children were nurtured by *both* parents. When their six-year-old daughter struggled to climb into the van, Brad Riley scooped her into his strong arms and plunked her into the vehicle. The child's delightful screams mingled with his playful growls and sent a lump to Tanya's throat.

She rested her elbow on her knee and plunked her chin in her hand. Brad Riley was exactly the kind of father Tanya wanted for Coty. His being smack across the street had to be some kind of Divine torture. Fortunately, Tanya wasn't the least bit attracted to the man. In the first place, he was married. But the short, stocky type had never grabbed her fancy. Her dream husband would be tall and lean while being exactly the kind of father Brad was—the absolute antithesis of Maurice Salazar.

Shivering, she gazed up one stretch of street, and then the other. Tanya didn't dare fully believe she'd finally shaken that jerk. But her hopes grew with each day that passed.

She curled her damp toes against her flip-flops and wiped at the moisture trickling down her cheek. Coty had discovered some intriguing enigma in the wet grass. When he lifted a long, coiling worm Tanya chuckled and shook her head.

"The boy's going to be a fisherman. I just know it," she mumbled and stood. "Put the worm down and come on in, baby," she encouraged.

Coty's immediate protest accompanied his streaking across the yard. Experience had taught Tanya not to let the little munchkin get too much of a head start; so before Coty had gone more than a few feet, she caught up with him. Still clutching the worm, he fought against Tanya's embrace.

"No!" he screamed. "Outside! Outside!"

"Inside!" Tanya countered and marched toward the water faucet. "After that monster lunch, we're just going to have a sandwich for dinner. Then, it's time for your bath."

"No bath!" Coty lunged back and forth in her arms. Tanya increased her hold while searching for any distraction that might get Coty's mind off the conflict. A shiny black Chevrolet trolling down the road proved the perfect option.

"Look at the pretty truck, Coty," Tanya enthused as if the pickup had just descended upon heavenly clouds.

The child stopped his struggles and relaxed in the face of this new distraction. "Truck," he repeated and rubbed at damp eyes with a grubby fist.

"Black truck," Tanya echoed and noticed a blond man behind the wheel.

"Black truck."

"You have a black truck inside," Tanya encouraged and subtly removed the earth worm from his grasp. "Wanta go play with it?" she prompted, dropping the worm without a flinch.

Coty nodded.

She reached for the hose faucet, but noticed the truck slowing. When it was parallel to Tanya's house, the driver looked directly at her and then glanced away just as swiftly. Tanya's grip on Coty tightened. The pickup slowed all the more and pulled to the other side of the road. She twisted off the water and hurried toward her door steps.

Don't panic! she insisted. *He looks nothing like Maurice! You're being ridiculous.*

Despite the logic, a pall of dread spread through Tanya as she fumbled with the key deep in her shorts pocket. The truck's door slammed. Tanya dropped the key.

"Truck!" Coty twisted in her arms and peered over her shoulder.

He's probably just a relative visiting the neighbors. She set Coty on the porch before snatching up the key. The droplets of moisture still clinging to her skin merged with a fresh rash of cold sweat. Tanya wrestled the key into the deadbolt, unlocked the door, and couldn't stop the compulsive glance over her shoulder. That only confirmed the tall stranger was striding directly toward her.

She fought the urge to bolt inside and slam the door until reason overtook fear. Scooping Coty back into her arms, she forced herself to face the stranger. Dressed in basketball shorts, a jersey, and high-top sneakers, he certainly looked harmless enough . . . almost like an old adolescent who had yet to find his way in life. Despite her better judgment, Tanya found herself responding to his warm, ready smile; and the knee-jerk fear eased but didn't disappear.

"I'm sorry to bother you," the man began. "But I noticed you have a garage apartment."

Trying to determine his reason for asking, Tanya mutely stared at him before rasping, "Yes . . ."

The longer Sonny watched Tanya O'Brien the more terrified she appeared. Shoulder's hunched, she clutched her son as if Sonny might be about to snatch him. Nevertheless, her wet hair coupled with the beads of water clinging to her cheeks made her look more like a beach model than the motherly sort. Slipping his hands into his shorts pockets, Sonny increased his smile. While he had expected some caution on her part, he hadn't predicted Tanya would act like he was a stalker either. *Unless she has been stalked*, he thought and recalled Kelvin's hungry eyes.

"I was wondering if you might consider renting the apartment— that is, if you aren't already renting it," he said. "I'm a photographer—actually, in my spare time. I own my own place not far from here on Lynch Street," he pointed east, "but I'd really like to have a studio and office separate from my house. I freelance for magazines and I'm out of space in my house. I was just cruising by and wondered if it was vacant. If so—"

"It's not for rent," she blurted and shook her head in a manner that invited no further discussion. When she whirled toward her front door, Sonny knew he had only a few more seconds to make a last effort. Coty's dark-eyed stare over his mother's shoulders gave Sonny the prod he needed to press forward.

He took several steps across the soggy grass and blurted, "I'd pay you well—and, hey, I'm a private eye in my real job. It never hurts to have someone like me around for safety and all."

She stopped.

"My brother's Jack Mansfield—the chief of police," Sonny rushed, sensing he'd scored a point. "I've got the best references in town." A distant siren underscored his claims.

She pivoted to face him, and Coty shifted to focus on Sonny as well. Narrowing her eyes, Tanya said, "So you were just driving around the neighborhood, looking for a garage apartment?" Her skeptical gaze traveled from his casual clothing to his sneakers and back.

"No, actually, I was coming home after meeting a client," Sonny truthfully stated and dared to wave and grin at the toddler.

With a coy smile, Coty put his head on Tanya's shoulder and turned his face into her neck. "I spotted your apartment and just thought I'd ask," he continued with a shrug. "I guess you could say it was on a whim." He added a genuine smile that underscored the validity of his claim. Even though every word was truth, he was leaving another story out; but Tanya O'Brien didn't need to know that now—or ever.

"I'm Sonny Mansfield, by the way." He extended his hand. "And you're?"

She eyed his hand and then shifted her attention back to his face. "Bring me your references first," she said. "As a matter of fact, bring me your brother first," she added. "If he really is the chief of police and you really are a private eye, then we might talk business." Patting her son's back, she glanced up one end of the street, then the other.

"Good!" Sonny tried to hide the smug in his smile. Some days he even surprised himself. Whether Kelvin Stuart really was her ex-husband or not, she acted like a woman with somebody on her trail. She'd obviously view Sonny as protection; and renting the apartment would give him time to decide whether or not he'd made a mistake in so readily giving Kelvin her location.

Of course, it also meant he'd only be able to pay two house payments. But Sonny wouldn't have to rent the apartment long . . . maybe a couple of weeks or just a month. That would give him time to find out what he needed to know. If Kelvin Stuart were telling the truth, Sonny would move on with his life. Tanya O'Brien would have to face the fact that she had to allow Coty's adoptive father into his life. However, if Stuart was up to no good, then Sonny would deal with that in a completely different way.

Deciding to push his luck an inch further, he dared to make one more suggestion, "If I call Jack now, would you be willing to meet him tonight?"

After another pause, she shrugged and said, "Why not?"

"Truck!" Coty said and pointed toward Jack's Chevy. "I play truck inside," he insisted and began to squirm.

That's when Sonny remembered Jack's second honeymoon—the one he'd promised Bonnie. He slammed the heel of his hand against his forehead. "Oh man! I totally forgot! Jack got married a couple of weeks ago. He took his wife and stepdaughter to Six Flags for the weekend. He won't be back until Tuesday, for cryin' out loud."

"That's convenient," she quipped in a way that dismissed the whole conversation.

A rash of heat raced Sonny's gut, and he struggled to hide his irritation. While he understood her hesitancy, Sonny had never enjoyed being labeled a liar—whether blatantly or subtly. Nevertheless, the longer he observed Tanya O'Brien the more swiftly the irritation diminished. Her heart-shaped face and peaches-and-cream complexion had probably upset more men than she ever comprehended. She most likely had to act frosty just to ward off all the advances.

If Kelvin Stuart did get sucked in, I can understand why, Sonny thought, and that realization made him harden his own heart against a similar fate. *I'm here just in case Stuart is trying to victimize her and her child*, he admonished, *and that's the end of it.*

He took a long, slow breath and counted to ten while gazing across her yard toward a small pile of limbs and dead leaves that appeared to have been raked from beside the house. As he inhaled the smell of wet earth, his nerves eased and he could talk without sounding stiff.

"I do have another brother," he said, forcing his voice to a natural tone. "His name's Ryan Mansfield. You might have seen his picture in today's paper. He's the highway patrolman who rescued the teenage girl from that sex trafficker."

"I saw it." She nodded.

"Would he do for now?"

After gnawing her lip a few seconds, she finally nodded. "Yeah. But I need to see his badge and ID . . . and yours too."

"Truck! I play truck inside!" Coty demanded and began to thrash in Tanya's arms.

Sonny pulled his billfold from his hip pocket, stepped closer, and flipped it open. "Behold my driver's license and my private eye license. I don't have a badge, but Ryan will. Note, I am bonded." He pointed to the number at the bottom of the card that also featured his photo and thumbprint.

Momentarily distracted from his pursuit of the truck, Coty gazed at Sonny's billfold, then leaned down to touch the photo. An unexpected paternal instinct arose in Sonny, and he stopped himself from tousling Coty's hair.

Tanya eyed the identification and finally shook her head. This time, when she looked into his face, most of the doubt had vanished. In its place was a hint of relief. Her casting another glance down the road only intensified the impression that she was afraid of something . . . or someone. Sonny tucked that fact away as the first evidence that he'd most likely made the right move.

"Now, you never told me your name," Sonny said with an encouraging grin.

Tanya smoothed at her wayward hair, now falling into her eyes. "I'm Tanya O'Brien," she said. "And if you're as legit as I'm beginning to think you are . . ." She trailed off and simply gazed up at him.

"I'm as legit as all-get-out," Sonny quipped with an assuring grin.

"Okay," she said and nodded. "Give me a day or two to think about it and I'll let you know for sure. I don't make decisions like this on the spur of the moment."

"Of course not," Sonny assured. "Who would?"

"Can you call me tomorrow afternoon? I can let you know what I'm thinking then. We'll go from there."

"Sure," Sonny agreed and pulled out his cell phone. "Give me your number and I'll plug it into my phone."

She recited her number and then added, "That's my cell."

"I'll be glad to have Ryan with me if you decide to let me look at the place." Sonny put an extra punch into his smile as he peered into blue eyes that dominated her features.

"Yes, that would be good," she affirmed and shifted Coty to her other hip.

Sonny focused on Coty and once again squelched the urge to tousle his hair. Such a great age . . . just starting to talk, all personality. He couldn't help but wonder what Sonny Jr. had looked like at Coty's age. His gaze slid back to Tanya, who eyed him with curious anticipation. Hesitating, he searched for something else to say but came up with nothing.

With his protective instincts revving higher by the second, Sonny hated to leave the two of them vulnerable for even one night. He hadn't become a private eye to help *predators*, to abet their sniffing out victims, and he wasn't going to start now . . . especially after meeting Tanya O'Brien.

CHAPTER FIVE

Tanya stood at the living room window, shivering against the impact of air conditioning on wet clothes. With unsteady fingers, she discreetly pulled the blinds apart and watched Sonny Mansfield stroll toward his pickup. Barely aware of the puddle she created on the carpet, Tanya marveled at the conversation she'd just had.

"Truck!" Coty's bellow echoed up the hallway as he trotted to his bedroom in search of his beloved toy.

"I've got to call Mom and Dad," Tanya breathed and hurried toward the cordless phone. She bumped the Chippendale end table while trying to retrieve the receiver and then dropped the phone. "Ah man!" she exclaimed before grasping the phone and hitting her parents' speed dial number.

"Daddy," she breathed over the line the second her father answered.

"Tanya? Is everything okay?" he rushed. "You sound—"

"I'm shocked," she answered. "And I think it might be a good thing."

"What's going on?"

"You're never going to believe who just walked into my yard and asked to rent my garage apartment."

"Who?"

"The police chief's brother. His name is Sonny Mansfield."

"Whoa!"

"He's a private eye. He showed me his license and everything. He says he's looking for a place to rent for a photography studio. He's a freelance photographer on the side." She nearly sat on the polished cotton sofa, but remembered her moist clothes.

"Are you sure he's for real?" Ed O'Brien asked.

"That's exactly what I thought at first," Tanya admitted. She moved into the hallway and gazed toward Coty's room, catching a glimpse of his shorts as he pushed the truck near the doorway. "But I can't argue with a license, and our police chief's last name *is* Mansfield.

"Maybe this is an answer to prayer," she rushed. "I hate to bother you and Mom, but I'm always looking over my shoulder. If there was a private eye in my garage apartment some, maybe I could finally relax. And knowing he's the police chief's brother." Tanya rolled her eyes and said, "What a bonus!"

"But are you sure he's legit?" her father pressed.

"I'm going to spend the next twenty-four hours thinking about that. He's offering to bring his other brother for me to meet for validation. His other brother's a highway patrolman. He was just in the Bullard newspaper. I think you mentioned seeing him in the Flint newspaper too. His name is Ryan Mansfield. I guess all three brothers are in law enforcement."

"Why can't he bring over the chief of police?" Ed asked.

"He's out of town with his new wife and stepdaughter. He got married not long ago. After Sonny left, I remembered that being in the paper too. You know Bullard is so small, if the mayor sneezes it goes in print."

"Maybe this is a godsend, Tanya," her mom's soft voice floated over the line, and Tanya deduced they had turned on the speaker.

"I said the same thing." Tanya covered her heart with her hand, leaned against the wall, and breathed a prayer for guidance. "I wonder if he'd consider sleeping in the apartment some," she said. "It's at night when I go to bed that I get the most antsy."

"Us too," her parents admitted in unison. "We're still willing to let you move in with us," her mom added.

"I know. And I really appreciate it, but . . ."

"You're still too independent for your own good," her dad injected.

"Yeah. Something like that," she said through a chuckle.

"Would you mind if I meet him before you agree to his staying?" her dad asked with a protective edge.

"That's fine," Tanya agreed. "I'd like that too. I'll call you tomorrow afternoon and let you know if I decide to have him come back."

"You know we're just a phone call away," her mom assured.

After bidding her parents adieu, Tanya hung up. When she was in college, her father's overprotective ways had driven her to the brink of berserk. He'd backed off once Tanya had secured a good job and moved into an apartment complex with a security guard. It wasn't until Maurice began breathing down her neck that Tanya appreciated her dad's sacrificial willingness to protect her. Even though she wanted to go back to those days when she never gave a thought to stalkers and threats, Tanya knew those days were over. She'd never be the same.

And this evening, she was thrilled her dad still wanted to look out for "his little girl." Even though she'd started out skeptical of Sonny Mansfield, the man was close to convincing her he was for real. However, she still wanted her father's scrutiny on the situation. If anyone knew how to sniff out a rat it was Ed O'Brien.

Tanya walked to her room and changed from her wet clothes

into a pair of lounging pants and a matching shirt. The soft cotton warmed her skin, still cool from the romp through the sprinkler. Before heading for the kitchen to prepare their sandwiches, she took a detour through the living room.

Tanya pulled out the end table drawer, retrieved the phone book, and flipped to the yellow pages. Within seconds, she'd found the "Private Investigator" heading and ran her finger down the short list. Her eyes widened the second she spotted Sonny Mansfield's name. The small ad featuring his photo underscored everything he'd told Tanya. A driver's license and even a private eye license could be fabricated; but his being in the phone book validated that the license was authentic.

"At least it looks like he really is who he says he is," she whispered and replaced the phone book.

Sonny threw the covers aside, swung his legs out of bed, and was standing in one fluid movement. "This is crazy," he mumbled and stomped down the hallway toward his kitchen. He'd seen midnight come and go, then one, two, three, now four—and still, no sleep.

"It's five after four," he told himself, "you need to go to sleep!" His yawn was big enough to take him under, but did nothing to encourage his gritty eyes to go heavy. Instead, a raw nervousness ate away the possibility for slumber.

From the second his head hit the pillow at eleven thirty, Sonny had thought about Tanya O'Brien and her son . . . whether Kelvin Stuart would be on their trail—tonight, or any other night. The more time that lapsed between his last encounter with Stuart, the more of a threat the man became. Sonny had lived and relived Kelvin's hungry expression so many times he abhorred it. Even though Tanya's taking her time to consider renting the apartment was reasonable, he'd wished a thousand times she'd agreed to lease it to him on the spot.

He opened the fridge and perused the contents while the cold air chilled his bare legs. After a lazy once-over, Sonny grabbed a bottle of water and twisted the lid. By the time the bottle was half empty, his stomach felt as if he'd emptied a whole tray of ice in it. On the heels of a hard shiver, he grumbled, "This ought to help me sleep," and rolled his eyes. "Yeah, right."

Sonny slammed the refrigerator and leaned against the kitchen counter. Fat Cat meandered into the kitchen, sat in the middle of the room, and blinked up at him like he'd lost his mind.

"Yeah, I've lost it," Sonny said and motioned toward the over-sized tabby. "I've totally lost it. I'm even thinking about getting in my truck and driving around her neighborhood just to make sure there's no one watching," he mumbled.

Fat Cat yawned and then gazed toward his mother, Mamma Cat, who strolled into the room and stopped beside her offspring. The two began lazily licking each other while Sonny continued his monologue.

"I fully understand why you'd both think I was off my rocker. After all, I barely even know the woman. It's not like she's my responsibility or anything. But look at things from my angle." He set the water on the counter and placed both hands on his hips. "I'm the one who gave Stuart her information. If he somehow hurts her, then I'd feel responsible."

He rested his fingertips against his chest. "And I don't want a repeat of Lola Briones either. I just did what the guy paid me to do," he grumbled, "and the next thing I know, I'm being assaulted by a purse-packing maniac." He tried to imagine Tanya O'Brien being as volatile, but couldn't. Nevertheless, Sonny didn't want her on his conscience.

Fat Cat meowed and meandered toward his food bowl; the gray female followed close behind. With a hopeful appeal, Mamma Cat gazed up at Sonny.

"It's four in the morning," Sonny said. "Munch on some dry food. You know the canned food doesn't happen until eight."

Fat Cat's protesting yowl did nothing to influence Sonny. Instead, he grabbed the bottle of water, switched off the light, and headed back to his bedroom. "Now I've started talking to my cats about this whole business," he mumbled all the way up the hallway. "I've *got* to get some sleep."

CHAPTER SIX

Tanya's eyes lazed open, and she turned in her bed. Morning's gray light oozed through the blinds, and she predicted it was nearly 6:30 A.M. A glance toward the digital clock on the nightstand validated her assumption. *Time to get up and start the day*, she thought while turning off the alarm clock before it ever buzzed. She was always the first medical professional to arrive at the clinic and was available for early morning emergencies, should they arise. That meant an arrival time of eight o'clock. Her mom would be here to pick up Coty in an hour.

"What would I do without you guys?" she whispered and thanked God for her parents before reaching for her Bible on the nightstand. After a quick trip to the restroom, Tanya embraced what she called her morning encounter . . . ten minutes of reading Scripture and five minutes of prayer. She spent half of her lunch hour in silent meditation and what she called her "listening time."

It was during one of those times of listening for that still, small voice that she had been prompted to leave Dallas. At the time, she hadn't seen Maurice for over a week and wondered if he'd given up on her. But during her prayer time, she'd been overtaken with an urgency that she should take advantage of his absence to move as soon as possible. From that point on, God had miraculously guided her safely to Bullard, from the resignation of her job and the acquiring of another in Bullard to finding a home to lease. Tanya had followed her gut and stored her furniture after buying out her existing lease. She'd rented a hotel room until she could sell her car as well. She knew Maurice probably had her license number and she decided to start over with another vehicle once she moved. During that entire shuffle, she never saw Maurice and hoped he'd been out of the country so that she'd thrown him off her trail.

Once the car was sold, she booked a shuttle flight from Dallas to Tyler. Even though the flight wasn't quite an hour, she'd chosen it rather than have her parents drive her to her new home. It had been her last attempt to cover her tracks. The home God provided had been ready for her to move into. The moving company had been glad to handle the transport of her furniture. In retrospect, she could see God's hand in every step.

This morning, Tanya embraced the Bible, closed her eyes, and decided to do a little listening before the day started. "Dear Lord," she prayed, "please direct me what to do about Sonny Mansfield. I don't want to make a decision based on fear, but I also know I'm a woman alone . . ."

Tanya waited, but instead of the comfort she expected to experience, an eerie uneasiness spread across her spirit like a suffocating fog threatening to choke out her life. Opening her eyes, Tanya clutched the Bible tighter. Without another thought, she released the Bible and dashed down the short hallway into Coty's room, to the side of his toddler bed. When she spotted the top of his dark head protruding from beneath his Hot Wheels blanket, Tanya's shoulders sagged.

But seeing Coty did nothing to sweep aside the uneasiness. If anything the eerie fog seemed to be thickening by the second. Finally,

Tanya came to a firm conclusion she couldn't sidestep, "Something is wrong," she whispered, "and God is trying to tell me." *Oh God,* she silently pleaded, *make it clear—so clear I can't miss it.*

Blindly, Tanya went through her morning routine—shower, dress, feed Happy, prepare Coty's cream of wheat. She was stepping into the hallway to wake up the little guy when she heard the usual bicycle horn that announced the paper boy had thrown her daily news somewhere in her front yard. How he managed to get it in a different place every day continued to amaze Tanya. She'd begun to wonder if he was actually *trying* to do exactly that.

When Tanya opened the door to retrieve the paper, she peered across her yard. Even though everything appeared normal, her skin prickled. She stepped onto her porch and strained for any clue that would validate her nervousness, but found nothing. With a sigh, she spotted the paper near the big pecan tree in her front yard. After retrieving the daily news, Tanya scrutinized the yard once more, then the whole neighborhood. A shiver overtook her.

"Weird. Very weird," she mumbled and turned to go back into the house. That's when a flash of something black, snuggled near the flower bed, caught her eye. Tanya walked toward the object and identified it as a small flashlight.

"There you are!" she exclaimed and bent to pick it up. She'd spent nearly an hour one night last week searching for her little black flashlight and finally gave up. How it landed in the yard was anybody's guess. *Coty probably toted it out here one day when I was working outside,* she thought.

She pushed up the switch and was satisfied that it still worked as sufficiently as always. Before she dropped it into her office smock's pocket, she noticed a thin gold line around the rim. Squinting, she couldn't remember hers having that touch of gold. With a shrug, she dropped it into her pocket.

"Oh well," she breathed. Since she got Coty Tanya was so distracted, she did well to keep up with her own name—let alone details about a flashlight.

Before heading back in the house, Tanya snapped at the newspaper's rubber band and eyed the street once more. The eerie feeling was gradually dissipating, and Tanya decided she had no choice but to get on with her day—which would include a decision in favor of or against renting to Sonny Mansfield.

By the time she pulled her Honda into her spot at work, Tanya decided that if she could find no reason not to sublease the garage apartment to the private eye, then she would go ahead and lease it to him. *He'll be protection when he's there*, she thought as she put the car in park. After the way she'd felt that morning, Tanya was thinking she could use all the protection she could get.

She opened the car door, got out, and closed the door. After pressing the lock button on her remote, she strode toward the Victorian home Dr. Dan had turned into a children's clinic. Today was crammed with back-to-back appointments. She had no more room in her brain for Sonny Mansfield.

When she stepped through the back door, Tanya spotted her good friend, Dolly Lennon, just arriving as well. Some time today, she'd mention Sonny's offer to rent the apartment to her new friend. Even though the gray-haired RN was thirty years older than Tanya, the two had formed a friendship that Tanya already appreciated.

But for now, Tanya closed the door on the clinic . . . and on Sonny Mansfield. She'd only allow herself to think of him again when she asked Dolly's advice.

By five o'clock Sonny stood in Tanya's garage apartment. Hands in his jeans pockets he gazed around the dusty room and feigned as casual expression as he could muster. Ryan stood nearby, his chiseled features impassive. No one would ever guess that he'd looked up

Kelvin's license plate number for Sonny and discovered the Cadillac was registered to Lone Star Transport, located in Ft. Worth. Ryan had agreed to do some more digging. For now, the guy was standing by his brother, as calm and steady as always.

Their mom always said that if the house was on fire Ryan would nonchalantly stroll out while Sonny bounced around like a crazed Ping-Pong ball. Now, Sonny felt exactly like that crazed Ping-Pong ball. He hadn't been this nervous since he tried out for the basketball scholarship at Texas Tech.

He scratched at the back of his neck beneath the stiff collar of the blue business shirt he decided to wear instead of his first choice, a T-shirt. He'd wanted to make a good impression, and for once in his life Sonny was glad he'd dressed up, considering Ed O'Brien's presence.

Ed had been in the apartment when Tanya led Sonny up the stairs. Presently, he studied Sonny like he was some predator after his daughter and grandson. Despite the fact that he and Ryan both had shown the man their IDs, his wary eyes suggested he wasn't free with his trust; and Sonny suspected that the man sensed something else was going on.

Nevertheless, he refused to allow Ed or his daughter to see that his motives were as ulterior as all-get-out. Feigning a casual air, Sonny strode toward the front window and pulled the cord on the blinds.

They wheezed up and released a puff of musty-smelling dust. Fighting a sneeze, Sonny squinted against the blast of evening sun illuminating the room. This window gave him exactly what he wanted—a clear view of most of Tanya O'Brien's front yard. While the view of the front door was blocked because the apartment was recessed in the driveway, at least Sonny could see the yard and the street.

Tanya moved to his side, and Sonny cut her a sideways smile.

"It's not very big," she admitted with a shrug. "I was just using it to store a few things, but I'll move them down to the garage." She pointed toward several boxes and a stack of paintings leaning against the wall.

Sonny stepped toward the paintings and squatted beside one breathtaking landscape. "Who's the artist?" he asked and eyed the bottom, right corner until his suspicions were founded: Tanya O'Brien's name claimed the author's corner.

"These are mine," she pointed toward the stack Sonny began looking through. "Those are my grandmother's." Tanya motioned toward another stack leaning against the wall. The top one was of a magnificent iris that was as arresting as Tanya's work.

"My grandmother taught me to paint when I was a teenager. Before I adopted Coty, it was a rather consuming hobby. We worked together a lot. But now grandmother's gone and there's not much time."

Sonny stood back up and couldn't stop the admiration from warming his smile. "You're quite an accomplished woman."

Her gaze shifted from his and then fleetingly returned like some shy butterfly, not certain where it should land.

He concentrated on a painting of the iris, every bit as dazzling as Tanya's big blue eyes, and wondered if she were feeling the buzz between them as strongly as he.

In a pair of walking shorts and a simple T-shirt, Tanya looked closer to twenty than thirty-something. Her auburn hair framed her face in a curly cloud that only accented her skin's translucent glow. While Sonny had appreciated her beauty yesterday, he hadn't expected any sort of serious attraction.

He thought about his experience with Karen, and Kelvin's story popped into his head. If Tanya was the coldhearted female Kelvin had described, then Sonny would chalk up these feelings to his sick preoccupation with women who were going to rip out his heart. But the longer he was in Tanya O'Brien's presence, the more convinced Sonny became that there was way more to the story than Kelvin related; and the parts he left out would make Kelvin look bad. Really bad.

"So how long do you want to rent the apartment?" Ed asked from nearby.

Sonny hid his jump and turned to see that Tanya's dad was only a few feet away. He'd been so distracted with Tanya and her paintings he failed to notice.

Ed peered up at Sonny like he was finally starting to let down his guard.

"Well, I thought I'd try it for a month or so and then go from there," Sonny quipped and attempted to sound respectful. Somehow, he didn't think flippant would fly with Ed O'Brien. Tanya had mentioned he was a retired accountant, and the exact cut of his short hair coupled with the perfect fit of his slacks and shirt suggested the man was as exacting as they came.

He probably never lost a penny . . . or a clue, Sonny thought.

"A month-to-month basis is fine with me," Tanya agreed. "I like it best that way, actually. Then, neither one of us is tied down." Her smile was all business, and Sonny took the hint. She was willing to make a go of it the first month. If it didn't work out in her interest, then she was as free to cancel the agreement as Sonny would be.

"So what do you think?" Ryan asked and glanced at his watch. "I don't want to rush you, but I've got to pick up Sean from his friend's in half an hour and then I've got to get to that city council banquet." The guy already wore a pair of tan slacks and a sport coat. Whatever this banquet was about, Ryan was certainly dressed for it.

"I'd like to go for it," Sonny said and eyed Tanya.

Tanya nodded and motioned across the room. "I'll get rid of the clutter and help you clean up," she said. "I've got an extra broom and some other cleaning stuff in the garage."

"Sure," Sonny agreed and turned to Ryan. "Go ahead and take care of Sean. I'll stay here while you're gone. Since I promised to watch him tonight, just drop him off here. Maybe he'll enjoy playing with Tanya's little boy."

"Good idea," Ryan said. "He's very good with younger kids."

"Great," Sonny said and glanced toward Tanya for approval, but she and her father were talking near the window. He turned back to Ryan. "Then, can you pick me back up later, after the banquet, and help me get my camera equipment over here?"

"If you like, I can just run you home now and you can load your truck and come back over to—"

Sonny drew a fast, fierce line across his neck and nudged Ryan toward the door that led to the stairs. Another glance over his shoulder attested that Ed and Tanya's conversation had grown somewhat intense. Thankful they hadn't noticed Ryan's offer, Sonny closed the door and followed his brother to the top of the stairs.

"Have you forgotten why we came together in the first place?" Sonny whispered. "I don't want to bring my truck over here. If Kelvin's watching, I don't want him to see me here. I'll drive my motorcycle over later and park it behind the garage. But for now, I'll need to use your truck for hauling my stuff."

Ryan nodded. "Sorry 'bout that slip." His smile turned impish. "I was too distracted over the distraction."

Sonny narrowed his eyes and tried to assign a meaning to Ryan's cryptic comment.

"I guess this is the part where I'm supposed to ask what exactly you mean?" Sonny quipped.

"Well, you're wearing your long jeans for a start." Ryan stepped onto the top stair.

"So." Sonny glanced down at his pants. They'd been worn to a perfect shade of pale blue and were nearly as comfortable as pajamas. "This is my favorite pair."

"And a Sunday shirt that would make mom proud. Aside from the tuxedo at Jack's wedding, I haven't seen you this dressed up since—" He shrugged.

"What are you suggesting?"

"Not suggesting a thing," Ryan said, turning down the corners of his mouth. "Just wondering about your motives . . . and not so sure about her motives." He cut a glance toward the apartment.

"You're hallucinating again." Sonny waved away his comments and neared the flat's door. "If I've told you once, I've told you a thousand times—stop sniffing glue!" He threw the shot over his shoulder and turned for the apartment.

Ryan's laughter echoed up the stairwell in sequence with the tap of his shoes on wood.

His hand on the doorknob, Sonny glanced down at his jeans and shirt. Granted, he had taken extra care with his appearance tonight, but it was more because he wanted to seem trustworthy than anything else. Of course, the appreciative gleam in Tanya's eyes hadn't gone unnoticed . . . but neither had the businesslike lift of her chin when she admitted a month-to-month rental agreement suited her best.

There was no reason for Sonny to get interested in this woman and her son. He was here for one reason only. Once that reason no longer existed, Sonny would go back to his side of the world, and she'd go back to her life.

He stepped inside the apartment, cast a smile toward Tanya, and said, "Where did you say that broom was?"

CHAPTER SEVEN

Tanya walked toward her front yard with Sonny at her side. They'd spent the last couple of hours cleaning the apartment from top to bottom. She'd been impressed with Sonny's domestic prowess and wondered if that was the norm for him or if he'd just risen to the occasion. Whatever the case, the apartment now lacked one speck of dust.

The evening breeze eased Tanya's mind as much as it alleviated the sweat she'd worked up. She and Sonny had found a window AC unit in the apartment's closet and installed it, but that had been after they'd been working an hour.

"Do you mind if I move some of my things over tonight?" Sonny asked as they neared the front yard.

"Of course not. You've paid your deposit and the first month's rent. The place is yours now. Come and go as you please." Tanya smiled up at him and hoped she was projecting professional interest and nothing more.

"Good." He returned the smile, and Tanya couldn't deny that it was a tad bit too warm to be purely professional. They'd just spent the last couple of hours working together, and while conversation hadn't been constant, it had certainly become companionable. They'd even shared a few laughs when Sonny discovered a mouse skeleton in the bathroom closet.

He certainly didn't look as if he'd just been cleaning alongside her. If anything, his curly hair was better served. She'd seen male models in magazines whose hair didn't look half as fashionable as his. Given his carefree nature, she figured the guy did absolutely nothing but wash it and let it air dry.

The sounds of laughter floated from around the corner, and Tanya hurried toward the front yard. When she rounded the house, she spotted her father and mother playing with Coty and Sean. Ryan had arrived with his son soon after she and Sonny started cleaning the apartment. Sonny had explained that he promised to keep Sean for his brother tonight while he was at a city council banquet, and Tanya suggested that he play with Coty while they worked. The boys had pulled Ed and Shirley into a round of games shortly after Sean arrived. The sandy-haired seven-year-old didn't resemble his father in the least, and Sonny had mentioned that he was adopted. Coty had taken to him instantly and the two had included Ed and Shirley in a game of hide-and-seek.

Now, they were heavily into a round of croquet. Of course, at the ripe old ages of three and seven both of the boys were too young to really play the game. Presently, Coty was kicking his ball, rather than hitting it with the mallet, while Ed bent over Sean, instructing him how to hit. Shirley laid aside her mallet and pulled a camera from the pocket of her Capri pants just in time to snap Coty whacking the wire wicket with a small black flashlight.

Tanya wrinkled her brow and wondered how Coty had gotten her flashlight again. She'd placed the thing in the top of her closet this morning so he couldn't find it.

"What's he hitting the wire with?" Sonny questioned through a smile.

Not bothering to answer, Tanya hurried to her son, bent, and examined the flashlight. It appeared to be hers, but she lifted her gaze to her mother. "Did he somehow get this flashlight out of the top of my closet?" she questioned as Sonny's shadow fell across her and Coty.

"No . . ." With a concerned frown, Shirley pocketed her camera and neared her daughter. "It was in his toy box in his room. I wondered if it was yours, but he called it *his* flashlight."

"Mine!" Coty demanded. His eyes fierce, he pulled the flashlight to his chest and clutched it with a fury.

Just as Tanya had remembered this morning—the rim was *not* gold. Her gaze trailed to the place she'd found the black flashlight. She'd picked it up shortly after that eerie feeling had overtaken her . . . and after she'd prayed that God would show her if there was something wrong. Her heart began a hard pound, and Tanya now wondered if God had answered her prayer but she'd brushed aside the evidence.

"What's the matter, Tanya?" Ed questioned. "You're going pale."

"I . . ." she croaked and glanced from her dad, to her mom, to Sonny Mansfield, whose curiosity was as strong as her parents' concern.

Before she spoke, Tanya recalled the conversation she'd had with her father when Sonny stepped out of the apartment with his brother. The two of them had debated whether or not Tanya should tell Sonny about Maurice Salazar. After a brief discussion, they'd decided not to broach the subject so soon . . . at least until they were certain Sonny himself would prove to be a worthy renter. Meanwhile, Tanya had chosen to simply take comfort in knowing that someone from the right side of the law was on her grounds, at least part of the time.

Now, she wondered if not telling Sonny had been the right choice. If that flashlight was not hers, then it belonged to someone else—someone who had been in her yard.

But when? she thought. And that was anybody's guess. Tanya certainly didn't remember seeing the light before this morning, but it could have been hidden in the foliage.

Yes, but not for long, she argued. *It's like new. No corrosion. And it works well.*

"Tanya?" Shirley's concerned voice cut through Tanya's confusion. "Is something wrong?"

Her attention shifted to her mother, whose blue eyes held a wealth of motherly love . . . mixed with fear.

"Tanya?" Ed echoed. Her focus flitted to her dad and then landed on Sonny again. For some reason, Tanya couldn't drag her gaze from his. A haunting voice within urged her to speak . . . and speak the truth.

"I found a black flashlight in my yard this morning. I assumed it was mine and that Coty had dropped it outside. But now . . ." She shook her head, and a hard tremble started in her gut.

Sonny narrowed his eyes. "So do you think someone has been in your yard?" he asked.

"I don't know . . ." Tanya trailed off and silently beseeched her father for guidance. Perhaps she *should* tell Sonny about Maurice.

Ed O'Brien's slight nod was all the encouragement Tanya needed. She cast a worried glance toward Coty and Sean and then stood. "Sonny . . . can I talk to you for a few minutes, uh, inside." She pointed toward her living room.

"Sure," he agreed with a shrug.

Sonny followed Tanya into the air-conditioned home and welcomed the rush of cold along his neckline. He'd been sweating like a sow while they cleaned and had wished a dozen times—four dozen times—he'd worn a pair of shorts and a tank top.

Nevertheless, when Tanya closed the door, flipped on the light, and faced him, he dismissed his personal discomfort.

"I've debated whether or not I should tell you this." She rubbed at her forehead and then took a deep breath. "But I've decided I think I should."

"Okay," Sonny said and crossed his arms. Instinct told him this had Kelvin Stuart written all over it. Instead of projecting the intense interest that was eating at him, Sonny casually glanced around an immaculate room that was the stark opposite of his living room. This place looked like the "after" on one of those home makeover shows while his place was definitely the "before."

"I had a . . . bad experience in Dallas," she said and pulled at the hem of her T-shirt.

"Oh?" Sonny prompted.

She nodded and her lips trembled. "That's part of the reason I agreed to your renting the apartment. I like the idea of having someone on the right side of the law in the apartment."

"So . . . what happened in Dallas?" Sonny prompted as his mind aggressively pieced together the details he already possessed.

"A man began stalking me." Tanya tucked her hair behind her ear and crossed her arms.

"Oh, really?" Sonny asked as if he had no idea there might have been such an issue.

She nodded. "That's part of the reason Daddy was so—so intense," she admitted. "There for a while, we wondered if that man might even try to kill me or—or kidnap me."

Sonny's fingers curled into fists.

"He sat by me on the flight home from Korea when I adopted Coty." She motioned toward the front yard. "He told me I reminded him of an old girlfriend named Eva. The way he looked at me made me wonder if he thought I *was* Eva. He followed me home from the airport and then wouldn't leave me alone!" Her eyes widened as the composed professional slipped away and a haunted, helpless woman took her place.

"After months, we filed a restraining order and repeatedly contacted the police. The restraining order stopped the flowers and gifts, but not the watching." She shivered. "It's so unnerving! I'm sure you know, unless there's an actual crime the police can't do anything. Obsessively watching someone isn't against the law—or even against a restraining order."

She moved toward a wing-backed chair and picked at the top seam. "Finally, I got a license to carry a concealed handgun and took the required classes to learn how to shoot. I've still got several Glock safe-action pistols hidden around the house. But really, how much good is a scared woman with a gun against someone who's probably linked to the Mafia?"

Sonny's teeth clenched.

She waved her hand. "I don't know about the Mafia business for sure. That's just an assumption. He just seems so—so power hungry . . . a control freak . . . and so certain he can have what he wants. Like he's used to buying everything, and everybody," she rushed. "When he found out I wasn't for sale, he started breathing down my neck and wouldn't stop. I couldn't go anywhere without him watching me. I couldn't make him stop!" Her eyes reddening, she dashed at a tear.

"Finally, I realized one day he was gone. So I packed everything and moved. Even though I haven't seen him since I came here, I still can't shake the feeling he's looking for me . . . or that he might find me." Rubbing her upper arms, she stared at Sonny as a new cloak of dread masked her features.

Sonny measured her every word, assessed her expression, and drew a firm conclusion. The woman was telling the truth; and Kelvin had paved his lie with green to get what he wanted. He'd bought Sonny just like he'd tried to buy Tanya; and Sonny had never been more disgusted with himself than now. He should have recognized all the symptoms, but he'd been too influenced by that hard, cold cash.

How shallow have I gotten? he thought and remembered a time when he wouldn't have been so easily affected. Of course, that was B.K., before Karen—before he hit rock bottom and had to claw his way up.

I promise, if I ever drink another drop, you can strike me dead, he thought and realized he'd been more or less talking to God. The very idea of spontaneously doing such was enough of a distraction for Sonny to get sidetracked. But he refused.

Sonny dragged his wayward mind to focus on the issue at hand as a hard knot of resolution formed in his gut. "So you think the flashlight was his?" he asked.

"I—I don't know for—for certain." Tanya shook her head. "I just know it isn't mine."

"But you really *think* it's his, don't you?"

A barely perceptible nod preceded her rush of words, "Is there any way you'd consider moving into the apartment full time, just until—"

"Yes," Sonny answered.

". . . I felt safer. I'd even be willing to waive the rent." She lifted her hand as if tossing aside the very worry. "It would be worth having someone here all the time. If there's any way you would consider—"

"Yes," Sonny repeated.

"I know it's probably an imposition and all," she worked her fingers into a knot. "You already own a home, but if you might even consider—"

Sonny stepped forward, gently gripped her upper arms, and looked her square in the eyes. "Tanya, I've already said yes," he said through a smile.

"Oh." She gazed up at him as if he'd materialized out of nowhere. "You mean you will?"

Sonny nodded and wondered how he'd ever live with himself

if that rat somehow hurt this lady. He also wondered how Tanya O'Brien would ever forgive him if she found out *he* was the one who led the stalker to her. He lowered his hands and decided that was one detail she never needed to know.

"You never mentioned the guy's name," he prompted and waited.

"Maurice Salazar," she replied, "but I wondered if that was his real name, you know." She shrugged and huffed. "Who even knows!"

"Yeah," Sonny mumbled and gazed out the window, "I can see why you'd feel that way."

A flash of silver caught Sonny's eye, and he recognized Ryan's Ford pickup pulling to the curb. A plan formed in his mind, and Sonny had never been so thankful to see the pieces of anything falling so readily into place.

"I'll get Ryan to take me home and then I'll send an air mattress and some sheets and stuff over with him. After dark, I'll ride my motorcycle over and park it behind the apartment. That way, Salazar won't know you've got a bodyguard, and we'll be more likely to catch him if he tries anything funny. Does that work for you?"

"Whatever you think," Tanya said with a nod. She crossed her arms, and her shoulders straightened. The slumping victim disappeared; the composed woman was back. "Do you believe in God, Sonny?"

"Sorta." He shrugged.

Narrowing her eyes, Tanya gazed up and him, and Sonny wondered if she was trying to read his mind.

"Yeah, I believe in God," he finally admitted. "I'm just not so sure He believes in me."

Her brows lifted, and Sonny squirmed inside like a six-year-old trapped on the back pew in the middle of a long sermon. "I haven't exactly been the best pupil," he muttered. Averting his gaze, Sonny decided this wasn't the time or place to go into his spirituality—or lack of it. That was none of her business anyway.

"Well, I think He believed in you enough to send you here," she claimed. "I'm beginning to think your asking to rent the apartment is totally of God."

"Really?" he asked and wondered how her perception might change if she knew the whole truth.

CHAPTER EIGHT

Sonny downed the final drop of the bottled beverage labeled "Mean Bean." Even though the chilled coffee was as loaded with caffeine as it was sugar and this was his third one, his eyes still drooped. Presently, Sonny couldn't recall how long he'd been staring at the portable DVD player's blank screen. He'd gone through three Clint Eastwood movies and as many bags of microwave popcorn. Sonny had loaded the compact microwave on a whim when Ryan picked up the rest of his stuff. Now that he'd crunched through three bags of popcorn, he was glad he'd gone to the extra effort.

He peered around the tiny apartment. The gray haze from the DVD player proved the only lighting in the place, and the sparse furnishings blurred together in the shadows: an end table, the microwave, another end table, the DVD player, a small refrigerator he'd nagged Ryan out of.

When his gaze slid to the air mattress and the tumble of sheets wadded in the middle, Sonny could resist no longer. Playing babysitter all night had seemed like the only logical thing to do. But after his bout with insomnia yesterday morning, Sonny's groggy mind was going on strike.

I haven't heard a thing all night anyway, he mumbled and dragged his heavy body from the lawn chair. *And Tanya has my cell number if she needs me*, he reasoned and recalled the grateful glow in her eyes when he "checked in" for the night.

"She has nice eyes," he drawled and tried to remember why he shouldn't be appreciating her eyes—or any of her better qualities—but couldn't come up with one reason.

With a lazy smile, he set the Mean Bean bottle next to the other two near the DVD player and reminded himself to bring a trash can over soon. Eyeing the bed, he nearly flopped on top of the wadded sheets, but resisted. Despite a yawn that nearly swallowed him whole, Sonny decided to take one last look out the window before he crashed.

He'd left the blinds up on purpose and scanned the area during the evening. As with the other times he'd checked out the scene for any danger, Sonny saw nothing unusual. Though he could see most of Tanya's front yard from the garage apartment, the outer one-third was blocked from his vision. And that handicap left Sonny debating whether or not he should take a final stroll around the yard as he had twice between movies. Another yawn insisted he yank off his tank top and flop in his shorts, so Sonny decided to do exactly that.

But a last, hard appraisal made him pause. Blinking his gritty eyes, he strained to identify the shape protruding just past the edge of Tanya's house. Perhaps it was in the street . . . or not.

Sonny wrinkled his brow and then widened his eyes. "It's a bumper," he whispered. *Maybe on a truck . . . or a van. And it wasn't there the last time I looked.*

He bolted to the refrigerator, grabbed his 9 mm pistol from the top, and dashed down the stairs as quietly as the creaking old wood allowed. Once he merged into the night, the warm concrete against his soles reminded him he'd forgotten to put on his shoes, but it was too late to go back.

The shadows embraced him in balmy humidity as he slunk to the house's corner and peered toward the street. Just as he'd assumed, a lone van sat on the side of the road. Gripping the gun, Sonny hugged the corner and waited while his mind processed the van's presence.

Common sense suggested the van could have broken down and the owner had walked to the nearest gas station for help. *Or it could even belong to someone visiting the home across the street,* he reasoned. *But why wouldn't they have parked in that driveway . . . and why on Tanya's side of the road?* He noted the long, empty drive that wound to the home across the street.

The main issue is Tanya and Coty's safety, he told himself and forced his rapid breathing into an even cadence. His heart rate thumped a fraction slower. Sonny glanced down at his bare feet and bit back an edict.

Focus, focus, focus, he chanted instead and forced himself to step around the front of the house. Crouched low, he pointed his pistol upward and moved forward.

Tanya flopped onto her stomach and punched at her pillow. After dropping into the bed at ten, she'd gone to sleep with little effort. But a dream had awakened her at one thirty, and she hadn't convinced her mind to shut back down. The dream had centered upon the tall, blond man now staying in her garage apartment. Strangely, the two of them had been waltzing across her front yard, dodging croquet wickets, and laughing like carefree teenagers. The exhilarating laughter had only been topped by the invigorating energy that flowed from Sonny Mansfield's smile.

She huffed, turned onto her side, and squeezed her eyes tight. When she prayed for a father for Coty, she'd had a certain type of man in mind . . . one like some of the men she'd dated in the past. Perhaps a bank president whose dark suits are as distinguished as the slight gray at his temples. Or a pediatrician who is as committed to understanding children as he is to being a good father. Or even a minister whose walk with God could rival the saints. Any of those types would do.

"Private eyes are not on the list," she insisted through tight lips. Tanya shoved aside the sheets, rolled to her back, pressed fists against her temples, and squelched a scream.

She'd watched as more than one girlfriend fell for the wrong guy. A couple of them had been taken by men who were, in her father's southern vernacular, squirrelly. Tanya had secretly scorned her friends' poor judgment and couldn't fathom succumbing to any such attraction. She'd always been too logical to allow one fanciful molecule to even flit through her brain . . . so logical that she'd ended several promising relationships simply because the men didn't measure up.

"Now I'm having dreams about a flaky private eye I've known for less than a week!" *It's probably just because he's protecting me!* she thought and refused to be influenced by such a factor. "Forget it!" Tanya threw off the covers and stood.

Happy, sleeping in his bed by the doorway, stirred and yawned. Tonight, she'd let the dog stay inside because she liked the extra security he offered. He wasn't the most ferocious creature on the planet but he did know how to bark. He'd at least alert her if she needed to retrieve the Glock from atop the armoire.

"Go back to sleep, Happy," Tanya said and rammed her feet into her house shoes. "I'm just on a tear. Nothing more." She grabbed the terry cloth robe from the end of her bed and shrugged into it. Since Coty had begged to spend the night with her parents, Tanya didn't have to worry about waking him. Therefore, she didn't squelch stomping toward the kitchen in pursuit of a scalding cup of cranberry tea.

Maybe it will knock some sense into me, she thought, *and help me relax enough to go back to sleep!*

CHAPTER NINE

By the time Sonny neared the house's corner, something he couldn't explain insisted that all was not well. He'd heard Jack talk about his "danger sensor" often enough, and Sonny began to think Jack's gift had transferred to him—at least this once. All sleep was forgotten, every muscle tense. And Sonny was ready for whatever might wait in the shadows. The chorus of crickets cheered him on like an energized crowd at a boxing match.

At first, the faint creak that came from around the corner sounded as if one of the crickets might have gotten out of sequence. Nevertheless, Sonny stopped, held his breath, and waited. The second squeak proved too sharp to be any cricket. Frantically, he glanced around for a place to hide but only spotted the area between the house and the back of the bushes. Since shimmying behind the bushes would make too much noise, the whisper of footsteps on grass drove him to choose the only option available.

Sonny crouched low, in front of the last bush at the home's edge. He peered around the house just as a shadowed figure rounded the home and stumbled into him. The invader's grunt accompanied Sonny's shout and preceded the tumbling of bodies. The sprawling man toppled Sonny backward and sent his Smith & Wesson flying. Sonny turned over to get up as the heel of a shoe rammed his eye. He released a pain-filled roar and flailed for his pistol.

The front door banging open . . . a gun's firing . . . a dog's frantic barking . . . all spun in his head with the realization that a second man emerged from around the house. Tanya's screaming, "Help! Help!" before the gun went off again made Sonny forget his own pain.

"So help me, you jerks!" he bellowed, "if you've hurt her . . ." Abandoning the search for his gun, he grabbed the invader's legs, but they slipped from his grasp like the tentacles of an octopus. Another kick directly in the cheek popped Sonny's head back and left him reeling.

Now dizzy from the blows, Sonny was scrambling to all fours when the invader delivered another kick to his side that drove him into the prickly bushes. He attempted to trace the man racing toward the van but his image swam in and out of focus in sequence with the gun's firing. The van's back door slamming suggested the second guy had crawled into the back. The back window shattered as a bullet met its target.

Groaning, Sonny fought the pain stabbing his side and cheek while his injured eye watered. The screech of tires propelled him to sit up. He strained to read the license plate, but soon learned it had no light. With a moan, he fingered his swelling eye and figured the light had been removed on purpose.

Tanya's startled voice jolted Sonny from his stupor. "Are you all right?"

"Me?" he questioned and somehow managed to drag himself up. That's when he realized his right knee was burning as badly as his cheek. "I was worried about *you*. Are you okay? What about Coty?" A new onslaught of pain pierced his side. Gasping, he couldn't stop the hunch. "What about the shooting? Was that you shooting?"

That's when he noticed she held a handgun and remembered her preference for Glock safe-action pistols. "They didn't hurt you, did they?" he added.

"No, not at all, and Coty spent the night with my parents. He does that a couple times a week." A phone's faint ring nabbed her attention. "That's probably a neighbor—probably the Rileys," she said and turned for the door with the cocker spaniel on her heels. The dog's occasional growl laced with a worried whine indicated *he* wasn't fine. "And I'm going to shut you up in my bedroom for a while," she crooned and bent to gingerly scoop up the dog while managing the handgun.

Eyeing her pistol, Sonny hobbled behind and also recalled her mentioning that she'd been licensed to carry a handgun. He tried to struggle up the steps while she zipped inside. By the time he made it to the top step, she was back outside with a cell phone to her ear.

"Yes, it was me, Brad," she said. "Yes, I—I did have some invaders . . . maybe robbers. I don't know. Please do. Yes, that would be such a tremendous help."

She stopped near Sonny. "No, that's okay. The man who's renting my garage apartment is here with me now." She darted him a glance. "I'm safe. Coty's fine. He's at my mom and dad's tonight. Just—just call the police for us, okay?"

After saying her goodbyes, Tanya disconnected the call. "That was Brad Riley from across the street," she explained. "The Riley's are good people. He heard me shooting."

"So it *was* you?" Sonny confirmed.

"Yes. I couldn't sleep and was in the kitchen making myself some tea when I heard the skirmish. I grabbed my gun. Remember, I told you I have several of them hidden around the house. Actually, there are four."

"You mean that's *all*?" he mocked.

"I went for the one in the kitchen cabinet," she sheepishly stated, "and . . . you know the rest, right?"

"Yeah," Sonny affirmed and wondered why the woman acted so desperate for protection when she was a virtual brigade.

"Did you get a good look at them?" she asked, her eyes that of a hunted animal. And that answered Sonny's question. No matter how many hidden guns she had, she still didn't feel safe. Salazar had messed with her psyche to the point that she was trapped by the web of fear he'd knitted around her.

And that's probably the exact effect he wanted, Sonny scoffed.

"So did you see them?" she prompted.

"No," Sonny said, but his gut instinct insisted he'd been kicked by Maurice Salazar, not a generic robber, and that they were after more than material items. "Sorry. It was all such a scramble and then I was blind in one eye and dizzy in the other, and I just couldn't see him." Sonny rubbed at his forehead and realized he was swaying.

She moved closer and slipped her arm around him. "Come on. Lean on me. Let's get you inside," she persisted.

"I'm okay," Sonny argued but couldn't break her hold.

When they stepped over the threshold, Tanya's fearful eyes grew concerned. "You really took a beating," she said. "And that's only what I can see."

"All in a day's work," Sonny drawled.

"Did he get you in the side too?"

"Yeah," he admitted. "Right below the ribs, I think. I'm normally more fightworthy than this, but he took me by surprise and had me sprawled before I knew what hit me."

"Come on in, and let me get some ice on your eye and we'll see about your side too. I'm as good as a doctor for stuff like this," she claimed.

"Does this mean you'll charge me an office visit?" he quipped.

"Ha, ha, ha," she responded with a sarcastic twist to her lips.

Sonny squinted against the room's overhead lighting. "I'm going back out there to see what they were up to around the house as soon as I can."

"Did you get the license number?" she questioned.

"No," he admitted and rapidly blinked against his eye's fresh watering. "The light on the plate was out, and I don't think it was an accident."

She kicked the door shut, pulled away from Sonny, set the phone on a nearby table, and turned to engage the deadbolt lock. The lack of support sent Sonny into a sway, but he regained his balance and even straightened his spine.

"Oh no!" Tanya gasped and reached for him again.

"Really, I can stand on my own," he said and pulled away. Although he wasn't immune to a sleepy-eyed damsel in distress offering her arm, Sonny's need for independence drove him to insist this time. "I'm supposed to be the one rescuing you—not the other way around," he said with a firmness he didn't know he could conjure. "Now first, let *me* call the police and then I'm gonna go investigate."

"No!" she said and stomped her foot.

Sonny's brows lifted, but he paid for the effort and wound up in another wince.

"Brad Riley's calling the police," she said.

"But I know the police. I've got Payton's cell number memorized. He took over while my brother's gone. He'll get somebody here quick or come himself if he knows it's me."

"They'll get here soon enough," she admonished. "I'm worried about you. And you're not going anywhere until I get some ibuprofen in you and check out your side. Whoever that was—they're gone. It can wait until you get some treatment. You might need to go to the ER."

"I don't need to go to the ER," he scoffed.

"I'll be the one to decide that. Now sit!" She pushed him toward the couch.

"If you let me call the police, I'll let you doctor my chewed-up carcass without fighting, okay?"

Narrowing her eyes, she looked up at him like he was the most ornery patient on the planet. "Okay," she finally muttered and retrieved the cell phone from the table.

Sonny fought a shiver against the effects of air-conditioning on perspiration and tried to look stronger than he felt.

Phone in hand, she focused on his eye again, and her face filled with nothing but compassion and a trace of something else Sonny couldn't quite compute. He wasn't used to computing at three A.M. anyway, so he didn't even try.

"I can't believe this has happened like this," she said. "I'm so glad you were here. Thank *God* you were here! He had to have sent you."

"Uh . . . with that gun of yours, looks like you might have done just fine without me."

"No, oh no," she insisted and shook her head with a vengeance. "You're the one who did the fighting. I just shot enough to scare them away."

Once again, Sonny wondered how her whole view might change if she knew that *he* was the one who led Salazar to her. He decided not to think about that right now. There was nothing he could do about it anyway . . . except continue to be there for her.

She grabbed Sonny's arm and gave him another shove toward the couch's corner. "Sit," she repeated and nudged him into the soft folds. After his side's initial protest, the comfort was well worth the pain. She punched at some pillows and shoved them close.

"I've *got* to call Payton," Sonny insisted.

Tanya gazed at the phone like she didn't quite know what to do with it. "Here." She thrust it at him. "You call. I'll go get you an ice pack and some ibuprofen and then I'll examine your side."

"Maybe you should just admit me to the ICU," he joked while pressing the numbers. Sonny glanced up in time to see a sour, although humorous, expression scurry across her face.

"I'm a trained professional," she said with a shrug. "What do you expect?"

"Right. You take care of the ER, and I'll call the police. Maybe I won't be dead when you get back." He threw in a saucy wink with his good eye, but his stinging cheek protested and the wink ended in a grimace.

CHAPTER TEN

Tanya stood at the refrigerator and waited for the plastic tumbler to fill with ice. With every cube that dropped into the cup, her grip increased, her fingertips grew whiter. She rapidly blinked her gritty eyes against the sting that would not abate. Somehow, she'd miraculously held the tears at bay, and she refused to give in to one drop. Presently, Tanya didn't know what was shaking her most: the fact that Maurice must have found her or the presence of this man she barely knew who'd risked his life to save her.

Once the tumbler was full, she retrieved a ziplock bag from the cabinet and dumped the ice therein. By the time she was closing the bag and reaching for the bottle of ibuprofen, Tanya wondered what had alerted Sonny to the danger. In the upheaval to get him inside, she'd never heard his side of the story.

He'd hinted last night when he arrived that he planned to sit up all night. Tanya had insisted that that wasn't necessary. Now she figured he must have done exactly that and perhaps had seen the van at the road.

Tanya wondered if there might be more substance to him than she'd given him credit for. His carefree appearance, self-assured strut, and easy personality certainly leant themselves to a more shallow interpretation.

But sitting up all night to protect someone isn't the stuff shallow is made of, she reasoned. Tanya glanced at the oven's digital clock that proclaimed it was three thirty-two. *You don't need to be making judgment calls about any new acquaintance at this hour,* she admonished herself, *especially not after he just rescued you.* She knew enough about humans to know that most women had a propensity toward admiring men who rescued them. And Tanya was feeling human right now—exceedingly human.

Hardening her resolve, she retrieved a serving tray from the bottom cabinet and topped it with a glass of water, the ice bag, the ibuprofen, and her first aid kit. By the time she reentered the living room, Sonny had pulled her coffee table close enough to prop up his bare feet. One arm rested on the stack of pillows and the other on the couch's armrest. At this angle, he resembled some self-assured sheik who'd taken up residence in her home.

The threat of irritation nibbled at her heels . . . until Sonny turned to look at her. The sight of his swollen eye and puffy cheek dashed aside the sheik impression and left nothing but compassion. Nevertheless, cold logic overruled her humanity, and she stopped herself from showing more concern than she would for any patient.

"Here's your ice pack," she said, setting the tray on the table. "Keep this cloth around it, and it won't get too cold." Carefully, Tanya wrapped the bag in a thin washcloth and handed it to him.

"I'll take it without the cloth for now," Sonny said. He placed the bag against his eye and tossed the cloth onto the tray. "It hurts like the dickens, and the cold feels good."

"Suit yourself," she said before retrieving the ibuprofen. "I'm giving you four of these." She dumped the brown tablets into her palm. "Wait." She looked up. "Are you allergic to any aspirin products?"

"Nope. I'm too ornery to be allergic to anything," he said through a sassy grin.

Tanya refrained from smiling and concentrated on getting the medicine down him. "Taking four makes it prescription strength," she said. "You can take another four in about six hours for pain and swelling, but don't make a habit of taking this many all the time."

"Really, I usually avoid pills," he admitted. "I'm only taking these because I'm desperate and you're making me."

Tanya didn't make eye contact. "Feel like letting me look at your side?" she queried.

"Sure." He shifted and lifted his tank top, but not without a gasp.

Tanya's attention rested on his face. "How bad does it hurt?" she asked. "On a scale of one to ten . . ."

"Seven," Sonny replied. "He kicked *hard*. Last time I hurt like this, I was thirteen and Ryan and I fell out of a tree together—as in, he fell on me. But it's not as bad as the time I broke my ribs when I wrecked my truck."

"Does it hurt here at all?" She pressed against his rib cage, centimeters above the reddened area.

"No. It's definitely below the ribs."

"No skin broken," she mumbled and eyed the first aid kit on the tray. "I can wrap it tight in a bandage and it will give you some support—"

"Don't worry about it." Sonny waived aside the thought. "I don't think anything's ruptured. It just hurts."

Tanya gently pressed the area and felt no signs of internal injuries. "Probably just going to see some deep bruising. Your whole side will be pretty by this afternoon."

"Nice and purple, huh?" Sonny asked. "Like my eye."

"Right." Tanya lowered his shirt. "But make sure you let me know if it gives you any unusual problems—like an increase in sharp pain." She examined the wound on his cheek. "I can dress that," she offered and raised her gaze to encounter his steady appraisal. As much as she wanted to look away, Tanya didn't flinch.

"No, I'm good." He shook his head. "I'll move the ice pack over here some." He placed the pack on his cheek and smiled again. This time, Tanya noticed a brown star tattoo on the inside of his forearm. She strained to read the words under the star but failed, due to the angle of his arm.

"You noticed my star," he stated and lowered his hand.

"Yeah."

"It's the only tattoo I have. I did it in honor of my Uncle Abe. He got a Bronze Star in World War II for bravery. See." He pointed to the words beneath the star. ABE MONTGOMERY. GERMANY, 1943.

Tanya nodded and didn't tell him she hadn't thought the tattoo would involve something so honorable. The proud gleam in Sonny's eyes hinted that there might be some character beneath the surface. His putting his life on the line for her suggested he might carry some of Abe's bravery in his genes.

The lights flashing from outside jolted Tanya back to the danger at hand.

"That's Payton," Sonny said and pushed himself out of the couch. "I was about to head out there anyway. I need to see what those morons were up to."

"Are you sure you're ready to—"

"I'm *fine*," Sonny said and strode toward the front door with an assurance that only wavered when he reached to unlock the dead-bolt. Tanya started to rush to his assistance but stopped. No need to turn into his nanny.

He stepped outside and closed the door without a backward glance. Tanya rose, moved to the front window, pulled aside the drapes, and gazed toward the road. In the eerie shadows, Sonny was talking to a tall, dark police officer who didn't look like he'd take anything off anybody. Strangely, his crew cut and militant stance comforted Tanya.

"He'd scare the spots off a leopard," she mumbled and hoped he had the same effect on any criminals. Tanya stepped toward the front door. But glancing down at her robe and slippers, she decided to change before facing Payton.

Sonny turned toward the sound of footsteps brushing against the dew-laden grass and glanced around the corner of the house. As suspected, Tanya neared from the front yard. He flashed the light toward her path and noted she now wore flip-flops and jeans. He offered an encouraging smile when she stopped at his side.

Gazing toward Payton descending a ladder, she said, "What have you found out?"

"Looks like he was doing what I thought—disengaging your alarm system." Sonny pointed the beam toward the limp phone line. "He cut the phone line to stop the alarm company from getting the signal. Who knows what they were planning next, but I can bet it involved you."

Tanya's cold fingers clutched Sonny's arm.

"You're right," Payton said as he took the last step to the ground. "They cut the phone line for a reason." He pointed his flashlight toward the line that now sagged on the tree.

"I felt so much safer with the alarm," Tanya's voice wavered over the words. Sonny resisted the urge to wrap his arm around her. She didn't strike him as the clinging-vine sort, so Tanya had to be feeling fairly desperate to latch on to him.

"They do offer a measure of safety," Payton replied and his attention flitted to Tanya's fingers pressing into Sonny's arm. No telling what the guy thought. "But when you're up against a sophisticated criminal who wants what he wants bad enough, they have a tendency to get around alarms." Payton rubbed at his mustache, and his dark eyes were as intense as Jack's could get. The flashlight's glow only intensified the effect.

"I've already talked to Sonny, but I'd like to get your report as well, Tanya," Payton said. "Wanta go inside or stay out here?"

"Inside is fine," Tanya rasped, and her eyes reminded Sonny of a startled hoot owl who didn't know whether to fly or stay and fight it out.

Wondering if he should tell her everything, he allowed her to go first and followed close behind. Sonny had confessed all to Payton, but also informed the officer that Tanya didn't know Salazar had hired him to find her. Payton agreed she didn't have to know. He'd also said that unless they found some hard evidence that implicated Salazar there was nothing they could do. Sonny already knew that much. The law had so many loopholes—especially when dealing with stalkers—that it could be annoying at least and terrifying at worst.

As they neared the front door, Sonny recalled a nightly news headline several months ago. A gal in Austin, Texas, had begged police to arrest a man who'd been watching her, but they couldn't because watching someone was not illegal. When she came up dead and the man's DNA was all over the scene, they then arrested him for murder. Of course, it was too late for the woman.

I should be shot for letting Salazar get to me, Sonny thought.

When Tanya opened the front door, Sonny covered a yawn and could have sworn he smelled coffee brewing. *It wouldn't surprise me if the woman threw on a pot before coming out,* Sonny thought and hoped his assumption was correct.

But all longing for the hot liquid was obliterated when Tanya glanced up with a silent appeal that would have melted marble. A pool of vulnerability now blotted out all the sass she'd used to keep him in his place while she played doctor. And in the midst of the vulnerability was a plea that Sonny Mansfield would be worthy of her trust . . . because she desperately needed someone to trust.

He replied with a smile he tried to make kind, assuring—and couldn't remember a time he'd ever felt such a strong urge to protect a woman. Whether that was because he was partly responsible for her predicament or some other elusive reason was anybody's guess.

Sonny stepped through the front door and wondered if Payton sensed the undercurrent of who-knew-what between him and Tanya O'Brien. *It'd probably take somebody dumber than a box of rocks to miss it*, he thought and decided to stay with his original plan not to tell her Salazar had hired him—*ever*.

That little detail needs to go to my grave with me, he vowed and shut the door on even considering the subject again.

CHAPTER ELEVEN

A giant woodpecker the size of an ostrich pounded the roof, and Sonny couldn't figure out why the thing wouldn't stop. As much as he tried to stand from the recliner where he was watching the basketball game, he couldn't get up. The chair held him captive while the woodpecker drowned out the Maverick's game. It was a playoff game, one he'd waited to watch all week. Everything was perfect . . . including the butter-drenched popcorn in the bowl on the table.

The woodpecker grew louder. Sonny tried to yell at it, but nothing came out. And then the thing started marching across the basketball court, blocking his view of the game. Sonny's anxiety increased to a flood of frustration, but he could do nothing to stop the crazy bird. Somehow, the thing was still pecking the roof while it stomped across the basketball court.

The situation took on an even more bizarre turn when the woodpecker turned from the ballgame and began calling Sonny's name.

"Sonny!"

Frowning, Sonny tried to recall why the bird's voice sounded so familiar.

"Sonny! Are you awake?"

He reached to rub his forehead and found that his arm was tangled in some barrier that stopped movement.

"Sonny . . . it's me, Tanya. Are you okay?"

His eyes slid open, and Sonny was transported from the recliner and basketball game to the tiny garage apartment. As for the giant woodpecker with the familiar voice . . . that weirdo was gone. In its place was someone knocking on his door and a female voice calling his name . . . and hers.

Tanya O'Brien! he thought, and with the realization came an instant replay of the crazy night they'd just survived. After taking their report and finding no incriminating clues, Payton finally left at four thirty. Sonny had dragged himself back up to his air mattress. Still wearing his shorts and tank top, he'd eased his sore body onto the mattress. Tanya said she was going to send an e-mail to her boss, tell him what happened, and then wait until one to go into work.

If she's knocking, it's either nearly one or I slept until after she got off work. "Coming!" Sonny called. He threw off the covers and stood. That's when his aching side reminded him he'd been kicked senseless last night. He grunted and halted before holding his breath and forcing his torso straight. After the initial discomfort, he straightened and checked his watch on the way to the door. Fortunately, the digital numbers proved he'd only slept until twelve thirty.

Fingering his tender eyes, Sonny opened the door.

Tanya stood on the other side, wearing a smile and carrying a tray, laden with a carafe of coffee and some yogurt and fruit. "Sorry I was kicking the door so hard," she said, "but my hands were full, and I was getting worried." She lifted the tray as her focus rested on his worst eye. "Are you okay?"

"Yeah, just sore." He scratched at his unruly hair and wondered if he could put off the necessary trip to the restroom until after she left.

"I brought you some breakfast and also some more ibuprofen," she stated like a polite flight attendant.

"Oh, cool," Sonny said over a yawn. "Thanks." He closed the door and followed his nose to the top of the microwave where she deposited the tray.

"I also came up to check on you," she said and swiveled to face him. This time, she wore her doctor face. "How's your side?"

"Hurts like the dickens, but okay," he mumbled and reached for the mug and steaming carafe.

"I'd like to look at it again if you don't—"

"Have at it." Sonny broke off from filling the mug, replaced the carafe, and stole a sip of the brew before raising his arm and lifting his shirt.

Her cool fingers pressed his aching flesh, and he released a grunt.

"Are you having any sharp pains?" she questioned.

"Not that I can tell," he admitted, "but I haven't been up long."

"And your eye? Are you seeing okay?"

He looked down at her. "Yeah. You're the one with *two* heads, right?" he quipped before adding an impish grin and then downing a mouthful of the hot coffee.

"Oh my word!" she gasped. "Did he chip your tooth last night?"

Sonny ran his tongue across the chip that had been with him since childhood. "You just now noticed that?"

"Yes."

"That happened when I was fourteen. My oldest brother, Jack, accidentally hit me in the mouth with my new baseball."

"Sounds like you guys nearly beat each other senseless growing up."

"Pretty much," he admitted. "Get ready. You've got a boy of your own. As for me, I'm snaggletoothed now."

She smiled, but finally crossed her arms and got her doctor face back on.

Sonny's mind was starting to function enough for him to notice Tanya looked like some cover girl for a medical journal. She wore a pair of gray scrubs with her hair pulled into a ponytail. Fresh makeup gave her a pretty edge while her no-nonsense persona indicated she didn't really care whether she was pretty or not. Nobody would ever guess she'd had an invader and had been up until 4:30 A.M. Her present attitude was a long way from that vulnerable woman he'd left last night.

"Well, as long as everything stays about the same, I think you'll be all right," she continued. "I also brought another ice pack for your eye and cheek." She lifted a plastic bag full of ice from the tray and replaced it before picking up the ibuprofen. "Might not hurt for you to use it before it melts."

"Yes ma'am," he drawled.

Her face impassive, she extended four of the brown tablets, and Sonny accepted them. "Take these now and then again in—"

"About six hours. Got it," he stated before dropping the pills into his mouth. "He chased them with a generous swallow of coffee and set the mug on the tray. "I'm sorry to be rude, but nature's calling and it won't shut up."

"Right," she said, "and I've got to get to work. Just so you know, Dad's here. He's arranging for the phone company to replace the cut line, and then he'll wait on them to get here. So feel free to head on back over to your house. There's nobody here to get kidnapped for the rest of the day."

She walked to the door and paused with her hand on the knob. When she made eye contact again, her self-assured guise had weakened. "Thanks again," she said, "for last night and all."

"Oh, sure." Sonny smiled, then winced. Fleetingly, he wondered if he'd ever be able to smile again without the wince.

Tanya was on the verge of shutting the door when she remembered the envelope in her smock's pocket. She'd been so focused on maintaining a professional air she forgot about Sonny's refund. He'd probably saved her life last night, and the longer she thought about it the more her decision not to charge him for staying in the apartment made sense.

She stepped back inside just as the restroom door closed. Tanya smiled and made a major ordeal of coughing so he'd know she hadn't left. Meanwhile, she walked to the window, pulled up the blinds, and eyed the section of her front yard she could see. Sonny said he'd noticed the tip of a bumper protruding past her house, and Tanya experienced a fresh rush of certainty that God must have been in the midst of everything that happened. Although she had been up last night when the intruder arrived, she may not have had time to grab her gun when he broke in. Even if she'd screamed when they nabbed her, Tanya seriously doubted any neighbors would have heard her. If Sonny hadn't been outside, Tanya could have been history by now.

Images of Maurice bombarded her mind. Closing her eyes, Tanya tried to blot out the image—and the fear. She'd told Payton everything, but he found nothing to point to Maurice, or anyone else for that matter. He was supposed to come back today and dust for prints. But he'd said that unless there were prints already on file that matched any he found it did them little good, unless they actually caught the culprit.

The click of the bathroom door preceded Sonny's saying, "Still here?"

Tanya pivoted to face him while trying to hide her momentary dismay. "Yeah," she said with a smile she hoped didn't look as wobbly as it felt.

Sonny wore the same pair of floppy basketball shorts and tank top he'd been in last night. His curly hair, still rumpled from sleep, gave him a little boy appeal—despite the stubble. And Tanya couldn't deny there was something about Sonny Mansfield she liked—too much for logic.

Under any other circumstances, she'd have put some serious

boundaries on him and kept her distance. But these weren't normal circumstances, and Tanya's usual mode of operation was significantly handicapped by her need for protection.

After he'd retrieved his coffee and was taking a swallow, Tanya extracted the envelope from her pocket and extended it. "I forgot to give you this," she said.

He accepted the envelope and said, "What is it?"

"Your rent and deposit," Tanya replied without a blink.

Sonny squinted, and then the memory of the conversation from last night flitted across his features. "So you were serious about letting me stay for free?"

"Yes. And I'm getting more serious by the hour. The more I think about it, the more I know I can't keep the money," she explained. "You saved my life last night. Besides that, after Payton left I don't think I'd have gotten one wink of sleep without knowing you were in the apartment and just a speed dial away on my cell." She shivered and remembered that phone line, so skillfully cut.

A veil of indecision descended upon Sonny's features. He examined the envelope only a few seconds then nodded. "Okay. Truth be known, I can use it."

"It's the least I can do," she said and tried to keep her voice cool yet kind. "My dad also wants me to confirm that you are still willing to stay for a while—at least until we're sure there's no more threat. We're willing to pay . . ."

Sonny eyed her with an intensity that didn't match his flippant personality. "I gave my word last night," he finally said. "And I don't go back on it. I can stay most nights, I guess. Except I will have to take some other cases along the way."

"That's fine," she said. "As long as you're here when the sun goes down."

"I'll do my best to sleep here," he affirmed. "But sometimes I have to prowl around at night." He shrugged.

"Understandable," Tanya affirmed and noticed when she caught his eye that his blue tank top made his pale gray eyes take on the tinge of an azure ocean—the disturbing variety of azure that could disrupt a woman's life. Even though one eye was swollen and the other was marred by a scraped cheek, Tanya couldn't stop the warm appreciation that fluttered through her spirit.

Tanya forced her attention outside to the grass simply because it was green. She liked green. Green was a good color. Nice and safe.

Sonny cleared his throat and said, "Uh . . . how would you feel if I brought my cats over? They really like having me home at night. If I'm gone too much they start getting irate."

"As long as they use their litter box, I'm fine with it," Tanya said and couldn't walk toward the doorway fast enough.

"They're so committed to their litter box, they come in from outside to use it. Drives me crazy!"

Tanya's chuckle sounded as strained as it felt. "That's my kind of commitment," she agreed and checked her watch. "Well, I should have already left." Her smile felt so stiff she knew it probably looked fake. "I guess I'll see you tonight?"

"Yeah, I'll be here," Sonny agreed with a cocky grin that merged into another yawn.

Tanya didn't even try to analyze that grin. Instead, she dashed down the stairs and didn't slow until she retrieved her purse from her living room.

Tanya exited the final patient's room just as Dolly was walking up the hallway. Tanya smiled and hoped she and Dolly would have time to chat now that the day was winding down. The years had seasoned Dolly with a wisdom that was absent in most women Tanya's age. The effect was a no-nonsense relationship that Tanya found refreshing.

"Hey, sweet lady! Are you still doing okay?" the RN questioned and eyed Tanya from her face to her knees.

"A little tired, that's all," Tanya admitted and hugged the older woman who'd hovered over her ever since she arrived.

"You still look as gorgeous as you did when you came in—like nothing ever even happened last night—better than I've seen you look all week."

"Thank God for that," Tanya breathed. "I guess middle-of-the-night stress is good for me." She covered a yawn. "But looks can be deceiving. I'm beat."

The matron moved close and squeezed Tanya's shoulders. "Maybe it's just that man you've got stowed away at your place," she teased. "I guess having him in the middle of that big police raid was terribly exciting."

"Dolly!" Tanya whispered and glanced up and down the hall-way. "First, it wasn't a police raid. And second, remember to whisper." Yesterday, she'd consulted Dolly about Sonny's offer to rent her apartment and had called her friend last night to tell her of the final decision. She'd given Dolly no indication that the association was anything but business.

"Oh, don't worry about it, darlin'," Dolly crooned. "You know Dr. Dan is nearly deaf," she waved toward the aging physician's office, "and Trish is so scatterbrained she can't answer the phone and pay attention at the same time." She motioned toward the front desk where the secretary/receptionist was on the phone.

Tanya sighed. Dolly was right, but the house-turned-clinic was too small for her to be discussing personal matters in the hallway. Aside from what she shared with Dolly, Tanya preferred to keep her private life out of public view. And at the very least a stray patient might stumble into the middle of it.

"Come on," she whispered and tugged her friend toward the break room at the end of the hallway. "I need someone to talk to anyway." The wooden floors creaked as the women entered the small room. Like the other four rooms that lined the hallway, the break room was a bedroom seventy-five years ago, when the house was first built. Now the walls, covered in eighties wallpaper, were in need of some remodeling; but no one but Tanya seemed to recognize the blatant fact.

She closed the door behind Dolly and pulled two chairs out from the Victorian table that came with the house. Dolly took Tanya's cue and settled into the chair.

"I need advice," Tanya began and plopped into her own chair.

"Of course you do," Dolly said and eyed Tanya through her bifocals like she was some kind of specimen under a scientist's slide.

Tanya stared at her friend a full five seconds. "How do you know?"

"You've got a single man living in your place, and you're a single woman. Anybody in that situation is going to need advice."

"I shouldn't be attracted to him," Tanya admitted. "He's not my type."

"But you are anyway?" Dolly questioned.

Swallowing, Tanya nodded. "I think it's got something to do with the rescued-female syndrome."

"The what?"

"The rescued-female syndrome," Tanya stated and checked her watch. It was just past five and she'd need to pick up Coty soon. Nonetheless, Tanya still wanted to know if Dolly had any practical ideas to thwart the syndrome. "You know—when a woman goes all mushy over someone who saves her life."

"He *did* save your life," Dolly reiterated. "And that's something a lot of women find appealing."

"Exactly," Tanya said. "And he's agreed to stay there indefinitely as protection."

"But he's not your type?" Dolly queried. "Are you *sure*?"

"Yes, I'm sure," Tanya stated. "He comes across, well, a little flighty and not all that spiritual. When I asked him if he believed in God, he said he guessed and that he wasn't sure God believed in him because he hadn't been the best pupil. What does *that* tell you?"

Dolly simply stared at her; and her large brown eyes seemed all the bigger through her thick glasses.

"Well?" Tanya prompted.

"Well what?"

"What do I do?" Tanya pleaded. "I need him to stay, but I don't need him to stay." She removed the stethoscope from her neck and tormented the ear pieces while Dolly chuckled.

"This isn't funny," Tanya insisted and wondered why she ever thought Dolly Lennon would be the source of any sort of common sense. Now that she considered it, the woman devoured Christian romance novels in her spare time and usually ate lunch with her nose in a book. She undoubtedly had some sort of a romantic streak that wouldn't quit—if the current spark in her eyes was anything to go by.

"Tell me how you came to adopt Coty," Dolly said.

"What?" Tanya queried, wrinkling her forehead.

"Coty." Dolly lifted her hand. "Why did you adopt him?"

Not following the logic, Tanya decided to answer Dolly's question in hopes that there was a solid answer to the original question somewhere in her friend's mind. "Well, when I was a teenager a Korean missionary came to church and spoke about her work in Asia. She talked about a lot of things—including the need for adoptive parents. I knew when I saw the pictures of all those orphans that I'd adopt when I got married. Even if I had my own kids, I still wanted to adopt. My parents really encouraged me to stick to my dream." Tanya rested her elbow on the table, placed her chin in her hand, and continued with Dolly's rapt attention. "The problem was my dream was always linked to marriage."

Dolly nodded.

"I thought I'd met the right guy a couple of times, but it just never worked out. One was even planning to be a minister . . ." Tanya trailed off and swallowed the sigh.

"What happened with him?" Dolly prompted.

"Dave and I were a good match, I guess, but I just never felt the same spark for him he felt for me. I don't know. He just wasn't as mature as I wanted. I really thought he should have been deeper if he was going to be a pastor. No matter how hard I tried, I couldn't get over that and it affected my ability to love him somehow. So finally, I knew I had to let him go or wind up hurting him worse than I did."

She eyed Dolly and waited.

"What about the other one?" Dolly questioned.

Tanya slumped into her chair, crossed her arms. "Right after I was licensed to be a PA, there was a doctor—"

"A doctor?" Dolly's brows rose. "You certainly know how to nab the good ones, don't you?"

"I guess." Tanya shrugged. "But once again—"

"Something was wrong?" Dolly questioned.

"Well . . ." she hedged.

"So you finally got tired of waiting for a perfect husband and just decided to adopt?"

"I wouldn't say it like that, but I *did* find out that single people can adopt, and I decided that I might not ever find the right man so why keep waiting?"

"That's all about what I figured." Dolly drummed her fingertips against the table, and Tanya straightened.

"What do you mean?"

"Sometimes the Lord works in mysterious ways," she said as if Tanya had never even asked the question. "The way I see it, He put that Mansfield man on your place for protection, and apparently, it's already working."

So we're back to Sonny, Tanya thought and struggled to connect Dolly's conversational volleys.

"If you're getting the warm fuzzies for him then I'd ask the Lord why. Maybe if your visitor isn't all that spiritual it's time he gets that way and maybe God has put you in his life to help him along the way. As for his being flighty . . . he's acting *very responsible* if you ask me, and anything but flighty."

Tanya's gaze slid from Dolly's candid eyes to the window where the hot, evening sun bathed the yard in the promise of a sweltering evening. "Or maybe I should just go to Wal-Mart and buy some warm fuzzy insecticide," Tanya mumbled in a fit of sarcasm, "and spray those little rascals before they take me under."

"Yes, that would work too," Dolly encouraged. "Then you can spend the rest of your life alone, raise your son alone, and go to your grave . . . alone."

The edge in Dolly's words rankled. Drawing her brows together, Tanya focused on her friend again and tried to hide her irritation. She sat there in her flowered smock like some misplaced sage and observed Tanya as if she were ready for some kind of an answer. Unfortunately, Tanya had nothing to say and didn't appreciate her brand of wisdom this time.

Finally, she scraped together a few lame words and spilled them, "I'll be glad to marry the right man when he comes along. I just don't think a cocky private eye is the right one. I'm waiting on someone more stable and . . . and . . ."

"Predictable?"

"Yes. So why even indulge the warm fuzzies for someone I just met—"

"When he doesn't fit the mold?"

"Right."

"What if the guy who does fit the mold never shows up?" Dolly challenged. "What if your mold is too demanding? You've already turned down a minister and a doctor."

Touché! Tanya thought and no longer questioned Dolly's conversational strategy. "But I wasn't in love with either of them," she defended and stood.

"Maybe you wouldn't let yourself fall in love with them like you don't want to let yourself be attracted to Sonny."

Tanya squirmed and looked for an easy way out that was also respectful.

"Now, here you are a beautiful, successful woman who many men would *die* to marry."

"Well, I wouldn't say *that*," Tanya injected.

"You've even got some man so fascinated with you he's stalking you."

Tanya shivered. "And that's a positive?"

"No, but it proves my point. There's no reason you shouldn't be able to find a man. And you're still single."

"Well, it's not *my* fault. There are lots of men and women these days who wait awhile before they get married," Tanya defended and wished she'd never even brought up the subject.

"There are no perfect men, Tanya," Dolly continued. "If you keep rejecting the ones God brings in your path, pretty soon He might stop sending any." Dolly stood and patted her arm with motherly affection that softened her words, but Tanya was still hard-pressed not to jerk away.

"Dolly, I need my husband to have a strong relationship with Christ," she insisted.

"Who says Sonny doesn't have a relationship?"

"If he does, he's about this deep by his own admission." She held up her index finger and thumb and measured half an inch.

"I'm not saying do anything rash," Dolly conceded. "But at least have a another conversation with him about spiritual matters before you strike it all up as helpless. Maybe he's never been given a direct opportunity to accept Christ. Or maybe he has, and something happened to stunt him."

Tanya sighed, rubbed her eyes, and decided not to reply this time.

"Well, I've got to go," Dolly added like she'd never dropped the verbal grenades. She walked toward the doorway while Tanya mutely stared at her.

"I just want what's best for you," she said with a warm smile.

"Thanks," Tanya grumbled and plopped back into the chair the second Dolly closed the door. She'd hoped the woman would help her resist the attraction that was coming out of nowhere. Instead, Dolly had encouraged her to go with the flow. But that was something Tanya O'Brien had *never* done . . . and she wasn't about to start now. She far preferred to live in the land of careful, logical choices, based on careful, logical plans and never allow her life to take a path that she couldn't see the end of.

CHAPTER TWELVE

H̶ang on, Coty!" Sonny exclaimed. "Here comes a big push. Ready?"

"Weady!" Coty cheered before Sonny gave the toddler swing a swift shove.

Coty sailed into the air, laughing all the way up and back while Happy chased the swing, ran in circles, and barked like the most delighted dog in Texas. That only upped Coty's joy.

"Do it 'gin! Do it 'gin!" he begged the second the momentum slowed.

"Okay, here goes!" Sonny warned before another shove.

Coty's squeals increased with Happy's every bark. Despite the evening heat and the rash of perspiration, Sonny couldn't remember an evening . . . or a month he'd enjoyed more. He'd stayed at the apartment every night and wound up interacting with Coty and his mom. It started when Tanya had been pulling the child in his wagon along the sidewalk for a seven P.M. stroll. Sonny had arrived on his motorcycle and was holding the wagon handle before he ever knew what possessed him. Then, there'd been the wild romp in the water sprinkler the next evening while Tanya unloaded her groceries. That had led to a month full of playing and laughter.

Yesterday, Sonny found the high quality swing set at a drastically reduced price, due to some dents in the legs caused in shipping. When he called Tanya about the deal, she'd insisted on paying for the set. Sonny hadn't argued, but had set it up for free, despite her offer of an assembly fee.

No one could ever say Tanya O'Brien wasn't independent enough. Of course, the fact that she'd gone all the way to Korea and adopted a child said enough within itself. The more Sonny was around her, the more he recognized her as a quiet force. Whoever became her man, in the end would have to be willing to allow her to have her space and respect her logic. Even though Sonny and she seemed to be striking up a friendship, and even though there was a buzz between them, he wasn't so sure about anything more.

And she's not either, he thought, *if the wall she's had up all month is anything to go by.* The few times she let her guard slip, he'd recognized a womanly interest that was far more than professional. Watching her fight it had kept Sonny more intrigued than if she'd readily given in.

"Do it 'gin!" Coty insisted, and Sonny realized he'd allowed the child to slow beyond what any sensible toddler would tolerate. Happy now sat at his feet, tongue lolling, looking up with an expectant air that insisted he was as ready as Coty. Sonny shoved the swing anew and reveled in the child's laughter. For the laughter alone, it had been worth being displaced a month.

"You'll be out here all night if you don't finally say no," Tanya said.

Sonny tried to hide the moderate jump. He'd been so distracted by his thoughts . . . and Coty . . . he'd not heard Tanya's approach.

Tanya was wearing a sundress, carrying a tray laden with iced tea, which she set on the nearby picnic table. "Did I startle you?" she asked.

"No." He smiled and then shrugged. "Okay, a little. But I'm like a jumpin' bean most the time anyway."

"Yeah, me too," she drawled and glanced over her shoulder as if Maurice Salazar were watching her every move.

"I wish we had more solid evidence against Maurice," Sonny said.

"I know." She sighed. "But I appreciate all you've done."

In the last month, he, Ryan, Jack, and Payton had taken turns seeing what they could dig up. The only lead they had was the fact that Maurice's car was registered to Lone Star Transport. While that company was a legitimate business, there was no listing for Maurice Salazar or Kelvin Stuart in the Dallas–Ft. Worth area. Ryan, Jack, and Sonny had taken turns spying on Lone Star Transport, but neither of them had spotted Salazar yet.

Presently, Sonny was considering driving to the business and watching until he spotted Maurice—even if it took a week. From there, he could follow him and hopefully discover something that would incriminate him—whether it related to Tanya or not. Sonny didn't care why the man spent time in jail, as long as he did. The longer he was in jail, the safer Tanya would be.

"Do it 'gin!" Coty squawked like a parrot who only knew one phrase.

"Coty!" Tanya admonished. "You're going to wear out Mr. Sonny. He's been pushing you for half an hour."

"Ah, that's okay," Sonny said with a smile. "I don't mind." He didn't bother to tell her that playing with Coty had been his chance to develop the memories he'd never made with his own son.

"I really appreciate all you're doing," she said and served him a white envelope along with his tea.

Sonny took the tea and downed half the cold, sweet liquid before accepting the envelope. He already knew what was inside and had been surprised that Tanya had given him more than he'd suggested as a weekly fee since he'd been here. Even though they had a business agreement, Sonny debated whether he should take the money. Somehow, the business deal was slipping into a friendship of sorts, and Sonny never had minded helping out a friend in need. But the truth was, babysitting Tanya O'Brien had turned into a part-time job and was cutting into his other income. He really didn't have a choice but to accept her payment.

"I wouldn't take it, but I have to have it," he admitted.

"Of course," she stated. "At this point, I wouldn't have you here any other way. Dad and Mom are helping with the fee as well. We're all convinced that you're the reason I haven't had a repeat visit. As long as you're here, I'm safe. Do you mind staying indefinitely?"

Her guard slipped for the first time in weeks, and Sonny encountered the vulnerability that stirred his masculine instincts. Her question hung between them as Sonny realized the instincts involved more than just the protection of Tanya and her child. During the last month, Sonny became involved on a personal level. Presently, he wasn't sure whether the pull was more for Tanya or Coty. A few times he'd found himself thinking of the toddler to the point of distraction.

And he admitted to himself what he'd never tell Tanya: *I'll never forgive myself if Salazar gets to Coty and her.* Even if he never remained more than a family friend, Sonny would rather go blind than see her name in the headlines as yet another victim.

"Sure, I'll stay," he finally answered before taking another long draw on the sweet tea. Somewhere along the way, he'd stopped worrying about Salazar spotting him with Tanya. Like she said, he thought that maybe the guy was taking the hint and accepting defeat. Nevertheless, that speculation didn't release Sonny from his sense of responsibility.

"Do it 'gin! Do it 'gin!" Coty crowed and swiveled in the slowing swing, adding a big-eyed appeal to his request.

"Come on, sweetie," Tanya said. "It's time for you to go in and get a bath and get ready for bed."

"No!" Coty wailed. "Swing! Coty swing!"

"Bath, bath, bath," Tanya countered.

Sonny smiled and set his tumbler on the picnic table. "Look at Happy!" he crooned and pointed to the cocker spaniel, now collapsed beneath a huge oak. "You've worn him out."

"Coty swing!" the child demanded and rocked back and forth.

"Come on, Coty," Tanya said in a singsong voice. "You can play with your boat in the bathtub."

"Swing!" Coty repeated while Tanya tried to unhook the toddler lock.

"I don't know how you've done it all this time by yourself," Sonny admitted and couldn't hide the tinge of admiration coloring his words.

"It's been a dream come true," Tanya answered over Coty's wails. "He's got me so wrapped around his finger, I barely notice the struggles. He's stretching the terrible two's to the three's. Can you tell?"

"Hadn't noticed," Sonny quipped.

"Yeah, right," she said and struggled to unfasten the swing amid flailing arms.

"Here. I'll help," Sonny said. "Just hold the swing and I'll get him out." He bent to the task while Tanya steadied the swing.

Distracted by this new development, Coty stopped thrashing and gazed into Sonny's face as if he were Superman. "Sonny give me bath," the child said when Sonny gathered him in his arms.

"No-no," Tanya protested, reaching for her son. "We've monopolized Mr. Sonny long enough."

Not holding her view, Coty wrapped his arms around Sonny's neck and wailed, "Sonny bath!"

Rather than loosening his hold, Sonny's arms tightened. And his heart stirred in a way it hadn't since he discovered Karen had placed their son for adoption. "I don't mind giving him his bath," Sonny offered and wondered if his plea was reflected in his expression.

Her lifted brows and widened eyes answered that question. So far, they'd kept their relationship—if that's what you wanted to call it—outside the house. Sonny had simply been available to play with Coty and chat with Tanya in passing. They'd discussed the lack of progress in finding Salazar . . . along with the weather . . . and the price of jalapeños in Mexico. But Sonny hadn't been in her home again since the night of the invader. Now, with his offering to bathe Coty, the acquaintance moved to a new level—something Sonny refused to label as intimacy.

"Sonny, bath!" Coty insisted again and swiveled in his new position to face his mother.

"That's fine," Tanya agreed and averted her gaze.

Thirty minutes later, Tanya had brought in the tea service, loaded her dishwasher, and washed down her cabinets. She'd also opened a roll of cookie dough and popped some peanut butter cookies in the oven. Still, Sonny and Coty celebrated bath time. What usually took Tanya fifteen minutes had morphed into a laughter-filled splash-fest that was probably turning the bathroom into a pond. Nevertheless, she hadn't tried to stop the party. Even with her father's presence in his life, Coty could soak up every ounce of Sonny's attention too. And that only drove home their need for a man in the house all the more.

Her cell phone rang. Tanya pulled it from her sundress pocket, checked the tiny screen, and answered with, "Hi, Mom."

"Hello there," Shirley O'Brien replied. "Your dad and I were just checking in this evening to see if everything's okay."

"Yes. Coty's getting his bath, and I'm baking cookies," Tanya said before sizing up the implications of her statement.

"Is Coty bathing himself now?" Shirley asked.

Tanya pressed her fingertips against her temple and wondered how best to answer. She finally realized there was no getting around the absolute truth and wondered why she was hesitant to spill it anyway. While her father had always been somewhat overprotective, her mother had never pried in Tanya's private life.

"Tanya? Did I lose you?" Shirley prompted.

"Uh, no," Tanya said.

"Coty's bathing himself now?" she repeated.

"No, Sonny Mansfield's giving him his bath," Tanya said, trying to sound as casual as possible.

"Oh," Shirley said.

"He was pushing Coty in his swing," Tanya rushed, "and—"

"Coty has a swing?"

"Well, yes. Sonny found it on sale yesterday and I bought it. He set it up, and . . ." She meandered to the living room and yanked a few magazines into place. "And tonight, Coty threw a fit for Sonny to give him a bath, so I went with it. It gave me a break," she added and wondered if the excuse sounded as lame to her mother as it did to her.

"I see," Shirley answered as if nothing was out of the ordinary.

And Tanya's appreciation for her mother increased tenfold.

"Well, your dad and I wanted to let you know we bought an above-ground pool for our backyard, especially for Coty to play in. The men are coming tomorrow to set it up."

"Wonderful!" Tanya exclaimed and wondered how long it would take for Coty to be irrevocably spoiled. As her mother continued with details, she moved to the window and watched Brad Riley run across the yard in quest of a Frisbee his daughter had thrown. Tanya couldn't deny the longing it created. Sighing, she recalled the advice Dolly had given her a month ago. Tanya had been too aghast to consider her friend might have been right and had avoided the subject ever since. Strangely, Dolly hadn't asked about Sonny either. Now

Tanya wondered if she should at least consider Dolly's advice, for Coty if nothing else.

The boy needed a full-time father. His growing attachment to Sonny proved it. Maybe Tanya should at least introduce the subject of faith and see where Sonny stood before assuming he had no spiritual life at all.

Perhaps there was more beneath his flippant surface than he was showing her. When Coty clung to Sonny near the swing, a haunted man had emerged. The longer she pondered what she'd seen, the more intrigued she grew. Something about Sonny didn't add up. Idly, she wondered if he might have been married and didn't have custody of his child. Something was certainly on his mind.

"Tanya? Are you there?" Shirley's voice pierced Tanya's wandering thoughts.

"Y-yes," she stammered. "Sorry. I got distracted. What were you saying?"

"I was just going on about the pool," Shirley admitted. "Don't worry about it. We'll let you know when we get it set up. Ed is eager to teach Coty to swim."

"Okay, what now?" Sonny asked from behind.

Tanya yelped and whirled to face Sonny, now holding a drowsy Coty.

"Yikes! Sorry. Didn't mean to scare you," Sonny said.

"Dear? Are you okay?" Shirley asked.

"Fine," Tanya answered and covered her heart. "Sonny's here with Coty. I didn't hear him coming. He scared me, that's all."

"Well, I'll go then," Shirley said. "Tell him Ed and I said hello."

"Sure thing," Tanya answered and flipped the phone shut.

"I didn't notice you were on the phone," Sonny said with an apologetic grin.

"No problem. I guess turnabout's fair play, huh?"

"Yeah," he said through a chuckle. "You scared me at the swing and I got you back."

"I was just talking to my mom," Tanya explained and avoided eye contact. "She said to tell you hi." Tanya observed Coty, dressed in the pajamas she'd set out for him. With his head resting on Sonny's shoulder, she never remembered his looking so content. When his eyes slid shut, she took the cue.

Silently, Tanya motioned Sonny to follow her. Sonny's footsteps fell in sequence with hers as she led him to Coty's room. "Shhh," she said, pressing her index finger against her lips. Then, she pointed to the toddler bed and pulled back the covers.

Sonny moved forward with the grace of a pro and gently placed Coty into his bed. The child stirred and released one mild whimper before slipping deeper into the folds of slumber. Tanya covered him and then gestured toward the hallway. After closing the door, she offered Sonny a silent high-five before she ever considered the consequences.

When their palms touched, a shimmer danced up her arm, and Tanya yanked back her hand. The warmth in Sonny's gaze suggested she wasn't the only one who felt the charge. Tempted to run, she stammered, "I—I made cookies," and scurried up the hall without a backward glance.

Tanya was pulling the cookie sheet out of the oven when Sonny entered the kitchen. The spatula trembled as Tanya plopped the fragrant cookies onto the platter one by one, and she prayed he didn't realize just how affected and confused she was becoming.

"Yum," Sonny approved. "Peanut butter is my fave."

"Yeah, Coty's too. I thought he'd enjoy one before he went to sleep but it looks like it didn't happen that way."

"No, I wore him out in the tub," Sonny explained. "Thanks for letting me bathe him. I really enjoyed it." Again, Tanya glimpsed that haunted soul she'd seen at the swings. Her trembling stopped.

She moved four of the cookies to a saucer and offered them to Sonny. "I've got milk," she added.

"Sure. We can't do cookies without milk." His jaunty smile revealed that chipped tooth, which was becoming more endearing every time he grinned . . . right along with his ever-present basketball shorts and that swagger that wouldn't stop.

Her stomach flipped. The trembling started all over again. And Tanya was tempted to beat her head against the refrigerator. None of this was going as she'd planned. She was supposed to be keeping Sonny at arm's length. Until tonight the plan had worked. But tonight, something was crumbling between them, and it was more than the cookies.

He found his way to the breakfast nook that overlooked Tanya's backyard. She settled across from him and poured a glass of milk for each of them. Feeling like a sixth grader on an afterschool date, she dunked her cookie in the milk and enjoyed the first bite.

After downing half a glass and devouring two of his cookies, Sonny said, "I guess you're wondering?"

"Wondering?" she echoed and laid aside her unfinished treat.

"Yes. It's all over you. I guess I slipped, huh?" He stared past Tanya toward some apparition, visible only to him.

"Do you have a child, Sonny? Or . . ." Tanya hesitated and tried not to sound insensitive. "Did you lose a child somehow?"

"Yeah to both," he admitted.

Tanya's mind whirled with the conversation that was unfolding as naturally as if they'd known each other for years. The man sitting before her was miles removed from the overconfident dude who strolled into her yard a month ago and asked to rent her apartment. This Sonny Mansfield had a heart . . . and that heart had been broken. At least, the pain in his eyes suggested as much.

"What happened?" Tanya prompted.

"First, I was an idiot—a young idiot. I got a girl pregnant. But I never even knew it. She hid it from me," he blurted and then gazed past her once more. "When the baby was born, she placed him for adoption. I never got to see him."

"So how did you find out?" Tanya breathed.

"Her sister," he said. "I saw her in the store. It was one of those chance meetings . . . I guess," he added. "She let it slip. When I confronted Karen, she admitted it. I went nuts. I'd have never released my son if I'd known. For all that matter, I'd have even married Karen, but she didn't want any part of that. She had a career to chase, and she didn't want me . . . or our baby to stop her."

"I'm so sorry," Tanya said.

"Yeah." Sonny grimaced. "I was too. I went off the deep end—got into alcohol—finally had the sense to get sober and stay that way. All of it's my own fault, though. If I'd just acted more like Uncle Abe and less like a selfish jerk, I wouldn't have ever had to deal with having my heart ripped out." He stroked the star tattoo with his thumb. "Now I've got a son out there who I'll never see and I bet he wonders if I even care." His fist curled into a tight ball near his cookie saucer.

Tempted to wrap her hands around his, Tanya knotted her fingers in her lap. "How old is he now?" she asked.

Sonny lifted his gaze to hers. "Twelve," he answered and stared at her as if he didn't see her. After a hard blink, he shook his head, pressed his fingertips against his eyes, and straightened his shoulders.

"I don't know why I told you all that," he rushed and fumbled with nothing. "Sorry. I guess Coty just got to me. It's odd. I can go months without even thinking about it and then all of a sudden it hits me."

"That's understandable," she agreed and grappled with something to say that would calm his agitation.

"Well, I've taken up too much of your time." He hurried toward the front door as if he couldn't leave fast enough. "Remember . . . same routine as always," he said over his shoulder. "Call me if you need me. You've got my number."

"Right. Same as always," she repeated and watched him exit without a backward glance. Tanya rushed to the front window and craned her neck to catch a final glimpse of him, but what the shadows didn't hide her angle did. Before she even realized her intent, Tanya found herself standing at her bedroom window, peering through the blinds. Head bent, Sonny strode toward the garage apartment. This time, the strut was gone. All that remained was a man who'd made wrong choices, now eaten up by regrets; and Tanya doubted she'd ever view Sonny Mansfield the same again.

CHAPTER THIRTEEN

Sonny revved his Harley and zipped out of the driveway with a velocity that left the back tire snaking. After ensuring his balance, he hunkered low and steered the bike from Tanya's neighborhood, toward Jack's house. He needed someone to talk to, and Jack was as good as anybody.

He and Charli had been home from their second honeymoon three weeks, and Sonny had tried to leave them alone. They needed to get used to each other without a pesky younger brother to complicate matters. But tonight, Sonny needed someone to give him a kick in the seat of the pants, and Jack was always good for that.

Sonny was letting things with Tanya O'Brien get way out of hand. *I'm telling her stuff my own family doesn't know,* he thought and could only imagine how his mother would react if she discovered she had a grandson she'd never get to meet. Of course, his dad was still so wrapped up in his trucking empire he probably wouldn't care much. But Sonny didn't even want *him* to know.

He could only hope Tanya wouldn't share his secret with anyone in the area. Bullard, Texas, was too small for any secret to be kept safe once it hit the grapevine. He should have known better. But tonight, Tanya's wall had collapsed; and she had observed Sonny with a pair of baby blues that got past his defenses and left him babbling about a past he never intended to tell her . . . or anyone.

He slowed before hanging a right onto Highway 69 and then gassed the motorcycle with a vengeance that sent the bike leaping into the oncoming night. The setting sun smeared the western horizon with splashes of fading red and orange and gold; and the promise of darkness eased away the heat that had baked the concrete all day. But not even the comfort of night could diminish the heat in Sonny's gut.

The little family he was determined to protect was getting to him, and Sonny didn't know who was more alluring: Coty or Tanya. He at least had the presence of mind to know that he shouldn't develop a relationship with Tanya simply because he enjoyed playing daddy to Coty. Nevertheless, Coty was coming to expect his presence, and Sonny also couldn't see ending the budding relationship with the mom and disappointing the child.

Five years ago, Sonny would have run from the whole blasted ordeal. But this wasn't five years ago. It was today. It also involved his leading a stalker straight to Tanya's door. Whether he wanted to be or not, Sonny was trapped by some twist of fate he couldn't escape.

He pulled into Jack's driveway, and the smell of fresh-cut grass added a mellow welcome to the cozy cabin, emitting a warm glow. As Sonny braked and rolled to a stop, he realized more than one truck sat in the driveway. Ryan's Ford claimed the spot by Jack's Chevy.

He snapped the kickstand into place, removed his helmet, and was halfway to the lighted house before he spotted both brothers sitting on the porch. Each claimed a corner of the creaking swing and watched his approach while Jack's blue heeler, Sam, sprawled near his master's feet.

"Yo!" Ryan finally said when Sonny started up the steps.

"Hey," Sonny replied, his voice sounding as encouraging as Sam's drowsy tail wag.

"Whazup?" Jack said over a yawn.

"Not much. Just came to see what you were up to. Looks like you've already got one beggar on you, though." Sonny doubled his fist and tapped Ryan's knee before straddling a straight-backed chair and sitting.

"Right," Jack said through a chuckle.

A whippoorwill whistled at the oncoming night, and Sonny sensed the mood on the porch was every bit as melancholic as the whippoorwill's forlorn call; so he figured he was in good company.

"You seem awfully cheerful," Jack drawled, and Sonny sensed his scrutiny without even looking at him.

"Yeah," Sonny replied and never took his attention from the distant woods. Whether he told them all or not, just hanging out with his brothers had a way of easing his nerves. In retrospect, Sonny realized that their dad's constant working throughout their childhood had caused them to develop a deeper bond with each other in a pathetic attempt to replace what their father didn't give them. Tonight, it was mighty good to have the comfort of that bond.

"What are you here for?" Sonny finally asked and shifted his focus to Ryan.

He shrugged. "Charli cooked dinner for me, and I was just talking to Jack some."

"Hey!" Sonny exclaimed and pressed his fingers against his chest. "Why wasn't *I* invited?"

"We tried," Jack claimed. "I left a voice mail on your home phone and your cell, but you didn't return the calls."

"Oh," Sonny said. "Yeah, I think I remember seeing you called earlier, but I, uh, got busy and wound up not returning it. Sorry."

"You're the one who should be sorry," Ryan chided and pulled his

T-shirt out of his jeans. "We're talking chicken fried steak, mashed potatoes, gravy, green beans. That woman can cook!"

Sonny's stomach growled, and he picked up a whiff of the southern meal. Whether it was the power of suggestion or the aroma still oozing out of the kitchen was anybody's guess. Tanya's cookies were the only thing he'd eaten since that sad apple he'd grabbed on his way out of the house midafternoon. Now he was ready for some real food.

"How's it going with the woman and kid?" Ryan asked.

"Yeah," Jack echoed.

"No more break-ins," Sonny affirmed.

"I don't guess you or Payton have made any new discoveries about Maurice Salazar?" Sonny asked.

"No. He still can't find any proof of the man's existence. I'm thinking the guy has numerous aliases and uses them in layers." Dark worries clouded Jack's sharp eyes, and Sonny noticed the circles underneath them. While Jack's jeans and boots and western shirt were the same as always, something else lurked beneath the surface that had the man less-than-cheerful.

"Any more info on Lone Star Transport?" Sonny directed the question to Ryan and didn't add that he was seriously considering holding a vigil at the business.

"I did swing by the place again yesterday," Ryan said.

"Oh?" Sonny leaned forward.

"Nothing new." Ryan lifted his hand, shook his head. "I mailed an empty package to myself and got good service—just as good as UPS. No sign of Salazar, though."

Hunching forward, Sonny rested his knees on his elbows, stared at the tops of his Converse high-tops, and decided he liked the idea of mailing a package. He'd use that excuse to get in when he went. "I just hope he doesn't come back—assuming that really was him who tried to break into Tanya's place."

When Payton investigated the next day, he'd found one drop of blood near the curb. Tests showed it was Type B and the person actually had Hepatitis C. They assumed Tanya must have hit one of them during her wild shooting spree. Whether the victim had been Salazar or the man with him was still to be determined. Having the forensics on the blood might prove useful later; but for now it did nothing to give clues toward the immediate case. Idly, Sonny wondered if the wound might have been fatal. If so, and if the victim had been Salazar, they might never see or hear from him again.

"So how long are you planning on babysitting her?" Jack asked.

"I guess as long as she pays me," Sonny quipped with a carefree edge he was far from feeling.

"Nice cover," Jack mumbled.

Sonny's head popped up. "What?"

"Oh, nothing." Jack's mischievous smile hinted that he'd read Sonny's mind, which could be very annoying—especially if Jack was guessing right.

Looking for a subject change, Sonny shot a glance toward Ryan, who stared into the night like he was in a completely different dimension and heard nothing. "What's with him?" he asked.

"Shelly," Jack responded, looking more and more like an abandoned pup.

"And what's *your* deal?" Sonny asked. "You look like you lost your best friend."

"I'm in the doghouse bad," he affirmed.

"Not with Charli!" Sonny exclaimed.

"Oh, yeah." Sam's groaning yawn blended with Jack's admission for an effect that nearly sent Sonny into a fit of laughter.

"What gives?" he asked, keeping his lips from quirking upward.

"Forgot her birthday," he admitted. "Smooth forgot it." He slowly sliced the air with his flattened palm in sequence with Sam flopping to his side and rolling his eyes.

Sonny laughed out loud.

"Not funny." Jack glowered, and the distant pond frogs' croaking only added to his censure. "She was expecting me to take her out to eat, and I invited my brothers over and asked her to cook for them and never said a word about her birthday." Jack shook his head.

Sonny snickered again and thought Jack was going to snarl.

"What's so funny?" Ryan asked.

"We're a fine bunch," Sonny replied. "Jack's in the doghouse big-time." He pointed toward Ryan. "You're singing the blues over Shelly." He turned his index finger toward himself, "And I . . ." Sonny stopped while both his brothers waited for him to finish. In a fit of weakness, he wondered what they'd think if they knew they were uncles to a child they'd never met.

"You know," Jack observed, "you looked like you were ready to howl at the moon when you came dragging up here. Are you and Tanya on the outs?"

"Uh, no," Sonny admitted and wondered if his denial implied that they were an item. "I wish it was that simple." He stared across the shadowed pasture, and his gaze slowly trailed toward the indigo sky, studded with evening's first stars. He wondered where Sonny Jr. was . . . if he was looking at the same stars and thinking about his biological father. Sonny wanted to be the one to teach him to fish and swim and camp and ride a motorcycle. But he'd probably already learned all that and more from the man who adopted him.

Sonny felt both brothers watching him, and he sensed they knew something significant was up. That only increased his urge to confide in them. Why he hadn't ever told them everything before was anybody's guess.

"Probably just too painful," he mumbled aloud before realizing he'd spoken his thoughts.

"What?" Ryan prompted.

Sonny sighed and focused on his brothers, who were only one step removed from bug-eyed.

If not for the seriousness of the moment, he'd have laughed at their expressions, but the humor couldn't get past the wad of tension in his gut. "I just told Tanya everything, I might as well tell you too," he admitted, and even the idea of sharing again unraveled the knot within a bit more. "But I'd really rather Mom not know. I don't know if she ever needs to know."

"Okaaaaay," Jack dragged out the word like he wasn't so sure *he* wanted to know. "It doesn't involve anything illegal, does it?" he worried.

"Nooo!" Sonny waved aside the concern. "It goes back to right before I graduated from college—about twelve years ago. I don't even know why I'm bringing this up," he admitted. "I guess Coty's just getting to me to the point that I'm turning into a blabbermouth." Sighing, he blurted the truth, "You two don't know it but you're uncles to a child you never even met." He lifted his hand in resignation. "But don't feel left out. I never got to meet him either."

Jack blinked, and then squinted.

Ryan leaned forward. "Are you saying—"

"Yeah. Remember Karen? My girlfriend in college?"

"Yeah, Mom wanted you guys to get married," Jack said.

"Well, we should have," Sonny admitted. "Or I *would* have if I'd known she was pregnant. She placed the baby for adoption. I didn't find out until right before I graduated. All I know is he was a boy."

Ryan's low whistle mingled with the whippoorwill's constant chant.

Sonny peered into Jack's eyes. "You thought I started drinking because I didn't make the NBA, but . . ." He shook his head and tried to tell himself his eyes weren't stinging.

"Holy Toledo, Sonny," Jack breathed, and the swing creaked. "Why didn't you tell us before now?"

"I don't know why I even told you now." He stood and walked to the porch railing, leaned against it. "I guess I'm going soft in my old age," he said, but still sensed that sharing with his two best friends had somehow lightened the load.

"You should have told us before now." Jack's voice close behind accompanied a supportive hand on Sonny's shoulder. Glancing back, he realized Jack had gotten up . . . and that Ryan was nearing.

"Maybe we could have tried to hunt him down—or maybe we should now," Ryan offered.

"I don't know," Sonny hedged. "It's not that I haven't thought about it. When I confronted Karen, I told her I wanted to find him then. He would have been just over one at the time. But anyway, she said it was supposed to be a closed adoption and that she'd signed an agreement that she wouldn't pursue contact. He can go to the agency and ask for info if he wants, but we're supposed to wait and see if he ever does. Really, I thought about trying to find him anyway. But then I worry that maybe he doesn't *want* to hear from me." As much as Sonny dreamed of meeting his son, he also wanted to avoid even the chance of rejection.

The silence that settled between the brothers ushered in a camaraderie that went soul deep. Even though Ryan and Jack said nothing, their support meant everything. And for the first time in years Sonny sensed that his older brothers understood him. He remembered this feeling when they were younger. They'd stood up for each other no matter what, and Sonny never doubted his brothers' loyalty. Somehow, his trip into alcohol had affected their relationship, but his coming clean was as good as wiping the slate and starting over.

"I'm really sorry, bro," Ryan said. "It's been a killer not living with Sean, but at least I'm still in his life. I can't imagine . . ."

"You've probably done better than I could have," Jack admitted and punched Sonny on the arm.

Sonny turned to face his brothers, leaned against the railing, and crossed his arms. "Like I said, I don't really want anybody else to know, okay? Mom probably wouldn't ever get over it."

"Yeah," Ryan agreed, shaking his head. "I don't know if she'll ever recover from my divorce. Finding out about your son would probably kill her." He settled back into his spot on the swing, and Jack joined him. "You know she always wants to believe everything is perfect, and it makes her crazy if she has to admit it's not."

"Sometimes, I wish she'd just accept reality," Sonny said. "Our family is a long way from perfect."

"Try to tell her that," Jack drawled. "Remember what happened a few years ago when I tried to hash through just how dysfunctional Dad is, and she defended him to the hilt."

"I know." Sonny sighed. "That's why it's best just not to tell her. It would create an ordeal, to say the least."

"She'd blow a fuse if she knew Shelly had a boyfriend. She's so determined we're going to get back together." Ryan's eyes took on a haunted shadow.

"I thought you were too," Sonny said.

"Believe me," Ryan admitted, "my determination is slipping. Everyone's impressed with my rescuing that kidnapped girl . . . except Shelly. I can hardly get her to even have a conversation with me. And tonight, when I dropped Sean off, this new boyfriend was there. I got her cornered and asked her if she thought she could trust him with Sean, and she told me she trusted him with Sean more than she could ever trust me with our wedding vows."

"Low blow," Sonny groaned.

"Yeah." Ryan rubbed his face. "Until tonight, I kept hoping that maybe I could somehow win her back. I agreed with Mom that God was going to somehow work a miracle. You know"—he shrugged, and his eyes took on an intense sincerity—"since I recommitted my life to Him, maybe He'd go the extra mile for me. But I'm starting to lose hope. Her boyfriend drives a Mercedes, for cryin' out loud, and Sean *really likes* him. He's that new dentist in town," he added as if the very word tasted of decay.

"Sorry, man," Sonny said and wondered what had caused Ryan to go so religious. Jack had been there for years and had been trying to drag Sonny down the straight and narrow with him. Sonny hadn't thought he'd ever go that way again . . . but then he heard himself telling Tanya he should have acted like Uncle Abe. That man had been a saint. If ever a person had religion it was him. Sonny doubted he'd ever measure up to Uncle Abe, but he was beginning to think he should have at least tried a long time before now.

It sure would have simplified my life and saved me a lot of grief, he thought. His stomach growled again, and Sonny figured that ravenous beast would demand its share even in the face of death and dismemberment. He straightened and pointed toward the door. "Think Charli could scrounge me up some scraps?"

"I guess," Jack drawled. "Just don't tell her I suggested it."

"Why don't you go on to Wal-Mart and at least get the woman some roses and a card," Sonny suggested. "Maybe that will at least get your snout and front feet out of the doghouse. And when you promise to take her to the best restaurant in Tyler tomorrow night, that ought to get you a one-way ticket out of bow-wow land for a long, long time."

Jack lifted his brows. "I was thinking it would probably be too late. Like, it doesn't count if she has to *tell* me it's her birthday."

"When a woman loves you like she does, it's *never* too late," Sonny said and pointed toward the pickup. "Now get your carcass in your truck and go do some flower buying, man! The night is young!" He wiggled his brows.

Jack chuckled and stood. "Okay, you convinced me. Come on Ryan," he said. "Let's go get some flowers."

"I think I'll pass," Ryan drawled and stretched into a stand. "I've cried on your shoulder long enough," he added.

Jack offered a thumbs-up. "Any time," he said. "You know I'm praying like crazy."

"I know. And I appreciate it, man."

Sonny neared the door and said, "I'll hold down the fort until you get back, then."

"Is that another way of saying you're going to eat me out of house and home?" Jack quipped through a smile.

"You got it," Sonny shot back.

Both brothers turned for the truck. But as they neared the porch light's outer glow, Ryan paused and swiveled to face Sonny again. Soon Jack followed suit. Several seconds loaded with silent communication passed before Ryan spoke, "Call me if you want to talk more later, okay?"

"Same here," Jack added.

Their expressions reflected their support . . . and their love; and Sonny had never been so glad to be a Mansfield.

"Will do," he said and nodded. Folding his arms, he waited until his brothers were pulling from the driveway before he decided to grab a burger rather than disturb Charli. Besides, he didn't want to be in the way here when lover-boy came back.

Sonny meandered toward his motorcycle and marveled at how much lighter his load felt after being with those two guys. Ryan had certainly come around to Jack's way of thinking on the God business. Sonny wondered if he'd be better off to move in that direction himself.

Straddling his Harley, he recalled that year at youth camp when he'd made a commitment to Christ. He'd planned to stay true, but life had gotten in the way and distracted him. Soon, he didn't even consider God. Sonny slipped on his helmet, revved the engine, and figured Christ had probably given up on him, considering the mess he'd made of his life.

CHAPTER FOURTEEN

Sonny stepped into the air-conditioned apartment and closed the door. The street light filtering through the blinds cast an eerie glow upon the tiny room and stirred a haunting echo in his soul.

He flipped on the light. The shadows scurried to the farthest corners. Fat Cat and Mamma Cat, curled in the middle of the air mattress, lifted their heads and blinked in accusation.

"Hey, you two," Sonny quipped and moved to pet them. Mamma Cat appeared on his doorstep over a year ago with a litter of half-grown kittens. Sonny found homes for all but Fat Cat, who'd been the size of Goliath even then. He lowered himself to the mattress's edge and rubbed them both. "Whatcha been up to tonight?"

Fat Cat yawned and then playfully swatted Sonny's hand while Mamma Cat resumed her sleeping. Sonny pulled Fat Cat into his lap and gazed around the room while he scratched the feline into a purr.

Sonny thought about Tanya, the worry marring her eyes, the way she looked over her shoulder every few minutes. Tanya O'Brien was trapped. Maurice Salazar had driven her to the point of hiding guns everywhere and paying a bodyguard. She didn't feel safe, even in her own home.

The same desperation that hounded Tanya began seeping into Sonny's spirit. As long as Salazar was at large, Sonny was as trapped as Tanya. This tiny apartment could become his cage if he didn't stop that maniac and ensure Tanya's safety.

After tonight's spill-your-guts session with her, Sonny knew that if he didn't get some space Coty would single-handedly snare his heart. And even though Tanya's guard collapsed, the usual doubt in her eyes cautioned him against falling headlong in love with her . . . and her child.

Besides, Sonny wasn't so daft that he couldn't see the stark differences between him and Tanya. She probably wanted a man like Shelly's dentist friend—someone who drove a high-dollar car and lived a life of prestige. With her looks and education she could no doubt have all that and more. While Sonny certainly didn't think he wasn't good enough for Tanya, he also knew there were some molds he could never fit. Despite the fact that he was educated, he still wasn't suit-and-tie material and never would be.

Sonny was a free spirit. He'd been born a free spirit. And he would stay a free spirit until death.

Now he was forced to live part-time in this claustrophobic apartment and interact with an enchanting woman who would probably never choose a free spirit for a husband—no matter how much her son loved him. The end result could easily cost Sonny's very soul. He'd vowed to never again set himself up to be hurt as much as Karen hurt him. He'd already lost one son. He didn't want to lose another—even one that he *wanted* to be his.

When his cell phone's beeping broke into his thoughts, Sonny automatically walked toward the microwave and picked up the phone. He'd left the cell when he went to play with Coty and hadn't looked to see if he had any messages all evening. Now the screen displayed

a text message from Tanya sent over an hour ago. He pressed enter
and read the note:

> **Sonny? Are you there? I saw you leave a few minutes ago
> and just hoped you were still planning to spend the night
> tonight. T.O.**

Sighing, Sonny wondered if she'd heard him arrive. If so, he
didn't need to respond. He told himself Tanya's concern stemmed
only from her need for safety and nothing more. Nevertheless, a
rivulet of hope threatened to swell into a flood of optimism.

Maybe she's warming to me as much as Coty is, he thought.
Sonny squelched the wish in its infancy. Until Tanya gave him
more encouragement than one evening with her guard down,
Sonny was playing it safe. Finally, he decided to go ahead and
respond, just in case she hadn't heard him arrive. He pressed the
respond button on the text message and tapped in his reply:

> **Yo, T.O., I'm here again and will be all night. As usual, if you
> need me, call my cell. And one more thing . . . forget every-
> thing I told you tonight. I don't want anyone 'round town to
> know. My mom would flip if she found out. I should have kept
> my big mouth shut. S.M.**

He'd barely laid down the phone when it beeped again. He
picked it up and read Tanya's reply:

> **Your secret is safe with me. C-U. T.O.**

A wad a tension unraveled in his gut. Sonny figured Tanya
O'Brien was a woman of her word and that his secret really was safe
with her. But that didn't mean his heart was.

"I've got to find out if Salazar is still alive," he whispered and flipped the phone shut. "And if he is, I've somehow got to stop him from ever coming after her again. That way, she's safe, and I can leave this trap."

Sonny went to sleep with that decision entrenched in his psyche and woke up with it fresh on his mind. It drove him through his morning and afternoon while he submitted a selection of freelance photos to several magazines.

Before heading toward Tanya's for the evening, Sonny decided to start the next day early and keep it focused. The goal was to find Salazar. He'd set up a vigil at Lone Star Transport and stick to the deed until he spotted Salazar or uncovered a lead to him. If it meant getting more assertive than merely watching, then so be it. Sonny didn't know what he'd do with Salazar once he found him, but he was determined to begin the journey.

Tanya inserted the last brick on the edge of the flower bed and then pulled a stray root from the soil. Satisfied, she rocked back on her heels and observed the benefits of her labor. The new bed she'd created around the oak only lacked the bag of peat moss sitting near the house. Then Tanya could add the wood fern she'd purchased at the nursery after dropping Coty off at her parents.

The child had been so excited to spend the night with Gran-da and Ma-Ma he'd barely noticed when Tanya left. As Tanya retrieved the peat moss, she'd never been more thankful for her parents' support. There had been an outbreak of an upper respiratory infection in the schools, so the week at the clinic had been wild, and there was still one more day to go. Having the evening to herself had helped Tanya relax and rejuvenate for Friday. It had also given her the freedom to keep an eye on the apartment and to know when Sonny Mansfield arrived.

Tanya set the bag of peat moss near the flower bed and tore into the top as the earthy smell pleased her senses. After dumping the bag onto the soil, she evenly distributed the contents around the bed. When a passing vehicle slowed, she glanced up in hopes that this one was Sonny. Instead, she noted Brad Riley pulling into his driveway. He waved. Tanya tossed aside the empty bag and waved back. Then, she sighed.

Earlier today, Dolly had mentioned Sonny for the first time in a month. Up until last night, Tanya hadn't wanted to talk to Dolly about him; but all that had now changed. Tanya had briefed her friend on last night's encounter. While she hadn't divulged Sonny's secret, she had hinted that he'd suffered a loss and that perhaps there was more substance to the guy than Tanya had originally assumed.

That's when Dolly had issued the challenge, "Ask him to church. See what happens. I'd wager my last nickel he'll accept."

So, Tanya had screwed up all her courage to do exactly that. She'd planned to casually wave at him when he arrived—which was usually by seven every evening. If he approached for chitchat she'd smoothly suggest he attend services with her and Coty Sunday morning and see what he said. But seven o'clock had now come and gone, and there was no sign of the man.

With a huff, Tanya eyed the flat of wood ferns. Fleetingly, she recalled Sonny's saying that some nights he might have to prowl around, as he put it. But Tanya had at least expected him to check in. After all, she was paying him to be her bodyguard. She worked the final bit of peat moss into the rich dirt and didn't try to analyze her true motives for wanting him to check in. The guy had a way of worming his way past a woman's defenses, whether he was the best choice for her or not.

And Tanya was determined to bring their relationship—if that's what you wanted to call it—to a crossroads. If there was no chance of Sonny Mansfield growing spiritually, then Tanya would limit their interactions to a professional level only. But if Sonny did show some interest in spiritual matters, then that could put a new spin on the whole situation. After last night, she'd been far too disposed toward the possibilities of deepening their friendship. However, Tanya needed to get *un*-disposed if there was no chance he'd ever be a spiritual partner.

She rocked back on her heels and gazed toward the setting sun. A late-August breeze danced around the yard and promised September would bring a relief to the Texas heat. Forecasters were predicting a colder than usual autumn and winter. Presently, Tanya had perspired all she wanted and cherished the thought of a cold autumn. On top of that, her back was aching with the constant bending.

"The fern can wait until tomorrow," she mumbled as a long, relaxing bath called her name.

When Sonny steered his truck into Tanya's driveway, he was simultaneously relieved and disappointed that Tanya and Coty weren't outdoors. However, he'd waited until nearly dark to arrive because he knew Tanya usually corralled Coty into a bath about now. He didn't want a repeat of last night's spill-your-guts encounter.

Despite that logic, a shroud of loneliness settled upon Sonny all the way up the creaking, wooden stairs that led to his apartment's door. Shouldering his backpack, he cast a last glance toward Tanya's yard before stepping inside the refrigerated room and encountering a couple of cats who were ready to engage with the great outdoors. Both Fat Cat and Mamma Cat darted out as he stepped in.

"It's getting too small for you too, huh?" he said over a chuckle.

Once inside, Sonny dropped the backpack on the air mattress and raided the fridge for a bottle of water. However, he'd barely flipped on the TV when his cell phone's bleep announced a text message.

He pulled the phone from his pocket and couldn't squelch the latent hope that Tanya's name might be on it. His hope found fulfillment when he pressed the button to retrieve the message. Expecting her to confirm that he was on guard, her simple request left his eyes widening:

Would you like to go to church with me this Sunday? I attend Bullard Community on 69. T.O.

Sonny jerked his head back and blinked. He hadn't been to church regularly since he left home for college. Once his mother wasn't in his space to force the issue, Sonny had broken away and never went back . . . except for holidays like Easter and Christmas.

While he searched for a way to squirm out of the invitation, Sonny gradually realized that this could be considered a date of sorts. That threw a new dimension on the whole request. With his mind jumping in several directions, he considered declining. His logical side reminded him that he didn't want to get hurt; but his other side—the side that never failed to notice her blue eyes—insisted he should accept.

Gritting his teeth, Sonny fought the battle of reason versus heart. Finally, the two came to a compromise. If he accepted, then perhaps it would bring their friendship to a crossroads, of sorts. Spending the day with Tanya would give Sonny the opportunity to determine if she was willing to take their relationship to something deeper . . . more promising.

Tanya refused to allow herself to hover over the phone after she sent the text message. Instead, she laid the cell on the bathroom counter and walked to her bedroom to change from her bathrobe into her night shirt. However, she'd only gotten halfway up the hall before she heard the phone's beep.

Spinning around, Tanya rushed back into the restroom, grabbed the phone, and flipped it open. Her hand unsteady, she finally pressed the appropriate button that revealed Sonny's response:

Sure. What time do we leave? S.M.

Tanya read and reread Sonny's reply before finally believing she wasn't hallucinating. Dolly was right. He *had* accepted her invitation.

Now she tumbled through a series of contradictory emotions that left her smiling and then wincing. *What will Mom and Dad think when I walk in with my bodyguard?* she wondered. Although both her parents had occasionally chatted with him and seemed to like him enough, Tanya hadn't even hinted that she and Sonny were more than professional acquaintances.

And now that she'd invited him to church, another issue posed itself: Tanya hadn't considered the Sunday lunch she shared each week with her parents. Her mother always cooked a meal that would make the angels sing and expected Tanya and Coty to eat until they could hold no more. Southern hospitality insisted that Tanya invite Sonny to go with her. If Tanya didn't invite him, she was sure her mother would.

"It's the only polite thing to do," she whispered before beginning a new message.

Sunday school starts at 9:45. Church at 10:45. I usually leave at 9:15. Can you join me at my parents' for lunch afterward? My mom will expect you to come as my guest. She always cooks enough for an army. T.O.

Tanya squeezed the phone and willed it to produce a new message soon. She was not disappointed:

I'm going to live dangerously and do both SS and church. This will make my mom happy—not to mention Jack, who's been trying to harass me into church for years. We can go in my truck. As for your mom's meal . . . I'll try to suffer through and pretend I like it. ;-) S.M.

Tanya chuckled and then was faced with a disturbing thought. *What if his going to church has nothing to do with spiritual interests and everything to do with pleasing his family . . . or me?* Tanya lifted her head and stared at her own reflection in the oval mirror. A wide-eyed woman with limp hair gazed back while the lingering smell of bath salts grew suffocating.

"Now what do I do?" She'd known of more than one man who attended church with their girlfriends until the wedding happened and then they never set foot in the sanctuary again. That wasn't the kind of marriage she'd always dreamed of.

Soon, Dolly's advice floated through her mind. *Just go with the flow.* At some point, she needed to stop analyzing all the *what if's* and simply wait and see.

"First things first," she whispered. "At least I know he's open to the idea. We'll just take it from there." She squeezed her eyes tight and prayed, *Lord, I'm going forward. Please stop this if it isn't Your will.*

Opening her eyes, Tanya tapped in her final message— "Works!"—and closed her phone.

CHAPTER FIFTEEN

Saturday morning Sonny pulled the rented SUV into the Arby's parking lot east of Lone Star Transport. Calculating the safest distance and smartest angle, Sonny chose a spot on Arby's east side and backed the truck into place. After lowering the automatic windows, he turned off the engine and shoved up the sleeves of his shirt. This was the second day in a row he'd chosen long sleeves to cover the Bronze Star tattoo. Sonny had no idea if Salazar had noticed it when they met at Spring Creek Barbeque, and didn't want to take any chances.

He retrieved his binoculars from the passenger seat and gazed toward the building's side entry, just as he'd done yesterday. Lifting the binoculars, he zoomed in on the small print along the parking curb. Yesterday, he'd noticed that a name was assigned to each of the six places nearest the doorway. He already knew Salazar's name wasn't on any of them, but Sonny had decided to jot down the names that were there for future follow-up. He grabbed the pen and notebook on his dashboard and scribbled down four of the names. Two of the parking places were occupied by a Mercedes and a Lincoln, so Sonny decided to retrieve those names later.

He gazed toward the loading area where a red, white, and blue truck was backing up to the dock. A single star claimed the door panel. Above it were the words Lone Star Transport.

Sonny slumped lower in his seat and tapped his fingers against the steering wheel. The morning sun already heated the breeze that whispered through the cab. He scratched at the fake beard that prickled anew with every degree the thermometer increased. He hated the feel of the beard as much as he despised the dark wig. But the black beard and hair together transformed Sonny's appearance to the point that he'd even fooled Jack once. The last thing he needed was to be recognized—because today he planned to stop the mere watching and get up close and personal. Something had to crack in this case, or Sonny was going to smash it open himself.

"God, if you're watching," he whispered, "please don't let today be another flop. You know Jack's been hassling me for years about You. Well . . . this is one deal I'm beginning to think Jack might be right about. I need Your help here."

Straightening, Sonny lifted the binoculars, and scanned the lot again. He thought about the prayer he'd just spoken and wondered why he hadn't prayed more on his cases. The whole experience certainly left him feeling more optimistic about the day that started at seven thirty.

He'd left the apartment after seeing Tanya let out her dog. Sonny sent her a text message, saying he had a case to deal with and was leaving early. She'd responded that she was going to her parents for the day and would be fine. He never told her that he'd spent all day yesterday in Ft. Worth. If not for the fact that he'd agreed to stay at the apartment every night, Sonny would have gotten a hotel last night. But his desire to protect Tanya had meant his driving home last night and a repeat trip to Ft. Worth this morning.

Sonny checked his watch. He'd left home three and a half hours ago. His lids growing heavy, he forced himself to stay awake and focus on the task at hand. He reached for the phony package in the passenger seat, but the sight of a black Cadillac rolling into the parking lot shook his plans. He stiffened and then shrank into the seat until he could barely see over the top of the dashboard.

The Cadillac glided toward the loading dock and stopped in an unmarked parking place. As suspected, Maurice Salazar emerged. Dressed in a gray suit, he glanced around the lot before slipping into the loading area.

Sonny sat up and strained for any signs of him but saw nothing more than what looked like a truck being packed. At this angle, he only caught an occasional glimpse of a workman's uniform. What they were putting inside the truck was left to be seen.

"Maybe it's time to find out," Sonny whispered and pulled his sunglasses from his shirt pocket. Sliding on the glasses completed his disguise. Last, he pulled down his sleeves until the Bronze Star was covered.

Sonny clicked the ignition key backward, rolled up the electric windows, and retrieved the package from the floorboard. He'd gone online, chosen a Seattle name and address for the recipient, and plugged in a fake Dallas address for the sender. He was sure the poor guy in Seattle would spend many nights wondering why someone in Dallas had sent him a block of wood.

"Whatever works," he said through a chuckle.

Sonny opened the door and stepped out. Once the door was locked, he strode toward Lone Star Transport and debated how best to make his entry. The concealed 9 mm Smith & Wesson, strapped beneath the leg of his loose jeans, offered an extra measure of support. He'd been licensed to carry a gun for years and had never been more glad than today. Sonny had no idea what might transpire once he entered the business.

A rash of perspiration erupted along his collar, and Sonny felt like a kid riding his first roller coaster. This venture was every bit as terrifying as it was thrilling. And he'd never loved his job more than now . . . because today he was putting his life on the line for Tanya O'Brien.

Maurice Salazar stomped into his office, slammed the door, and marched to the corner bar, loaded with as much alcohol as the walls were loaded with fine art. He'd downed two shots of Scotch before he paused long enough to get some ice from the refrigerator.

It's bad enough that the shipment is behind schedule, he fumed. *Now they bust a kilo on the floor!* Maurice had walked into the hidden room, reserved for the sole purpose of cutting cocaine, while the idiots were scrambling to clean up the mess. He examined his stinging knuckles and hoped the blows he'd given the fool who made the mistake would encourage him to never repeat it.

The whole operation had taken the first bad turn last week when Maurice received a call from Police Chief Rolf Whitaker, telling him they were being watched and to be extra careful. A few times, Maurice had seen too many patrol cars cruising the neighborhood. As long as Rolf was on Maurice's payroll, getting busted was more of an annoyance than anything else. Nevertheless, Maurice still heeded the chief's warning and curbed any unnecessary activities.

On top of that, his right hand man had nearly been killed in a surprise attack two nights ago. Drake's getting shot in the Rontelli raid had delayed the next cocaine shipment. During the raid, a bullet lodged near Drake's heart. Even though the surgery was successful, he was just now leaving ICU.

The family needed Drake too much for him to die. He knew how to negotiate the border . . . how to kill without a flinch. And even though he'd gotten himself shot, he'd never break a package of the fine, white powder that supported so many of Maurice's habits. Of course, Maurice had never touched anything stronger than Scotch and had no plans of doing so. But as long as there were idiots who paid for cocaine, he'd distribute it.

The final shot of Scotch flowed over the ice like liquid gold, and Maurice pulled a Coke from the fridge and filled the glass. This time, he drank slower and enjoyed more. While the whiskey wove its calming spell through his veins, Maurice stopped near the window. He yanked open the blinds and glared past the parking lot to the traffic zipping by.

"Stupid, stupid, stupid," he mumbled and then added a few more edicts against Drake's attacker. He'd depended on Drake to pull off the final delivery tonight. He was the best—the only one the family trusted with so much wealth.

Scanning the parking lot, Maurice hated to admit the inevitable. Tonight, *he* was going to be forced to drive to their central distribution center in Kansas. Despite the signs that Thomas was as trustworthy as Drake, Maurice couldn't allow him to be alone with over a thousand kilos of cut cocaine . . . or the millions that would trade hands.

Even in the face of his fuming, the whiskey began to ease his nerves and mellow his mind. As his thoughts turned toward Tanya O'Brien, a dark-haired man walking from the Arby's parking lot snared his attention. The guy wore sunglasses, carried a package under one arm, and strode toward Lone Star Transport with a confidence that struck Maurice as oddly familiar.

Deciding the man must be one of hundreds of the regular Lone Star customers, Maurice pivoted from the window, claimed his desk chair, and set his glass on a coaster. He pulled an aging photo album out of a drawer and opened it like a connoisseur of rare collectibles. Maurice had taken special pains to align the shots he'd stolen of Tanya next to the photos of Eva. Their resemblance still struck him as astonishing and still moved him to the core. Maurice had been so close to making Tanya his last month, but Sonny Mansfield had thwarted his and Drake's attempts at taking her. Poor Drake had even received a flesh wound that night as well.

"I didn't want to hurt you, Tanya," he whispered and stroked her photo as if caressing her cheek. "Once I got you, I'd make you love me. I *know* I could—just like Eva."

He turned the page and absorbed more of Tanya. Closing his eyes, Maurice dreamed of their first days together. He wouldn't rush her. He'd give her time to get used to him . . . to fall in love. And then, when she was ready . . . Maurice inhaled deeply and imagined the smell of her hair, the feel of her satin skin, the taste of her lips.

He opened his eyes and spotted the last photo he'd snapped while watching her house. This picture featured Sonny and Tanya together, and had been the final confirmation that the man Maurice had hired had turned bodyguard. Never had Maurice hated so fully. He'd thought about killing Sonny several times, and still hadn't completely dismissed the option.

After Maurice downed the final dregs of his drink and plunked the glass back on the desk, that familiar man walking across the parking lot barged back into his mind. Narrowing his eyes, he stared across the room while instinct insisted he not ignore that person. Standing, Maurice whipped back around and searched the lot for the man. He spotted the guy hovering near the loading dock.

He's had time to get to the front mailing desk by now, Maurice thought as the police chief's warning resounded through him with new intensity.

His gut going hard, he whipped out his cell phone and speed dialed Thomas. The second his voice came over the line, Maurice said, "Man with package near loading dock. Be ready," and hung up. He doubled-checked the Heckler & Koch Elite .45 strapped beneath his suit coat, and stormed the hallway.

* * *

Near the loading dock, Sonny debated his options. He could either attempt to slip by the men who'd yet to spot him, or act like an ignorant customer. When a balding man with sharp eyes appeared in his path, Sonny ruled out slipping by him.

"Oh, dude, you scared me," Sonny said in the singsong voice of a surfer. "I, like, have a package that needs to be mailed, man." Thankful his dark glasses hid his eyes, Sonny examined the area for any signs of foul play.

"Go to the front desk," the man barked. "Can't you see this is the loading dock? We only load packages that are already paid for."

A metal door banged open and Salazar rushed the dock.

Sonny stopped a flinch.

"What do you want?" Salazar demanded.

"Oh, dude!" Sonny lifted his hand and stepped back. "I was just wanting to, like, mail a package here."

Maurice studied him like he should suspect something, but wasn't sure what. "Go to the front office if you want to mail something," he growled and pointed toward the building's main entrance. "You have no business back here."

Sonny looked down and mumbled something about UPS. Then, he noticed a streak of fine, white powder along the front of the dockhand's shirt. Keeping his face impassive, he adjusted his sunglasses and debated the source of the powder.

Looks like powdered sugar, he thought. That could mean the guy was eating a doughnut. Or it could mean he'd been cutting cocaine with the sugar. Imported cocaine was often brought into the United States pure, and cut 10 to 1 with powdered sugar.

Tanya had said she thought Salazar might be linked to organized crime. Owning a transport business to cover successfully distributing large shipments of cocaine was about as organized as you could get.

Sonny searched for a way to somehow get onto the dock . . . or at least glean a clue.

When Salazar stepped toward him, Sonny drew on his high school theater training. "Man," he groaned, "I don't feel so good now." Moaning, he hunched forward and staggered toward the dockhand. "I think I'm going to be sick." With a lunge, he ran headlong into the man and reached out as if he were trying to stop himself from falling. Purposefully planting his hand in the center of the white streak, Sonny continued stumbling past him while Salazar released a round of curses.

"Get away from me!" the dockhand bellowed and pushed at his arms.

"Get him out of here!" Salazar commanded.

Nevertheless, Sonny kept up his momentum until he crashed into the dock, dropped his package, and writhed in an attempt to see what was inside the truck. The vehicle's contents consisted of rows of neatly stacked boxes that could have held anything. Sonny flopped in the other direction and spotted a door ajar along the loading dock's west well. A startled man emerged, holding a plastic bag, half full of white powder. Then, the door snapped shut.

Hard hands shoved Sonny back the way he came. He lurched into giant strides to keep from sprawling face first onto the concrete. His package hit his back as the dockhand's cursing mingled with Salazar's command, "Get out of here! Take your box to the post office!"

"But I need a bathroom, man," Sonny demanded. Bracing his fists on his bent knees, he faked a heave.

"Not on my parking lot!" Salazar screamed and attempted to kick Sonny.

Maintaining his wobbly stance, Sonny sidestepped the kick. Keeping his fist curled to protect the traces of powder, he retrieved the box and staggered around the side of the building as if he had every intention of seeking a men's room.

But as soon as he saw the glass doorway, he glanced over his shoulder. When he spotted no one, Sonny turned and trotted back toward Arby's. Fist tight, he walked into the restaurant and went straight to the men's room. Once inside, he removed his sunglasses, locked the door, dumped the package in the trash can, and opened his fist.

A hard examination proved traces of the white powder still remained along the middle of his palm. Sonny touched the tip of his tongue to the powder and waited for the telltale powdered sugar sweetness.

"Just what I thought," he said with a nod before pulling out his cell phone and pressing Jack's speed dial number. The packages in the back of the van looked too uniform to belong to random customers; and the powder in that plastic bag he glimpsed looked too white. While he certainly hadn't expected to stumble onto a cocaine operation, Sonny would take whatever breaks he got. As long as Salazar was behind bars, he couldn't hurt Tanya. Sonny didn't care why he landed there, as long as he was out of circulation.

Jack answered on the fifth ring.

"Yo," Sonny said, his low voice echoing off the tiled walls.

"Yo, yourself!" Jack replied. "Whazup?"

"In Ft. Worth. At Lone Star Transport."

"Really? Have any luck this time?"

"Spotted Salazar," Sonny affirmed. "Remember that guy you went to police academy with? You told me the other day he was on the force in Ft. Worth."

"Dallas, actually," Jack replied.

"Looks like Salazar might be involved in cocaine distribution," Sonny explained, eyeing his palm.

"Cocaine?"

"Yeah," Sonny drawled. "I thought maybe if you made a phone call it would be better than a generic nine-one-one call from me," Sonny replied and eyed himself in the mirror. The scraggy beard and limp hair made him look like a society dropout.

"Are you sure it's cocaine?"

"Well, it's like this," Sonny said. "It looks like cocaine. It's as sweet as powdered sugar. I saw a man with a plastic bag half full of white powder . . . and a truck loaded with neat boxes all stacked in nice rows. And Salazar and his hired hand are both acting like mamma bears, protecting their den. You tell me what you think it is."

"Remind me of the address," Jack said.

Sonny recited the address. "I'll call Cooper and see if he knows anyone on the Ft. Worth force he can call to get out there pronto."

"Good," Sonny said. "And tell 'em to hurry. Looks like they might pull out soon."

"I'll call you back as soon as I know something," Jack replied.

"Thanks." Sonny hung up.

He debated whether to wait and see if the raid happened or make a swift exit. The chance that Salazar might get suspicious and come looking for him nearly drove him to hurry back to his truck and get out of Ft. Worth. But his curiosity demanded he stay for the inevitable raid. He'd like to be able to report an eyewitness arrest to Tanya and assure her that Salazar would no longer be a problem.

Sonny left the bathroom and spotted a wire rack holding free real estate guides that were the size of a newspaper. He grabbed one and then bought a cup of coffee. A corner booth waited on the other side of the trash bin.

Only when Sonny slid in and hid behind the paper did he notice his shirtsleeve was shoved up enough to reveal part of the star tattoo. Wrinkling his brow, Sonny tried to remember when the sleeve might have come up, but couldn't. He yanked it back down and assured himself that he must have subconsciously pushed up the sleeve in an attempt to alleviate the heat.

Sonny tried to read the paper, but the words blurred as his tension increased. His second glance around the paper confirmed that he should have left while he could. Salazar entered the restaurant, and his determined expression suggested he wasn't interested in a roast beef sandwich. He scanned the place with a keen eye that said he was looking for someone. The aroma of coffee that once enticed now smothered. Sonny had never felt more trapped . . . or more at risk. Salazar was probably packing a gun and wouldn't mind jeopardizing the safety of the whole restaurant to take down just one.

Sonny hunkered behind the paper and counted to ten before daring another glance around the edge. This time, he caught sight of Salazar walking toward the men's room. Sonny recalled throwing away the package and bit back a commentary on his own negligence. If Salazar saw the package, he'd know for certain Sonny had been in the restaurant and that he might still be there.

CHAPTER SIXTEEN

Tanya sat on her parents' porch, watching her dad splash with Coty in the new backyard pool. She'd started out in the water with Coty, who was now into his second hour. About forty-five minutes ago, Ed had joined them, and Tanya took a break.

Wearing a swimsuit cover and flip-flops, Tanya now enjoyed the lounge while her father was teaching Coty the first steps of swimming. Tanya had known how to swim as long as she could remember because Ed had taught her to swim nearly as soon as she learned how to walk. Presently, Coty stood on the ladder's top rung and jumped toward Ed O'Brien with a trust that couldn't be feigned.

Her parents' puppy, a full-blooded, animal shelter mutt the color of a dirty mop, ran around the pool and gleefully yelped every time a new surge of water splashed out. Squealing, Coty commanded his grandfather to take him to the side so he could splash the pup some more.

Tanya smiled, stretched in the lawn chair, and indulged the yawn creeping up her throat. Without the cooling relief of her damp hair and swimsuit, the heat would be almost unbearable. But as things stood, the warmth worked like a pleasant drug that left Tanya's eyes heavy. Fingering her hair, she enjoyed the relaxation.

She wondered what Sonny was doing. He'd mentioned a case, and Tanya hoped he wasn't in any kind of danger. Who knew where the man's job landed him. She wondered if he'd thought about church tomorrow or if he might be looking forward to it. With every hour that passed, Tanya anticipated their day together all the more. And every time Coty had asked "Where Sonny?" she'd hoped that all her logical concerns were soon swept away. Coty was ready for a father; and for the first time in her life, Tanya was ready for a husband. Looking back on the relationships she'd had, Tanya wondered if her hesitation might have involved her own independence as much as her search for the model husband. But during the last couple of years, her independence had been shaken by her stalker and she couldn't deny she'd gladly give up some independence for the feeling of safety of having someone like Sonny always by her side.

Her mother walked onto the porch, and the screen door snapped shut behind her. Holding a tray laden with two glasses of iced tea and a full pitcher, and wearing a long straight skirt and eyelet blouse, she personified the epitome of the southern hostess. "Have a glass," she said and extended the tray toward Tanya.

"Thanks," Tanya said and reached for her tea.

Shirley placed the tray on the patio table and settled into a lawn chair. "They're having the time of their lives," she said and waved toward the two.

"Yeah," Tanya agreed and sipped the sweet liquid.

"So . . . what's on your mind these days, girly?" Shirley questioned.

Tanya shot her mother a sideways glance. "Who says I've got something on my mind?" she said through a smile.

Her mom's auburn brows arched over curious, brown eyes that candidly revealed her suspicions—and the fact that she didn't buy

Tanya's stall tactic. Earlier, when Tanya had casually mentioned that Sonny Mansfield would be attending church and lunch with her tomorrow, Shirley never blinked. Now her appraisal suggested she'd assimilated all the clues and suspected there were more details.

Normally Shirley didn't ask, and Tanya told when she was ready. But Tanya figured the bath scenario coupled with Sonny's church attendance was simply too much for Shirley to remain silent.

Tanya picked at the hem of her swimsuit cover and finally admitted the stark truth, "There seems to be something between Sonny and me that I never expected to happen."

"Yes," Shirley stated with no hint of surprise.

Tanya cut her a glance to confirm her mother's knowing. "You aren't surprised?"

"Not in the least. I've only seen you together once when we were playing croquet with Sean and Coty, but—"

"We'd only just met then," Tanya defended.

"But there were already sparks between you—even then," Shirley said with an intuitive grin. "Then, the way you talked about Sonny after he fought those criminals for you . . . and if that's not enough, Coty mentions Sonny every time I'm with him. Now Sonny's setting up a swing set, giving Coty baths, and going to church with you. I put two and two together and figured he was in your lives far more than a typical bodyguard." She took a long draw on her tea and gazed toward Coty's splashing.

"He's not exactly the type I envisioned," Tanya admitted.

"But you like him anyway?"

"Yes," she admitted. "He walks to the beat of his own tune, and I've accepted that. But my main concern now is that he doesn't seem to be a spiritual giant by a long shot."

"And you always did want a spiritual giant," Shirley mused.

Tanya eyed her mother, whose attention remained fixed upon the swimmers.

"I wondered if you'd ever be content to settle for normal," she added.

"What?" Tanya exclaimed.

With a chuckle, Shirley patted her daughter's arm. "Sorry, dear, I didn't mean to be so pointed. It's just that you've rejected so many decent men that I'd almost lost hope. I've wanted to tell you for some time that most young men are, well, like most young women. There's plenty of room for growth." Shirley tucked an unruly lock into her hair clip.

Gazing at her mom, Tanya wondered if she and Dolly Lennon had been reading the same script.

"I guess you've really been staged for setting your standards so high, though." Shirley sighed. "Your father and I had you in our late thirties, and by that point, we'd both matured quite a bit. So you'd naturally want a man as deep as your dad. But sometimes, deep only happens with maturity, and maturity happens with time."

"But I don't even know if he's a Christian," Tanya defended.

"Yes, that *is* important. While you shouldn't expect him to be perfect, you certainly don't want to throw all standards to the wind either," she said with a sage nod. "I recommend you find out soon and then decide if you can live with his weaknesses. Because if Coty's half as in love with him as he seems, and if there's going to be a break-off, the sooner, the safer." This time, her gaze was as direct as her words.

"Yeah," Tanya agreed and sighed. *The sooner, the safer,* she thought and knew without a doubt that tomorrow would be a pivotal day.

The second Maurice disappeared down the hallway, Sonny deserted the paper and coffee and hurried to the nearest exit. While he wasn't daft enough to remain in the restaurant like some easy target, Sonny still wasn't ready to drive off either. Once outside, he scanned the area for options while the east Texas heat, radiating off the concrete, crept up his neck.

A Starbuck's Coffee shop, one business down, offered an option. A booth near the window would give Sonny a clear view of Lone Star Transport. *Or give Maurice a clear view of me,* he reasoned, then dismissed the idea. With another glance over his shoulder, Sonny finally decided to make the SUV his refuge. He darted toward the vehicle and was opening the cab door when Maurice rounded the building with a cell phone to his ear.

Wildly, he scanned the parking lot and then spotted Sonny the second he slid behind the wheel. Maurice snapped the phone shut, dropped it into his shirt pocket, and reached inside his suit coat.

Sonny's pulse thumped in his temples. He fumbled with his keys until the SUV key miraculously slipped into place. The engine purred to life.

When Maurice's hand slid from inside his coat, he held a hand-gun.

God help me, Sonny prayed and had never meant it more. He rammed the vehicle into drive and pressed the accelerator while steering straight for Salazar.

His eyes widening, the criminal fired a wayward shot before tumbling out of the SUV's path.

Sonny darted into creeping traffic midst a chorus of angry honking. A last glance over his shoulder revealed Salazar racing toward his Cadillac. Sonny's heart pulsed in sequence with Salazar's feet pounding the pavement.

"Come on," he growled as he neared an intersection. "We've got to make this green light." The light turned red. He slammed his fist against the steering wheel and looked into his rearview mirror. A siren's whine began as a distant threat but loomed closer by the second. Soon, an entourage of lights flashed in his mirror.

The light turned green. Sonny rolled through the intersection, pulled into a gas station, and positioned the vehicle for a clear view of the show. Presently, Salazar's Cadillac was being hemmed in by a team of professionals who weren't applauding his extracurricular activities.

Breathing easy, Sonny closed his eyes, rested his head against the seat, and realized his body was covered in a thin film of sweat. He cranked up the air-conditioner and soaked in the cool. Once his hands had steadied, Sonny retrieved his cell phone from his belt harness. After flipping it open, he pressed Jack's speed dial number and waited until his brother answered.

"Cooper said he was going to make the call," Jack said without a greeting.

"He did!" Sonny exclaimed. "There are black-and-whites all over that place already."

"Yeah. Cooper also called back and said there'd been a collective effort on that place for a while. They were close anyway—just waiting for something to give," Jack explained.

"Whatever . . . he's fried and Tanya's free. Thank God," he added without even thinking.

"Glad to hear you say *that*," Jack replied.

"I'm not half the heathen you think I am," Sonny retorted. "I'm even going to church tomorrow."

"Help! Murder! It's the sign of the apocalypse!" Jack teased. "Whatever possessed you?"

"Ha, Ha," Sonny chided and wiped at his damp forehead with unsteady fingers. "I happen to be going with Tanya."

"Now I'm getting the whole picture," Jack drawled.

"Well, maybe you could share it with me. I'm still not sure I've got the whole picture." Sonny eased back into traffic and cast a final glance in his rearview mirror. Straining, he caught a brief glimpse of Salazar, sprawled against the side of his car. Sonny smiled and gassed the SUV.

"And what church does Tanya go to?"

"Who wants to know?"

"The mouse in my pocket," Jack shot.

Sonny laughed. "Seems like she said it was Bullard Community. They're on sixty-nine, right?"

"Yep. I know *exactly* where that is. That's a good group of people, from what I understand."

"Great!" Sonny returned as a motorcycle cut in front of him. He braked and winced. "Listen, I gotta go. I'm in some traffic and not in the mood to be smashed because I was on my cell. I can't chew gum and walk at the same time."

"Gotcha," Jack replied and then added, "You know I'm still praying for you, right?"

"Yeah," Sonny said on a sigh. "And that's probably what just saved my hide. Salazar had drawn a bull's-eye on my forehead."

"Did he *shoot* at you?" Jack croaked.

"Once. But he missed because I was trying to run over him."

"I'm going to try to pull some more strings," Jack said. "We need to make sure he stays under lock and key. He might try to come after you again if he gets out."

"I'm in disguise," Sonny explained.

"We can't be too careful," Jack said before ending the call.

CHAPTER SEVENTEEN

Tanya covered Coty in his toddler bed and straightened. A surge of motherly love insisted she nudge the damp hair from his forehead and brush her lips where the lock had been. Coty had played in the pool until lunch and then played some more. After wearing out Gran-da, he'd nearly exhausted Tanya. The child had barely protested when Tanya loaded him into the car seat. He'd been asleep by the time she left her parents' neighborhood.

Now Tanya had tucked him in for an afternoon nap. Covering a yawn, she widened her eyes and commanded herself to stay awake. Tanya needed to pay some bills and straighten the living room. She'd taken a catnap after drinking the tea at her mom's, but the romp in the pool left her drowsy all over again.

I'm acting like a slug, she thought and eyed her bed as she entered her room. Still resisting, Tanya moved toward the window and sneaked a peak out the blinds to see if Sonny had arrived. A disappointed sigh accompanied her moving away from the blinds.

"You might as well be a lovesick teenager," she scolded and wondered if her attachment to Sonny was already deeper than she'd admitted to herself . . . or anyone else.

Settling at the desk, she picked up her pen and checkbook and hoped Sonny's case didn't keep him out past nightfall. After Maurice had cut her phone lines, she'd grown to hate the very thought of Sonny's not being on guard.

On an impulse, Tanya set aside the pen and checkbook and reached for the Bible resting on the desk's edge. Tanya opened the Word to Psalm 23 and read the familiar passage that had comforted her many nights since she arrived from Korea. After the words sank into her heart and calmed her nerves, she held the opened Bible against her heart and prayed, "Oh God, please continue to keep me safe. And thanks again for sending Sonny Mansfield."

An engine's low rumble tugged her gaze back to the window. Tanya dropped the Bible, rushed back to the window, and inched apart the blinds.

As suspected, Sonny's gleaming truck halted in the driveway. A sense of safety and peace mixed with the increasing spark that couldn't be squelched. When he slammed the truck's door, Tanya fully expected him to go into the apartment. Instead, he strode toward her house.

Gasping, she hurried to her dresser mirror. The woman who peered back looked like a damp-haired street bum. She grabbed a brush, whacked at her hair, and fished a tube of lip gloss from a cosmetic bag in her top drawer. Thankfully, her hours in the sun had christened her skin with a pink glow.

She huffed and rubbed at her rumpled T-shirt and linen Capris. "That'll have to do," she said as the doorbell rang.

By the time Tanya reached the front door, her legs were unsteady. As she opened the door, she understood why. Tanya had invited Sonny to church since the last time they talked; and that invitation could be viewed as a low-key date of sorts. The prospect changed everything. Sonny was no longer merely her bodyguard, he was now a friend . . . a potential boyfriend.

She smiled into his face and hoped her lips weren't as wobbly as they felt. "Hi!" she said.

"Hi, yourself," he quipped and responded to her silent invitation to enter.

When Tanya shut the door and turned to face him, she noticed the dark circles under his eyes.

"I've got some very good news," he proclaimed, his face animated despite the haggard veil. "You are *not* going to believe it."

"What?" Tanya asked, her mind racing in sequence with her pulse.

"Maurice Salazar." He drew an invisible line across the center of his neck.

"Dead?" she gasped.

"No, arrested. I think you know we did a trace on his license number a few weeks ago. It was registered to a business in Ft. Worth—Lone Star Transport. We've been watching it off and on. I went back yesterday and today and wound up stumbling into a cocaine operation. Short story—I called the police and whammy!" He clapped his hands. "He's been arrested."

"A-arrested?" she repeated and grappled with the full implications.

"Yep. In the slammer. Out of your life. Up to his eyes in *big trouble.*"

Dumbfounded, Tanya stared at Sonny as a slow tremble preceded hot tears. Then the stalking upheaval began replaying in her mind. Tanya had grown so accustomed to living in fear she wasn't certain she knew how to live in freedom anymore. She gazed up into Sonny's tired face as a wave of gratitude nearly overwhelmed her.

The desire to fling herself into his arms sprang out of nowhere. She wanted to hug him, to absorb his strength until every ounce of fear completely drained away forever. By some miracle, Tanya stopped the impulse. Instead of hugging him, she covered her face and surrendered to the tears that wouldn't be stopped. The terror, the sleepless nights, the worries, the nightmares . . . all of it drained from her body through the release of those tears.

And when Sonny's comforting hand rested on her shoulder . . . when he moved close and simply said, "Oh, Tanya," her desire for comfort overrode her former resolve; and she leaned toward him. Sonny's arms slipped around her and pulled her close. Tanya clung to him like the lifeline he'd been. She drank of his strength, reveled in his support.

"I'm so sorry all this happened," he said. "And I couldn't live with myself if he hurt you. I *had* to find him, and I'm thinking maybe God went before me and somehow pulled it all together. Like I said, Maurice Salazar is going to be so busy for so long, he'll forget you ever existed. I hope they put him *under* the jail."

"Thank you . . . thank you so much," Tanya hurried. Gulping like a child she tried to gain control of her emotions while fumbling for the box of tissues sitting on the coffee table.

Sonny reached for the box and tucked a tissue into her fist, balled against his chest. She mopped at her face and went for more, but Sonny beat her to the task and offered several fresh tissues.

Once she'd blown her nose, Tanya instinctively moved back to the source of comfort like a hurt child needing the assurance that all really would be well. She snuggled into Sonny's arms and rested her head on his chest. He stroked her hair, and Tanya closed her eyes and absorbed the new sense of safety.

Everything is going to be all right, she told herself. *Salazar is going to prison. Coty and I will be fine. I can get on with my life.*

A long sigh marked the moment Tanya floated back to reality . . . to the full realization that she was clinging to Sonny Mansfield . . . and that his heart was pounding as if he'd been running the block. Tanya's pulse leaped to the rhythm of his, and she recalled the few times she'd allowed a man close enough for a kiss. Never, had she experienced such a sudden rush of chemistry. Her eyes inched wider, and she wondered how she'd landed in this spot and how she could extract herself with some measure of dignity.

The issues in their relationship sprang to the center of her thoughts, and Tanya knew she shouldn't have let herself fall into this situation. She didn't even know where Sonny stood spiritually, and that was the most important element in her world. If it wasn't that important to him, then she was surely leading him on; and Tanya O'Brien *never* led men on.

She stiffened, despite her resolve to suavely extract herself from his arms. His arms loosened, and Tanya gently pulled away. By the time she'd put some distance between them and lifted her head, her face had heated past the point of hiding the blush. Her only hope was that her sun-kissed cheeks might camouflage the obvious.

"I'm s-sorry," she stammered. "I somehow threw myself at you."

Sonny observed Tanya and wondered if she even halfway suspected the effect she'd had on him. He certainly hadn't expected to feel her in his arms, but he'd enjoyed the moment and longed for more. Her warmth would fuel his dreams just as her floral perfume fueled his senses. The urge to kiss her had nearly been too great to resist. If the same situation had unfolded ten years ago, he'd have given in. But this wasn't ten years ago, and Sonny wasn't half as selfish as he'd been then. His growing respect for Tanya insisted he not take advantage of her. So he'd simply absorbed the hug and hoped it was the first of many.

Now she looked at him like she'd fallen into the most hideous of sins, and the whole situation struck Sonny's exhausted mind as humorous. He laughed and didn't even know why.

"What's so funny?" she challenged.

"I don't know." He shrugged and for once wished he weren't half so spontaneous. "Maybe the look on your face," he added.

Her fallen-angel awe was replaced by a pair of stiffening lips and sharpening eyes.

"I'm sorry," Sonny said and rubbed his eyes. "I'm loony, I guess. It's been a wild day. I stumbled into enough cocaine to sink a ship and then Salazar tried to kill me."

"What?" she croaked.

Sonny slipped his hands into his jeans pocket. "Yeah. He shot at me. Fortunately, I had a bigger weapon—an SUV I rented—and I tried to run over him." He told himself not to look at her lips, but looked anyway. Sonny still wanted to kiss her, whether it was honorable or not.

Tanya's baby blues spoke the thanks her voice didn't express, and that only upped the urge to better acquaint his lips with hers.

Sonny's straightened his spine, hardened his resolve, and stepped toward the front window. He opened the blinds, stared at nothing, and wondered if she felt the chemistry as strongly as he did. Whether she did or not, Tanya O'Brien was a good, Christian woman and Sonny would treat her that way. She was the kind of woman his mother would be glad he brought home, and Sonny was getting old enough to appreciate that kind of woman. He just wasn't certain he would ever be worthy.

"I'm not good enough for you, you know," he said and realized he'd actually verbalized his thoughts *after* they'd tumbled out.

The silence spoke her surprise, but Sonny figured she wasn't any more surprised than he was.

"I don't know why you think that," she finally said, and her soft voice was so close Sonny knew she'd neared.

He didn't turn around for the sole reason that he didn't want to flirt with temptation. Sonny wasn't sure he was strong enough to resist much longer . . . and was just as unsure that she'd resist. But if they did kiss, Sonny wanted it to be for the right reasons—not just because Tanya was upset and weak and grateful. When their relationship moved to that level, Sonny wanted her to mean it, not regret it.

"You're way more—you're just a better person than I am," he eventually blurted.

"By whose standards?"

Sonny cut a glance to the left and glimpsed her.

"If you're talking God's standards," she continued, "we're all on the same plane. I need a Savior as much as anyone. Without Christ, I'm bad news, Sonny. No telling what I'd do or where I'd be."

He turned to face her. Her candid appraisal surprised him as much as her words. "You really believe that?"

A simple nod was her only answer. He gazed past her, toward a massive landscape painting that hung above a loveseat. He strained to see if Tanya's name was in the signature corner but couldn't make it out. The woman certainly possessed ample talent . . . and class. On top of all that, she seemed to have a thing going with God that Sonny wondered if he could ever achieve.

"Sometimes I wonder if God gave up on me a long time ago," he admitted.

"God never gives up on anyone," Tanya said and rested her hand on his arm. This time, the touch held more support than spark.

Sonny covered her hand with his and raised it. He pressed his lips against her fingers in a salute to her virtue. Then he lowered her hand and said, "You're an angel, Tanya O'Brien. I'm sure God is proud of you." He squeezed her fingers. "Me? That's another matter."

"Have you asked Him how he feels about you, Sonny?" Tanya questioned, and the intensity in her eyes implied his answer was of utmost importance.

"No," he admitted and released her hand. "But maybe I need to, huh?"

"I'm praying you will," she said, and Sonny sensed an underlying meaning he knew would fully hit him later. For now, his mind was too muddled to think straight. He'd nearly kissed Tanya, and now they were somehow talking about God. The two encounters weren't mixing in his mind, and Sonny was growing more bewildered by the minute.

He yawned and recalled the last couple of days. Sonny had never been able to sleep much during an intense investigation. The stress of taking down Salazar was now descending on his mind like a dense fog.

"You're tired," Tanya said.

"Yes," he simply answered. "It always hits me like this—after an investigation is over."

"Are you going to stay in the apartment again tonight?" she asked, and her eyes begged him not to go home.

Sonny strained to make the leap to the new subject and finally connected. "Sure thing," he said, "if that's what you want."

Her silent nod affirmed her desires. "If you don't mind. I'd still feel safer, for a while anyway."

"Sure." He shrugged and yawned again. "Look, why don't I go take a nap right now."

"Okay, you do that." She nudged him toward the door. "And when you wake up, I'll have supper ready, okay? You deserve something special for all you've done."

"Don't forget you've been paying me," Sonny teased.

"Not enough. You've given my life back to me. I can *never* repay you."

CHAPTER EIGHTEEN

Sonny opened his eyes, blinked at the ceiling, and tried to recall where he was. He rolled to his side, sat up, and remembered when his feet touched the wooden floor. He was in Tanya's tiny garage apartment. He'd facilitated Salazar's arrest that morning. Tanya was so grateful she was cooking him dinner. Sonny had agreed to be there at six.

Bright sunlight squeezed through the half-opened blinds. Sonny rubbed at his puffy eyes and wished for a bottle of cold water to wash away the paste in his mouth. He checked his watch and noted he'd only been asleep two hours, but he felt like he'd dropped into a dark pit for days.

"I still have an hour till dinner," he mumbled and stood into a long stretch. Sonny stumbled toward the refrigerator, grabbed a bottle of water, and downed half the icy liquid before moving toward the restroom. He gazed at himself in the mirror and decided a shower was in order. He had the worst case of bed-head he could remember.

"Besides," he told himself, "I want to look good for my girl."

Sonny turned from the mirror and allowed the implication of

those words to sink in. Before he met Tanya, he'd convinced himself he was better off without a woman in his life. But something had changed all that. What, Sonny wasn't sure. Maybe now that the whole Salazar threat was off, Sonny no longer felt trapped; and Tanya still acted plenty interested. He was thinking in terms of what was best for her and calling her his girl. His goal in upping the heat on Salazar so he could get some space was somehow blurring in the face of Tanya in his arms.

He moved to the window and gazed toward her front yard. He was now free to go home. There was no reason to stay, except Tanya wanted him here. He figured after a few nights the reality of Salazar's absence would penetrate her mind, and she'd tell Sonny he could leave. But for some odd reason Sonny no longer wanted to go back home.

Pressing the heels of his hands against his temples, he tried to will himself into a logical conclusion for why he wanted to stay. Sonny squeezed his eyes tight and fought against the gut-level instinct that was suggesting the preposterous. Finally, the acknowledgment sprang from his lips, despite his attempts to squelch it.

"I'm falling in love with her," he blurted. "Good grief! I'm falling in love with her." He lowered his hands and realized his attempts to stop himself from doing exactly that had failed.

The evidence of his love danced before him like apparitions of the recent past. Up until today, Sonny had been more worried about protecting himself in their friendship. But when he held Tanya in his arms, he'd focused on what was best for her, rather than gratifying his desire for a kiss. Over a month ago, he'd wanted to protect her as the decent thing to do under the given circumstances—just as he would any person in jeopardy. But this morning, when he took down Salazar, Sonny had been motivated by so much more.

His heart began a hard, slow beat. His palms grew clammy. Sonny recalled her answer when he told her he wasn't good enough for her. "I don't know why you think that," she'd said. Then she had somehow pulled God into the equation . . . said something about her needing a Savior as much as anyone.

He downed another long swallow of the cold water and squinted. They'd gone from an electric hug to talking about God in about 2.5 seconds. Then two nights ago, she'd even invited him to church.

The clues began to fit together like the pieces of a shattered mirror, and Sonny wondered how he'd missed them before now. *Tanya O'Brien's interest in me hinges on my interest in God.* He squeezed the half-empty bottle until it crackled. She'd asked Sonny if he'd asked God how He felt about him. The thought had never crossed Sonny's mind until then. He'd assumed a long time ago that God no longer cared.

But maybe I'm the one who gave up and stopped caring, he thought and once again recalled the year at youth camp he'd made a commitment to the Lord. Somehow, the pursuit of basketball and the attractions of living with gusto had made him stray farther and farther from that commitment. Until two nights ago, Sonny hadn't recalled that camp experience. And now it hung in his thoughts like a fog-cloaked spectrum from another life.

He thought about the implications of renewing such a commitment . . . the changes in his life . . . in the way that he thought. He'd seen a marked change in Jack when he got right with God; and Ryan seemed to be just as different. Sonny recalled the times Jack vowed he was praying for him . . . the times his mom had asked if he was going to church.

All at once, he felt sandwiched between his family and this new woman in his life. He thought about telling them all he'd made the change just to get them off his back, and to get his girl. But he labeled the fleeting thought deceptive and deleted it from his mind. If he and Tanya did develop a relationship, it needed to be based on honesty.

And if I ever go back to that commitment, it needs to be for me, he thought. *Not just to get Tanya.*

With a sigh, he turned from the window, set the bottle atop the petite refrigerator, and thought about the success of this morning's sting. He'd told Tanya he thought God had been responsible for the success. The odd thing was, Sonny really believed that. Despite his struggles in the God arena, Sonny knew that this morning's arrest hadn't happened by accident. Nevertheless, he still struggled to imagine that his prayers had contributed to Salazar's arrest.

He headed for the shower while wondering how tonight's meal would go. Sonny hoped Tanya didn't bring up God again. He wasn't in the mood to be pressured. Jack had done enough of that the last several years.

Maybe it's just because he cares about you, a soft voice whispered. *And maybe Tanya does too . . . even more than you realize.*

Sonny shed his clothes as decidedly as he shoved aside the thoughts. He crawled into the shower, turned the spray to hot, and decided if he did renew his vow to Christ it would be all or nothing. And the decision would be for him, not Jack, his mom, or even Tanya.

The barred door clanged shut behind Maurice Salazar. He cut a departing glance toward the empty cell and chuckled under his breath. The negotiation took longer than he'd anticipated, but it was thorough. There'd be no permanent record of the arrest. All charges had vanished. And the local authorities heartily agreed that Lone Star Transport was a lucrative shipping business and nothing more.

While the arrangements had cost the family, these mishaps were to be expected. His father had certainly bought his way out of prison more than once. Maurice had learned from the best.

He followed the sergeant down the hallway lined with the caged human animals that jeered at him. One haggard old man released a stream of obscenities as filthy as his odor. Sneering, Maurice bit back a retort.

The sergeant opened a steel door. Maurice stepped into freedom and smiled into the chief of police's lined face. He handed Maurice a bag full of his personal possessions, offered his hand for a firm shake, and then waved the sergeant aside.

"Great to see you again, Rolf," Maurice said.

"I understand you're leaving the country for a month or so?" the chief queried.

"Yes, as a matter of fact, I am," Maurice's responded. "Thanks for asking."

"Good. It will do you good." He patted Maurice's back, leaned closer, and mumbled, "Get out tonight, and there won't be any trouble."

"And what about the goods?" he asked, peering into the chief's cold, dark eyes.

"Thomas has arranged a pickup tonight," he explained. "We arranged for those in the know to remain silent. They have children, you know." He shrugged and let the rest go unsaid.

Maurice nodded. They both knew the routine well. The only potential pitfall came in the form of the few honorable lawmen in Ft. Worth. A time or two, Maurice had even been forced to arrange for the "accidental" death of a couple of them. He'd also learned that threatening to harm a child could make an honest officer go mute. For now, Maurice would disappear for a while and give the chief time to make certain none of the honest men broke rank. They could be such a bother.

Silently, Maurice followed Rolf down a back hallway to a door that opened onto the parking lot, shrouded in nine o'clock shadows. He shot a final nod toward the chief and caught a glimpse of his shiny badge that supposedly stood for law and order. Maurice smiled. The door slammed shut behind him. His black Cadillac rounded the corner, and he stalked toward the vehicle like a panther, ready for an evening prowl.

This wouldn't be the first time he'd been driven to DFW for an international flight after dark. His home wall safe held counterfeit visas for any number of countries. Maurice would book the first flight that had a vacancy and stay gone until all loose ends had been dealt with.

When he got back, the first item on his agenda would be to kill Sonny Mansfield. Like the honest law officers who'd been removed, Sonny now knew too much and had thwarted Maurice's goals one time too many.

Sonny's Bronze Star tattoo had guaranteed his doom. Maurice had noticed the tattoo when Sonny pushed past Thomas. As Thomas shoved at his arms, Sonny's shirtsleeve slipped up enough to reveal a glimpse of the telltale symbol. While he knew the image was familiar, Maurice hadn't remembered where he'd seen it for several minutes. Then, he flashed back to that late-night meeting with Sonny at Spring Creek Barbeque. And that's when he'd stormed Arby's. Thomas said he'd watched the guy head that way. Maurice confirmed it when he found a package in the men's restroom identical to the one Sonny had been carrying. It contained nothing but a block of wood.

The Cadillac whizzed to a stop inches away. The back door popped open. Maurice slid into the black leather seat and closed the door.

Dalton twisted in his seat. The dash lights lent an eerie glow to his hardened features and pointed goatee. "To your penthouse?" he queried.

"Yes, and I need a cigar."

"Of course." The driver produced a thin brass box that Maurice snatched from his grasp. He rammed the tip of one of the Cuban masterpieces between his teeth, flipped open the gold-plated lighter, and ignited the end. The smoke permeated his senses as thoroughly as the murder plans penetrated his mind. By the time he arrived back into the states, he'd have perfected the deed, and nothing would stop him.

CHAPTER NINETEEN

Tanya eyed Sonny during the Sunday service's opening prayer. He'd left the garage apartment early this morning and arrived back at her place for church, as planned. She'd been impressed with his shirt and tie. Even though his jeans were fashionably faded, Tanya had been pleased that he was at least trying to dress up. They'd arrived in time for Sunday school, as planned. And Sonny had escorted Coty to his class, then later to toddler church.

So far the day had progressed without a hitch. But in the wake of last night's meal, Tanya had wondered if he'd keep their date. After that electric hug, Tanya had decided to be a little more cautious and was surprised when Sonny had seemed just as distant. The pasta Florentine and salad had been some of Tanya's best cooking. But their guarded conversation lacked sparkle. Sonny had focused more on Coty than Tanya, who smeared pasta in his hair before the meal's end. And when bath time came, Coty insisted on Sonny doing the honors. As Sonny left for the evening, Tanya had asked him if they were still on for church in the morning. He'd absently agreed, which led Tanya to wonder if he'd even show up.

Now Tanya observed his profile and wished she could read his mind. While the pastor's opening prayer continued, she studied Sonny's expression. His brows were drawn, his lips tense, his eyes closed tightly.

When he abruptly opened his eyes and stared into her face, Tanya was too stunned to look away. His jaunty smile held a cocky edge, and Tanya's chagrin merged into exasperation. Sonny had caught her watching him, and that grin said he liked it.

So much for being distant, she thought. Tanya broke eye contact and realized everyone else was sitting down. She plopped into her seat and noticed a few late arrivals as the praise team members took their places. Tanya recognized two of the men dressed in jeans and boots and carrying cowboy hats; and she eyed Sonny to see how long it would take him to realize his brothers had just entered the auditorium. When they settled across the aisle, Sonny glanced their way and did a double take. Jack discreetly waved while Sonny mumbled something under his breath, then leaned toward Tanya.

"Yesterday, I told Jack I was going to church with you, and now I know why he asked where you attend. I guess they came to see it with their own eyes," he whispered and wiggled his brows. "Maybe somebody needs to tell those two to get a life."

"Maybe they're just too glad to stay away," Tanya breathed.

Sonny sighed and focused on the front, only to grab Tanya's fingers. She thought he was trying to put a move on her until he released her hand as quickly as he'd grabbed it. Then Sonny leaned closer and whispered, "I had no idea my ex-sister-in-law attended this church. She's on the praise team!"

As the congregation started a resounding chorus of "Celebrate Jesus," Tanya asked, "Which one's your ex-sister-in-law?"

"Shelly Mansfield. Third singer from the end." He discreetly jerked his head to the left.

Tanya followed his gaze to spot the brunet. In a congregation of several hundred, Tanya had yet to meet everyone. While she certainly recognized the woman as a regular member of the praise team, they weren't acquainted.

She looked toward Ryan, and then her attention trailed back to Shelly. While Tanya was only an inch or two taller than most women and had never considered herself fat, Shelly's petite frame made her feel like an Amazon. Her cute ponytail and blissful lack of makeup gave her the appearance of an eighteen-year-old.

"He must have robbed the cradle," Tanya mumbled under her breath.

"She's in her early thirties," Sonny whispered.

"Certainly doesn't look it."

"Never has," he replied and eyed his brother again. He then leaned toward Tanya and whispered, "He's wanting to reconcile with her. Maybe *that's* the real reason he came."

Tanya tried to sing a few lines but could hardly pay attention to the words for fighting the temptation to watch Ryan. The glimpses she stole revealed little. Ryan sang to the song's end and never indicated he knew anyone on stage.

Once the song was over, the minister of music announced a special song by Shelly Mansfield and Dr. Tim Aldridge. A tall blond man stepped away from the praise team and neared the podium. As the couple picked up their mics, the minister of music broke into a mischievous smile and reapproached the pulpit.

"For those of you who don't know," she proclaimed, "Shelly and Tim announced their engagement last night at our praise team practice."

"Man, oh man, this is going south fast," Sonny drawled as the congregation broke into spontaneous applause.

Tanya shot another glance toward Ryan. His chiseled features were tight, his head bent slightly. And he stared at the pew like he was mad at it.

Shelly Mansfield beamed. She and her fiancé locked fingers and began singing "More than Wonderful" in a duet that reaped a standing ovation. The applause had barely begun when Ryan hastened up the aisle and left the sanctuary. Only a few seconds passed before Jack followed. Tanya sensed Sonny's tension rising before he leaned close and said, "I'll be back."

"Sure thing," Tanya replied and strained to watch him leave. Tempted to follow, she chose to remain. This was none of her business, and Ryan probably wouldn't want her intruding.

She took her seat with the rest of the congregation and absently listened to the adult ministries director begin the announcements while her mind wandered to the Mansfield brothers. However, even the Mansfields couldn't distract Tanya from the final announcement.

"If you're in the singles group, you won't want to miss the annual camp retreat," Roger Wilson exclaimed. "As usual, you'll be staying at Camp Cherokee, which is equipped with modern cabins, so it's not too rustic, ladies." The congregation laughed while Tanya snatched a pen and jotted down the first weekend in November— just over two months away. "Remember, this is a time of spiritual renewal that is unmatched!" Roger concluded.

Tanya tapped the pen against her notepad and decided to find out as much as she could about the retreat. *Sonny might even enjoy going*, she mused.

I give up!" Ryan steamed. "I was a fool to even think about coming to her church today!" He slammed his fist against his steering wheel and stared across the highway, his features hard.

"So that's the reason you came? To see Shelly?" Sonny stood near Ryan's opened truck door and propped his foot on the running board.

"I told him you were going to church here this morning," Jack explained, "and he knew Shelly attended here. So we just decided to come." He shrugged. "I wanted to witness the answer to my prayers, and Ryan wanted to see if Shelly would at least talk to him. Little did he know . . ." Jack focused on Ryan. "I'm really sorry, bro," he soothed. "If I'd known . . ."

"It's not your fault." Ryan shook his head and rubbed at his forehead. "It's nobody's fault but my own," he added. Shoulders slumping, he cranked his Ford pickup, switched the AC to high, and pointed a vent at his flushed face.

Jack sighed and slipped his hand into his back pocket. "I understand if you want to leave. I don't much blame you."

Sonny backed away from the truck.

"Yeah. I'm going home. I've witnessed all the drama I want for one day." He closed the truck door.

Jack edged backward while Sonny pulled at the neck of his stuffy shirt. He glanced toward the eleven o'clock sun broiling the east Texas hills, and watched Ryan's truck purr out of the parking lot.

"I hate this is happening," he said. "I always liked Shelly."

"Yeah," Jack admitted.

"Hey, where's Charli?" Sonny questioned.

"She went to our church this morning. You know she teaches Sunday school, so she's not as free as I am." He shrugged.

"Oh," Sonny said and didn't admit that he hadn't known. "So I guess you're out of the doghouse with her now?" he asked as the two brothers walked back to the sanctuary.

"All the way," Jack said and rubbed his chin in a suave salute to his current status.

"Good." Sonny cut his brother a glance and didn't bother to detail his own predicament with one particular female. After realizing he was falling in love, Sonny had been too stunned to even carry on a decent conversation with Tanya over dinner last night. Trapped in a fit of the awkwards, he'd focused on Coty and nearly ignored Tanya. Now he felt like a nervous seventh grader in a camp chapel service.

Jack arrived at the church's glass door and opened it wide. "After you," he said like some snobby butler and motioned Sonny into the cool interior.

"Maybe we oughta start praying for this Ryan and Shelly business," Sonny absently observed as they neared the sanctuary.

"Maybe so," Jack replied through a huge grin. "Maybe so," he repeated and fondly squeezed Sonny's shoulder.

Sonny hovered in the back of the sanctuary while Jack resumed his place. Earlier, when he felt Tanya watching him, Sonny had been overtaken by a magnetic presence he hadn't anticipated. It was almost as if God himself was beckoning him. The experience again took him back to fifteen . . . to the church camp where he'd first encountered God. Sonny remembered feeling as if the Lord was embracing him. He recalled telling his counselor, Joe Mack, he thought God had something special planned for his life. Joe had heartily agreed.

But once camp was over, Sonny had been so distracted by girls and cars and basketball that he forgot God and His plans. Sonny had gradually slid into living life by his own rules. Of course, that had led him to an existence full of empty relationships, broken promises, crashed dreams, and a dead-end road lined with alcohol. He thought about Sonny Jr., and wondered if God would ever bring the child across his path.

When he realized one of the ushers was watching, Sonny spotted an isolated seat on the back row and slipped therein. While the song service continued, he closed his eyes and absorbed the presence of God. He wasn't really sure about the right steps to recommitting his life. But he *was* sure of something this morning he'd been uncertain of yesterday: Sonny was ready to make that step, not for Tanya or Jack, but for himself and his God.

The longer His presence immersed Sonny, the more he became aware of the haunted, lonely shell of a man he'd become. Whether he and Tanya ever made a go of their relationship or not, Sonny knew Jack was right; he needed to go with God. He recalled all the times through the years that Jack had tried to influence him to take this step and how he'd resisted. Looking back at the vast improvement in Jack's life, Sonny now couldn't imagine why he'd been so blind to his own need for God.

I guess I was blinded by my own determination to do things my way, he thought and wondered why he ever thought that would work.

"Well, here I am, Lord," he whispered. *Like I said in the shower yesterday. It's all or nothing now. Nothing halfway about it. I'm sorry for messing up my life—for all the mistakes. Please just take the mess I've made and see if you can salvage any of it. As for Tanya . . .* He opened his eyes and strained through the crowd for a glimpse of her. *She's a wonderful woman, but this isn't about her. It's about us—You and me all the way—whether she lands in my life or not.*

When the congregation began the song "He Is Lord," Sonny closed his eyes and savored the final prayer song. His heart swelling, he sensed the fire of God's presence consuming his soul, and he knew there was no going back this time.

As the song ended, he opened his eyes and again gazed toward Tanya who was scanning the back of the auditorium. Sonny stepped into the aisle, and resumed his seat beside her.

Her smile, laden with curiosity, begged him to at least offer a hint as to what transpired in the parking lot. He leaned toward her ear and said, "Ryan left. More later."

She nodded, and Sonny held her gaze, then reached for her hand. Her eyes widened. She looked down. Thinking she might withdraw, he braced himself for the rejection. When she twined her fingers with his and gazed toward the pulpit as if they held hands every Sunday, Sonny's mind whirled with the implications. If not for his determination to listen to the sermon, he'd have never been able to focus.

After the service, Tanya hurried to keep up with Sonny who trotted across the church parking lot with Coty in his arms. The child laughed hysterically as he bounced up and down in sequence with Sonny's jog. When Sonny slowed to a regular pace, Coty patted his back and said, "Do it 'gin, Sonny! Do it 'gin!" So Sonny obliged.

By the time they arrived at the truck, beads of sweat dotted Sonny's forehead and he puffed for air. "Whew, Coty! You wear Sonny out," he exclaimed and pressed the remote lock.

Tanya opened the passenger door, reached for Coty, and said, "Here ya go, big boy! Let's put you in your car seat."

"No!" Coty wailed and clung to Sonny. "Sonny put me in! Sonny!" .

"Well, pardon me," Tanya drawled. "Looks like Sonny's the celebrity of the hour."

Chuckling, Sonny stepped toward the door and settled Coty into his booster, secured in the center of the truck's bench seat. "There you are, Coty." Sonny said, "Now, let's let Mamma click you in. I'm not sure I'll do it right."

Tanya hovered close behind with plans of crawling into the truck and securing Coty in the seat. But when Sonny turned around, she was trapped between him and the door. Gazing into his dancing eyes, Tanya held her breath and relived his taking her hand in church. She'd been initially shocked and had nearly disengaged her hand as swiftly as he'd nabbed it. But something deep within urged her to twine her fingers with his and hang on tight.

Tanya had spent the first half of the sermon confused by her ready acceptance of this simple sign of moving forward in their relationship. So many questions still remained unanswered. Tanya didn't know whether to bring up the issue of God now or wait until after lunch. Either way, the conversation had to happen *today*.

As the buzz between them warmed, Sonny's eyes danced with a determination Tanya didn't understand until he planted a quick kiss on her cheek and said, "Thanks for today. You'll never know what it has meant to me. I hope you don't mind if I tag along with you every week now."

Tanya gulped and peered into his soul. "N-no, I don't mind," she stammered and couldn't deny that something had changed within him—something for the better. She didn't ask. He didn't explain. But as they pulled away from the church, she touched her cheek and smiled.

CHAPTER TWENTY

What!" Sonny paced across the tiny apartment and was heading the other direction before Jack responded.

"Salazar has left the country," Jack repeated. "At least that's what his secretary told me. 'He's out of the country on business,'" Jack mimicked a falsetto voice.

"How? I *saw* him being arrested. I *saw* the cocaine!"

"There doesn't seem to be any record of the arrest," Jack replied, his voice as cold as steel. "My hunch is he never was booked—just put on hold until . . ."

"Until what?" Sonny demanded and answered his own question. "Until the right people were holding the right amount of green?"

"Bingo," Jack drawled. "As big as Salazar seems to be, I wouldn't be surprised if some of the top officials are in on it."

Sonny walked toward the window, slammed his fist against the frame. "Can't we *do* something?"

"Already have," Jack replied. "Called the FBI. Reported everything. If there's one thing I'm determined to uncover, it's corruption like this. It gives us good guys a bad name." His voice rose to a new tenor of frustration, and Sonny remained respectfully silent while he continued his pacing. "And I have no plans for letting anyone bluff me into keeping quiet. Who knows! A few honest officers might have come up missing in Ft. Worth or been conveniently killed in the line of duty."

Jack never talked much about the two years he was on the Richardson, Texas, police force . . . or how his former partner's blowing the cover on police corruption had cost his life. Determined to reveal the evil, Jack had miraculously been able to lie low and pick up where his partner left off. The results were a huge sting that made national news.

"If it weren't for the grace of God, I'd be dead myself," Jack stormed, the anguish in his voice evidence that his partner's memory was still alive and painful. "I promise, I wish I could go in and wipe the floor up with all of them right now, but the smartest thing is just to let the FBI know."

He huffed. "Sorry I went off."

"No prob."

"Anyway, the main reason I called was to tell you the FBI wants to talk to you Friday."

"Friday!" Sonny exclaimed. "That's six days from now."

"Yep. You know how slow they work," he added. "If there's corruption, they'll want to uncover as much as they can, and they don't do that by running in quick. Quick can get you killed and give some of the fish an opportunity to swim away. They'll be doing some preliminary work between now and then, but don't even start expecting overnight results. They have to plant a mole, and then—"

"Months! That can take months!"

"Right. And nobody is more frustrated over that than me, but they have to be thorough. Believe me, I know."

Sonny balled his fist and squelched the roar rising within. Three weeks had lapsed since the Sunday he held Tanya's hand, and in that time Sonny had watched Tanya gradually relax until only traces of that tense, watchful woman existed.

Furthermore, their growing relationship had taken on an easy rhythm that Sonny had never experienced before . . . almost as if another force was orchestrating the whole thing. They'd even met for breakfast a couple of times and prayed together. Sonny hoped the encounters continued and had even thought about suggesting greater frequency.

As for their romance, he only held her hand occasionally and had refrained from kissing because he didn't want to rush her. Sonny's desire to savor each step in their growth had surprised him and seemed to be scoring points with Tanya. A new respect sparkled in her eyes and mingled with the relief over Salazar.

Now, after all this progress, Salazar was still at large! "Do you know for certain he's out of the country?" Sonny asked and kicked at the suitcase he'd just finished packing. It toppled into the stack of bed linens folded near the flattened air mattress.

"I have no proof," Jack admitted. "Only what the secretary told me." Jack had been working to get particulars of the case ever since Salazar's arrest. When Jack told Sonny he was having problems gleaning details, Sonny had secretively thought his busy brother was procrastinating. Sonny hadn't pressed, but as of yesterday he'd decided maybe *he* needed to be the one turning stones. Now, he understood why the information had come so slowly. Apparently, there was corruption in Ft. Worth. And while Sonny hadn't been an angel by a long shot, he couldn't quite wrap his mind around police officers siding with the wrong team.

"I guess moving out isn't a question," he mumbled and slumped into the lone chair sitting in front of the TV.

"If you're talking about staying in the garage apartment, I recommend it," Jack grimly stated. "I called you as soon as I knew. He might be abroad, but he could slip back into the U.S. any time. Don't lower your guard, okay?"

"Right."

"I'll let you know if I hear anything else."

"Sure," Sonny replied. "Appreciate your work."

"Anything, anytime," Jack replied before Sonny flipped the phone shut.

Sighing, he gazed around the room and debated what he should tell Tanya. She'd finally gotten comfortable staying alone at night. Even though he'd enjoyed protecting her, Sonny had been looking forward to going back home. He'd all but abandoned his photography and needed to start submitting freelance photos again. Plus, he was ready to sleep in his own bed. Now Sonny knew he couldn't. He'd have to unpack and settle back in.

As for what he'd tell Tanya, he debated whether he should just say he'd had second thoughts about leaving or tell all. He didn't want to scare her, but wondered if there was any wisdom in cushioning the truth.

A bump on the door interrupted his mental vacillation, and Sonny suspected Tanya. "Come in," he called. "It's unlocked." He stood and feigned a casual expression while praying for guidance.

The knob rattled, slowly turned. The door eased open, and Sonny stared into a dispassionate face. "What are *you* doing here?" he blurted.

Um, Sonny," Tanya whispered while staring out the living room window, "do you remember at church they've been talking about—no, no, no." She shook her head. "Start over." She swallowed hard, took a deep breath, twisted her fingers, and said, "Sonny, the church singles group is going on a camping trip. I wondered if you'd like to go. The deadline for registration is Wednesday night. I can cover costs if—no, no, no." Tanya shook her head again. "No. Don't offer to pay his way unless he hedges," she advised, then nodded and repeated the approved invitation, "Sonny, the church singles group is going on a camping trip. I wondered if you'd like to go. We're staying in the cabins at Camp Cherokee."

Tanya nodded and gave herself a thumbs-up. After she arrived home from work, yesterday they'd talked about his moving back home full-time. Tanya agreed she felt safe on her own, as long as she knew she could call him any time. He'd readily agreed, encouraged her to call every day if she liked, and threw in a flirtatious wink.

She smiled. Their relationship had certainly taken a cozy turn in the last few weeks, and Tanya hadn't erected one barrier. While Sonny had been the ultimate gentleman, he gazed at her like a man appreciating fine art. And Tanya had never been so glad to be exactly where she was. When she asked him to join her for breakfast and a devotional a couple of mornings, he'd readily agreed. He even shared that he had recommitted his life to Christ during that first church service he attended with her.

Now Sonny seemed unusually timid about doing more than occasionally holding her hand. While Tanya certainly didn't want to rush their relationship, she'd caught herself daydreaming at work about their first kiss. Dolly had even teased her a time or two.

Maybe the church camp trip will up the romance, she thought. "That would make Mom and Dad happy anyway," she whispered over a smile.

Her parents had grown to like Sonny tremendously and fully expected him every Sunday for lunch. She'd begun to suspect that they hoped the budding romance might lead to marriage, even though Tanya hadn't suggested the likes. Nevertheless, her father told Sonny he had rested easier knowing Tanya had a bodyguard in the garage apartment. They appreciated his protection even after Salazar's arrest.

An impatient yap from behind sent Tanya into a spastic jump. She yelped and laid a hand across her chest before recognizing Happy's bark. Pivoting to face the cocker spaniel, Tanya bent and scratched his ears. "Happy-Happy," she exclaimed. "You scared me batty!"

The dog barked again, ran to the kitchen, then hustled back to Tanya.

"Oh! You want to go outside? Is that it? Outside?" she repeated.

Happy sat down, barked with a vengeance, and then dashed into the kitchen. His toenails clicked on the tile floor like tiny tap shoes before he ran to the living room's threshold.

"Okay, okay," she crooned. "I'm coming. You must have to really go." She hustled through the kitchen and stopped halfway to the back door. Tanya stiffened and stared at the ajar door as a myriad of possibilities rampaged her mind. The final one involved her child.

Happy raced to the doorway, stared into the backyard, and whined. He glanced back at Tanya and worriedly whined some more.

"Coty!" Tanya wheezed. She dashed to her son's room, only to discover his rumpled toddler bed was empty. "Coty!" she hollered and scanned his room. "Coty!" Tanya yelled and checked the bathroom—just in case—as hard panic clawed at her stomach.

Happy arrived at the end of the hall, barking anew. He scurried back to the door, and Tanya knew there was no other explanation. Coty was gone. He'd exited the back door, and Happy was trying to tell her. Initially, Tanya assumed he'd somehow escaped, but then another dread thought erupted upon her mind: *What if someone took him?*

"Maurice Salazar," Tanya cried. She flung herself out the back door, only to run headlong into Sonny with Coty perched in his arms.

Tanya gasped and stared at the two several seconds before she realized tears dampened her cheeks. Her pulse pounding her temples, she looked from Sonny to Coty and back to Sonny. "How did you—"

"He arrived at my door a few minutes ago and said, 'Sonny stay—not go,'" he explained in the voice of a three-year-old. His hair mussed from his nap, Coty wrapped his arms around Sonny's neck and squeezed until Sonny winced. "I guess you missed him inside?'"

"I thought—I thought—" Tanya forced her breathing into an even rhythm and talked herself out of an emotional reaction. She'd already crumpled all over Sonny once, and she didn't want to give him the impression she was an overemotional female who wilted at every turn.

While Happy circled them and barked up a celebration, Tanya's legs didn't obey her command to remain stiff. They betrayed her, and she flopped onto the back steps. Tanya propped her elbows on her thighs and covered her face with her hands.

"I thought maybe Salazar . . ." She left the rest unstated.

"Mamma sad?" Coty asked, and a small hand pulled at the knee of her sweatpants.

Tanya lowered her hands and gazed into her son's black, almond-shaped eyes while trying to decide if she should scold him or hug him tight. Finally, the hug won. She gathered him into her arms and savored the smell of the SpaghettiOs he'd eaten for lunch and smeared all over his shirt.

"I guess it's time to put toddler locks on my doors," she said.

"Why would you say that?" Sonny's windbreaker wheezed with the movement as he settled next to her.

Coty squirmed in her arms and landed feet-first on the last step. He rushed at Happy and squealed when the dog woofed and wagged his tail.

Tanya rested her head on Sonny's shoulder and welcomed the warmth when he slipped his arm around her. As September progressed, the nights were getting longer, the days cooler.

"Are you sure you're ready for me to move out?" Sonny asked.

"I thought I was, but maybe not," she admitted.

"Okay," Sonny agreed.

Tanya lifted her head. "So you're agreeing to stay? Just like that?" She snapped her fingers.

"Sure." Sonny's easy smile started with Tanya and shifted to Coty. "I've been summoned," he said. "How can I say no?"

"I didn't think Coty was listening last night when we were talking about your leaving, but I guess he was."

"He doesn't seem to miss much," Sonny replied.

Sighing, Tanya placed her head on his shoulder once more and blurted, "Maybe you need to just stay for good." Sonny's immediate silence accompanied Tanya's widening eyes. She hadn't intended to sound like she was subtly proposing, but the implication hung between them just as strongly.

"Maybe so," Sonny answered as his arm tightened around her.

Despite the nippy breeze, Tanya's face flashed hot. She jumped up, fumbled with nothing, and said, "I need to go inside for a minute."

Sonny stood and didn't budge when Tanya tried to whiz by him. Instead, he caught her in his arms, gazed into her eyes, and held her tight. "I'll stay as long as you need me," he whispered and rubbed her cheek with the backs of his fingers. "And as long as Coty wants me." His words held a wealth of meaning while his expression urged her to snuggle close.

Tanya's unsteady legs wobbled anew, and all else faded in the face of Sonny's warm appraisal. His attention rested on her lips, and the attraction sparked between them. He lifted his gaze back to her eyes and posed a silent question. Logic insisted she not be taken under by his magnetic appeal, but Dolly's words about her being alone for life squelched the logic. Truth was, Tanya *wanted* Sonny to kiss her, and she'd wanted that for days now. Her answer to his silent request could not be misunderstood when she tilted her head upward and moved a tad closer.

The kiss she'd expected to be slow, gentle, and short was anything but. He went in for a swift expression of his appreciation that left Tanya's eyes bugging; but soon they closed, and she drowned in the moment that shook her world.

At last, Sonny pulled away, lovingly trailed a row of kisses to her ear and whispered, "Wow."

Tanya closed her eyes and relaxed against him. His rapid heartbeat matched hers, and she hoped their relationship would never end.

Through jumbled thoughts, she recalled the church trip and figured this would be the best opportunity to ask him to go. Tanya eased away while he stroked her hair.

"The camp church is going on a trip singles." She gulped and wondered how the articulate woman she'd aspired to be had vanished. Frowning herself into better concentration she said, "I mean—"

"You mean the camping trip the church singles are planning for early November?" Sonny questioned.

She nodded.

"I was wondering if maybe we could go together," he said.

"I'd love to," Tanya agreed. "We're staying in cabins—guys on one side of the camp, ladies on the other. It's going to be a lot like going to church camp when we were kids."

"Some of the highlights of my life," Sonny admitted.

"Swing! Swing!" Coty's voice shattered their interlude, and Tanya and Sonny turned to face him.

"I've never been so well-chaperoned," Sonny drawled and eased away.

"I'll make tea if you want to do the honors," Tanya said and motioned toward her son.

"We're a team," he said and gently nudged her chin with his fist.

As Sonny strode toward the swing set, Tanya's dreamy sigh ushered in a reality she had yet to accept. *I'm falling in love with him*, she thought, and didn't even try to stop another sigh. *And so is Coty.*

Tanya never imagined when Sonny Mansfield appeared in her yard that he might be the answer to her prayers for a godly husband and father. He seemed so far removed from her ideal. But the longer she knew him, the more she saw that Sonny ran deeper than the flippant guy she'd first met.

While Tanya couldn't deny the reality of her feelings, she also knew she could not jump into anything as serious as marriage without giving their relationship the test of time. Nonetheless, she had no intentions of stopping the natural flow of their attraction. If this thing between her and Sonny grew into a lifetime, so let it be. Even though he wasn't the spiritual giant she had envisioned marrying, he had serious potential. As Tanya turned to make the tea, she decided to take her mom and Dolly's advice and accept him exactly as he was, exactly where he was. God and time would take care of his imperfections . . . and hers.

CHAPTER TWENTY-ONE

Sonny bought the ring the day before the church camping trip. He'd spent way more than he planned, but Tanya was worth it. The one-carat diamond cluster had at least been on sale, but he'd still be paying for it long after their first anniversary. He'd shown the ring to Ryan, whose eyes bugged.

"You sure she's ready?" he'd asked. "You've only known each other four months."

"I guess we'll find out," Sonny replied with confidence. "We don't have to set the date for six months or so," he'd added.

"Well, okay. Whatever!" Ryan had gripped Sonny's shoulder and said, "Break a leg!"

Sonny withdrew the ring box from his canvas bag's side pouch and stuffed it into his jacket's pocket. He zipped his pocket and set the canvas bag into the Jeep's backseat. This afternoon, the campers were free to hike or horseback ride, fish or play table tennis. While several groups had started outdoors, few lasted. The sunbathed, November day appeared as warm as April from the safety of the main lodge. But an icy bite laced the breeze, and Sonny was glad he'd packed his hooded jacket. He'd checked the weather online, just in case, and noted there was only a twenty percent chance of rain. He decided to take his chances because today was proposal day. The canvas bag contained everything Sonny needed, right down to a bottle of sparkling grape juice and two glasses. He couldn't put the question off another day. He simply could not.

Despite Ryan's doubt, Sonny was convinced Tanya was ready. The adoration in her eyes was only matched by that in Sonny's heart. He'd never felt so complete when he was with Tanya, and her every expression said she felt the same.

As for Coty, he'd irrevocably stolen Sonny's heart. Coty had christened Sonny as *the one* for bath time; and the bigger the role Sonny played in the child's life, the more he felt like his father. Being with Coty had become one of the highlights of Sonny's life . . . only rivaled by his time with Tanya. He could only imagine the fulfillment of becoming a full-time dad.

The image of a lanky, blond-haired boy played in his mind, and Sonny wondered what his biological son might be doing today. "Probably playing basketball," he said through a chuckle. In recent weeks, he'd stopped mentally beating up himself and Karen. Instead, he now breathed a prayer for his son every time he thought of him. He also added a plea that one day he'd get to meet Sonny Jr. Until then, Sonny would find comfort in parenting Coty and being the best dad possible . . . if Tanya agreed to marry him.

After crawling behind the Jeep's wheel, he gazed across the pine-laden hills and waited for Tanya to exit her cabin. When he'd knocked on her door not long ago, she told him to give her a few more minutes. Sonny didn't mind. He enjoyed the smell of the piney woods . . . the sparkle on the lake . . . the crunch of the leaves beneath the feet of those passing by. The older he grew the more he appreciated the great outdoors. These grounds reminded him of his childhood camp experiences, and he sensed that God was giving him the chance to start over. This time, he wouldn't blow it. This time, Sonny would make the right choices and live with God's blessings.

His phone emitted the tune from the old *Dukes of Hazzard* TV show, the distinctive ring Sonny assigned to Jack. A thread of worry reaped a frown. The last time Sonny talked to Jack, they'd discussed Salazar. Through his law-enforcement network, Jack had asked to be alerted at the first sign of Maurice's entering the country. Sonny dug his phone from his shirt pocket and flipped it open. Jack knew Sonny and Tanya were having a special weekend. He certainly wouldn't bother Sonny with any trivial matter; and that led Sonny to be convinced this phone call would in no way be trivial.

"Yo," he said and gazed toward the glistening lake.

"Salazar's back in the country," Jack said with no preliminary greeting.

"Afraid that was why you were calling."

"Are you at Camp Cherokee now?" Jack asked.

"Yeah."

"Good. Stay there."

"Hadn't planned on going home until tomorrow, when it's over."

"Might not hurt to hang there a few more days until we see what Salazar might be planning. It's nice and remote."

"Don't know if we can pull that off," Sonny said and tapped the steering wheel with his fingertips. "We both have to work Monday."

"Right." Jack sighed.

"Where was he spotted?"

"Ft. Worth. The FBI is watching the transport business. He went back like a dog to his vomit."

Sonny grimaced. "Let's not get so graphic."

"Just keep your eyes opened, okay?"

"Sure thing. So they're trailing Salazar?"

"Yes. Last I heard from them was this morning. They won't tell me everything. They can't."

"Understandable."

"Really, they're probably telling me more than they should. But given his history with Tanya, there's a leak that won't stop . . . and I'm very thankful."

"Me too." Sonny scanned the campground and spotted nothing but a few campers scurrying from cabins to the main lodge.

He'd certainly been glad to share all he knew with the FBI and hoped the information aided them in capturing Salazar . . . and ultimately the corrupt policemen. "Any news on the upright and honest officers in Ft. Worth?" Sonny asked, a sarcastic twist to his words.

"They're tight-lipped on that front—except I have deduced that they think the chief's involved," he growled.

"And I guess you're seeing red all the way to Canada?" Sonny prompted.

"That's putting it mildly. There's a special place *under* the jail for police officers who go bad—and I don't think a crooked chief even ranks that high."

"Oh, hi, Sonny," a familiar female voice called from behind.

Sonny swiveled to spot Shelly Mansfield, walking down the nearby path.

He offered a slight smile and a wave, then pointed to his cell phone.

"Oh, sorry." She winced and then paused near the Jeep.

Sonny cut her a glance and suspected she wasn't leaving. "Well, I gotta go," he said, his voice guarded. "Thanks for the info. Let me know if you hear anything else."

"Is someone listening now?" Jack prompted.

"Yeah." Sonny held up his index finger toward Shelly.

"Gotcha," Jack replied. "I'll call later if I need to."

When Sonny hung up, his first instinct was to search the path for Shelly's fiancé. The two had been almost inseparable the whole trip, and Sonny had chosen to block them from his mind. The group was big enough for him to enjoy such a luxury. And he believed his loyalty to Ryan demanded as much.

"Hi," he responded and decided Tim-the-Dentist must not be in the neighborhood.

"Are you enjoying the trip?" she asked.

"Yeah," Sonny responded and focused on the steering wheel covered in leather. He tugged on a loose thread and wondered exactly what Shelly wanted. The uneasy silence suggested their encounter wasn't an accident and she wasn't here for chitchat.

"Sonny, this is awkward," she began.

He lifted his gaze and noted the anguish in her brown eyes. Shelly had always stricken him as cute. Ryan, on the other hand, had thought Shelly was the hottest thing going the first time he met her . . . and still did, for that matter.

"What's awkward?" he finally asked as she tied and untied the string on her cardigan.

"I mean, about Ryan."

"Ryan?"

"I know he wants to give us another try, but I . . . I just can't." Her expression begged him to understand. "I tried to get him to reconcile when I found out about his affair, but he made his choices. Now, two years later, he's changed his mind—"

"No." Sonny shook his head. "God has changed his heart. There's a difference," he said and was mildly surprised at how firmly he believed this truth when months ago he'd been skeptical himself.

"But how can I be *sure*?" she prompted, her eyes filled with fear.

"Maybe you should give him another chance and find out," Sonny said, attempting to make his tone easier.

But her sizable engagement ring flashed in the sunshine and dwarfed the one he bought Tanya. Fleetingly, Sonny wondered if

Shelly's reasons for refusing Ryan went deeper than just the fear in her eyes. As a highway patrolman, Ryan would never be able to provide the lifestyle that a successful dentist could. Sonny's mouth hardened, and he stared straight ahead.

From an analytical angle, he could certainly understand Shelly's reasons for not trusting Ryan. While Jack believed Sonny had a way with women, he couldn't touch Ryan's finesse. And the very charm that nabbed Shelly hadn't stopped with her. Nevertheless, Sonny had watched Ryan's pain and remorse enough that the facts no longer held the strength they once did. Presently, Sonny couldn't get past his love for his brother and what might be best for him. If Shelly was his sister, he might see things differently. But she wasn't.

Finally, Shelly sighed and said, "I really don't think I can give him another chance, Sonny."

He didn't respond. The determination in her words matched that on her features. And Sonny began to embrace Ryan's resignation. After Shelly's engagement announcement at church, Ryan had said little about her. That had initially frustrated Sonny, since Ryan wasn't the sort to give up.

But hell has no fury like a woman scorned, he thought and hoped he never found himself in such a situation with Tanya. Even though Sonny couldn't imagine breaking his wedding vows, he hoped he never did something thoughtless that deeply hurt Tanya.

"Well, anyway . . . here we are now attending the same church, and I feel like there's this wall between us," she continued. "It's awkward."

"Yeah," Sonny admitted and spotted a dark cloud in the distance. He glanced toward Tanya's cabin and wished she'd hurry. Salazar loomed on the edge of his mind like the cloud on the horizon. Even her understandable delay left him edgy.

"I won't keep you," Shelly said and laid her hand on his arm. "I just wanted to say hello, I guess, and let you know . . ."

Sonny focused on her again.

She shrugged and stepped back. "Maybe we can still be friends?"

"Maybe," Sonny said but didn't commit to anything. "Ryan's really hurting," he blurted, "and it's hard for me to—" It was his turn to shrug.

Her eyes narrowed a fraction. After a huff, she focused on her feet, kicked at a pinecone. "Ryan always wants life on *his* terms, Sonny," she defended and lifted her gaze. "Our marriage was all about *him*. He ripped my heart out, and now I'm supposed to just go running back when he crooks his finger?" She rested her hands on her hips, and the fear in her eyes gave way to pain and anger.

"Nobody said that," Sonny mumbled. "It's just that—"

"Okay, I'm finally ready!" Tanya's cheerful voice floated on the breeze, and Sonny turned to face her.

"Oh!" She stopped at the Jeep. "I'm sorry. I didn't see you. I don't know how I missed you in that red sweater."

Shelly looked down. "That's okay. We were through," she said and hurried toward the pathway that led to the main lodge.

"What gives?" Tanya asked and crawled into her seat.

"Oh, her?" Sonny teased and hoped he hid the frustration. "She was hitting on me."

Tanya narrowed her eyes. "That was your ex-sister-in-law. She's engaged."

"Yeah." He cranked the engine. "Don't we all know *that*," he groused and decided to tell all. "You know Ryan wants her back and it's a no-deal?"

"Right." Tanya nodded and pulled the hood up on her jacket.

"Well, now she's decided we need to be big buddies, but that's really hard for me."

Tanya fell silent as Sonny steered the Jeep toward the narrow road leading into the hills. "I never heard what happened with them," she said.

"Ryan had an affair," Sonny stated and didn't know how to soften the truth.

"Oh," Tanya said.

Sonny cut her a sideways glance.

"That's a hard one for any woman to swallow," she admitted. "I guess he hid it well, and she was shocked when she found out?"

"Yeah." Sonny glowered straight ahead, focused on steering.

"He probably lied like crazy to cover his tracks," she mused.

Sonny didn't even bother to answer that one. So far, Ryan wasn't doing so well in this trial. "All I know is—he's had a heart change . . . like me," he added. "And he's my brother, and—"

"You're loyal."

He nodded.

"I guess it's just a hard situation," she said, the wind ripping at her words. "She seems really sweet."

"She is." He smiled and decided they'd focused on Ryan and his problems long enough. "But so are you, and *you* are what today is about."

"Me?" Tanya laid her hand on her chest.

"Absolutely." He winked and hoped she took the hint while praying she didn't. As much as Sonny wanted to surprise her, he also wanted to prepare her heart for the question.

Taking her hand, he steered the vehicle up the steep path that the kind camp guide said led to the perfect mountainside plateau. With a gleam in his eyes, the guide also said the place was replete with a picnic table, a natural spring, and a breathtaking vista.

Couldn't be more perfect, Sonny thought as an expectant silence settled between them.

But despite the special moment, Sonny discreetly eyed the countryside and then gazed into his rearview mirror. Logic insisted Salazar couldn't be on these campgrounds, but Jack's phone call still left him uneasy.

He glanced toward Tanya, gazing at the scenic hills, and toyed with the idea of telling her everything, including the fact that Salazar had never even been booked. Coty's coming to his apartment had given Sonny the opportunity to stay at Tanya's without explaining that Salazar was at large. Sonny had chosen to withhold the information because he hated seeing Tanya terrified. And as long as Salazar had been out of the country, he was no threat.

But that had changed. Now Sonny did think Tanya should know the truth—for her own safety. If that meant the fear engulfed her again, so let it be. She needed to keep her guard up when Sonny wasn't there to protect her.

Nonetheless, Sonny feared the mention of Salazar would ruin their moment. Deciding to tell her tonight, he scanned the area a final time and squeezed Tanya's hand.

CHAPTER TWENTY-TWO

Maurice Salazar sat in a Jeep hidden behind a grove of roadside trees fifty yards north of the plateau. He and Drake had followed Sonny and Tanya to the camp yesterday and evaluated the best way to capture Tanya and eliminate Sonny. Finally, Drake had volunteered to dress like a camp employee, disguise his appearance, and mingle with the guests as a camp guide while Maurice scouted the outer grounds. During his exploration, Maurice discovered a plateau that couldn't be more perfect for a romantic rendezvous . . . and a murder. He'd immediately called Drake, who managed to divulge the information to Sonny Mansfield, who seemed enthusiastic about taking his girlfriend to the plateau. Drake had then watched Sonny until he arranged for a camp Jeep. Now they waited.

If the plan continued as smoothly, Salazar decided Drake deserved a bonus. After all, the guy wasn't even supposed to be working yet. Despite the doctor's admonishment that Drake not work for a couple of months, Maurice had insisted upon his help this weekend. When it came to planning a murder, Drake was the best.

After Maurice showed Drake the plateau, he'd suggested they

drop Sonny's body into a cavern that appeared to stretch to the center of the earth. The plan couldn't be more simple or complete.

Now Salazar and Drake sat in the Jeep . . . waiting to see if Sonny would drive into their trap. While Drake still wore the khakis, he'd shed the hat, sunglasses, and fake mustache.

The icy breeze and bank of clouds building on the horizon whispered of a miserable, cold night. He thought he heard the hum of a nearing vehicle. Maurice's pulse increased to the hard, even tattoo of a suitor reuniting with the woman he worshiped.

After an adventurous ride that left her cheeks stinging and her pulse elevated, Tanya stepped from the vehicle and gazed at autumn's splendor. The hillside was alive with colors only God could create, and each vibrant leaf hung like a jewel, especially crafted by Him. Tanya inhaled the cold air, every bit as invigorating as Sonny's expression. Several trees dotted the area, giving the impression of a small, city park amid the hills. A metal railing protecting viewers from a dangerous cliff framed an even more impressive overlook.

Sonny grabbed the backpack from behind the seat and rounded the Jeep. "Come on," he said and tugged Tanya toward the picnic table near the center of the leaf-strewn plateau.

Tanya didn't resist Sonny's prompting. He had something on his agenda that might involve forever, but Tanya didn't allow herself to hope too much. However, if Sonny did plan to propose, she already knew her answer. She'd prayed nonstop since their first kiss and sensed no urgency to break off their deepening attachment. Finally, she told God that if their marriage wasn't His will to somehow intercept any potential. So far, God had done nothing of the sort.

Sonny dropped the canvas bag on the picnic table and pulled Tanya toward a craggy mound of rocks that stretched into the side of the hill. Soon, she noticed a gleaming mountain spring splashing from an opening in the rocks that resembled a cavern.

"How pretty!" she exclaimed.

"Right," Sonny practically agreed. "Now you stand right here and don't turn around, okay?"

"Okaaaaaay," Tanya said and swiveled to watch him as he walked away.

"I said don't turn around," Sonny said. Laughing, he grabbed her shoulders and pointed her toward the stream again.

"And if I do?" Tanya teased.

"Thirty lashes with a wet noodle," he vowed and kissed her cheek through a chortle.

"Yikes!" she said while her excitement soared to new heights. As hard as she'd tried to squelch her matrimonial hopes, Tanya realized the effort was now wasted. She'd gone beyond hope to certainty that Sonny must be going to propose.

She stared at the crystal water and recalled the first time she and Sonny kissed. Today's excitement was every bit as fresh and awestruck as then, only the stakes were much higher . . . more invigorating. The sound of an approaching vehicle proved the only possible hindrance to the electric moment, and Tanya hoped the motorist wasn't planning to stop at the plateau.

"Okay, you can turn around!" Sonny exclaimed on the first beat of Michael Bolton's classic hit, "When a Man Loves a Woman."

Tanya whirled to face him. Her attention was first snagged by the portable CD player sitting atop a white table cloth whose edges danced in the wind. The words, "When a man loves a woman . . ." spilled from the CD and filled Tanya's heart with as much love as the song proclaimed.

Matching goblets filled with burgundy liquid perched near the player like twin vessels of celebration, ready to be embraced. At the table's end stood Sonny, a velvet box in his hand, a question in his eyes. A slow tremble started in Tanya's legs as she realized her dreams really were coming true.

The vehicle slowed to a stop and Tanya caught sight of a bumper, reflecting the sun. Two doors slammed, and Sonny glanced toward the inevitable invasion. Sighing, he shook his head, slipped the velvet box in his jacket pocket, turned off the music.

Tanya's trembling abated. Her shoulders sagged. She strode toward the table.

"So much for privacy," Sonny groused and grabbed a goblet.

Turning her back on the approaching footsteps, Tanya picked up one of the goblets and feigned a casual stance before taking a long swallow of the carbonated beverage.

"Oh—no!" Sonny's low-toned exclamation sent a prickle of fear through Tanya. His fumbling to pull a gun from beneath his jeans leg made her go stiff.

"Sonny?" she whispered and pivoted to face the reason for his alarm.

But even before she spotted the men, Tanya's pounding heart insisted Salazar had somehow found them.

"Drop the gun now!" Salazar demanded as he aimed a pistol at Sonny, who'd just secured his firearm.

Sonny's pistol fell onto the carpet of leaves. Slowly, he straightened, raised his hands. "Okay, okay, I dropped it," he chimed in a smooth voice.

The plateau tilted, and Tanya fought the urge to collapse. Salazar's cohort, a lean, dark man who looked like he could crush a soul and never flinch, strode toward Sonny like a robot on automatic pilot. When he was within inches of Sonny, he placed the barrel of a pistol against his temple.

"What's wrong with you, Mansfield?" Salazar said his voice even and hard. "Did you think I hired you to find my woman so you could romance her? Did you really think you'd get away with this?" He waved toward the picnic table like some dictator, disgusted with his insubordinate subjects.

His words circled Tanya like gibberish while she tried to absorb the invasion. Like a trapped fox at the end of a hunter's gun, Tanya was assaulted by violent quivering. "Sonny?" she cried and dropped the goblet with no thought for the spill.

Sonny's desperate eyes and rapid breathing only heightened Tanya's terror.

"Eva—" Salazar shook his head. "I mean Tanya, you come with me," he commanded, his authoritative gesture demanding no argument.

She recalled their first meeting on the plane, how he'd initially seemed so polite and courteous. But soon, the good manners had been tainted with a desire that drove him to pursue Tanya for nearly two years. Now the manners were gone. Only the desire remained— a desire mixed with a hard determination that insisted he would find Tanya no matter where she hid. His dark eyes held her captive while she inwardly clawed against the idea of what Salazar would do to her.

"Come on, Tanya," Salazar insisted, his voice a tad softer. "You won't regret it, I promise."

The gunman's finger tightened on the trigger. "Go with him, woman, or watch me blow his brains out. Take your choice," he growled in a guttural voice.

Her stomach rolled. Her eyes blurred. Tanya sought Sonny for guidance. His only advice was a slight nod.

"What are you going to do to him?" she questioned.

"I'm sorry, Tanya," Salazar supplied, and this time his voice was closer.

Gasping, she whirled to face him and stared into a soul as dark as it was lonely.

"But Sonny's going to have to die." He shrugged as if he was talking about ending the life of a rodent. "I really don't have a choice anymore. He not only double-crossed me, he's seen too much. He can't live. Now, come with me." Salazar grabbed her arm and yanked.

With a garbled cry, Tanya stumbled to his side. He slipped his arm around her waist and squeezed. "You're going to be just fine," he mumbled under his breath, and the smell of cigars tainted his words as much as the lust tainted his expression. "You'll get used to me. One day you'll even love me. You'll see."

"N-no," Tanya whimpered. "You can't—can't do this."

"Oh, I can and I have," Salazar purred and dragged her toward his vehicle.

"No!" Tanya repeated. "Sonny! God help us! Sonny!" She dug in her feet and tried to wrestle from Salazar's grip.

With a growl, he whipped her to his side and snatched her off her feet, like an oversized bag.

"Tanya!" Sonny screamed. "Tanya!" His words mingled into a painful grunt, and Tanya glimpsed his falling to the ground with Drake going in for the kill.

Tanya flung her fists and kicked and screamed until her throat went raw, but nothing stopped Salazar's iron determination.

"You won't get away with this!" she bellowed. "The police—the police will look for me—"

He threw back his head and laughed. "I *own* the police!" he bragged. "They won't touch me."

He dragged her to the Jeep. The second he dropped her into the passenger seat, a pistol's explosion echoed among the hills. Tanya went limp.

Salazar's gratified laugh immersed Tanya in stunned dread.

He leaned close, peered into her eyes, and said, "You're all mine now, Eva. I'll never let you get away again." Salazar's gaze trailed to her lips before he lowered his face to hers. The smell of cigars engulfing her, Tanya groped for every breath. A second before Salazar's lips touched hers, she shoved against his chest and spat in his face.

His eyes widened. A red flush marred his features. His lips hardened in sequence with his eyes. "Well, you little . . ." Salazar lifted his hand.

But a pistol's explosion jolted him midstrike. The radiator's hiss reaped Salazar's expletive while Tanya ducked and covered her head with her hands. She squeezed her eyes tight as her confused mind tried to make sense of the turmoil.

"Mansfield!" Salazar roared.

"Sonny!" Tanya shrieked and spotted Sonny standing fifty feet away with a pistol aimed straight at Salazar.

"Get down, Tanya!" he commanded, and she heeded his warning.

"I'll kill you!" Salazar bellowed as another shot erupted. His grunt, the stumble of unsteady footsteps, preceded his crashing to the ground.

Tanya lifted her head, only to encounter Sonny mere feet away.

"I thought he killed you!" she whimpered.

"He did, but I'm like a cat. I've got nine lives." His smile resembled a grimace. "When he knocked me down the second time, I came back up with my gun. He wasn't expecting that." Sonny glanced toward Salazar and then hurried to the driver's side. "Get out this way," he insisted and opened the door. "The scenery's better."

Tanya scrambled over the gear shift and slid out of the Jeep. Sonny slipped his arm around her waist, and she didn't resist the support. Her legs unsteady, she stumbled toward their Jeep while Salazar's vulgar expletives filled the countryside.

Fueled by an aversion that was greater than her weakness, Tanya hurried ahead of Sonny and crashed into their Jeep. "Just get me out of here," she said.

"Give me time to make a call or two," Sonny said and squeezed her hand just as his cell phone began playing the theme song from the *Dukes of Hazzard*. "That's Jack now. I guess he read my mind."

Tanya covered her face and began to slowly rock back and forth in the seat. Part of her wanted to believe this nightmare really was over, but another part insisted that as long as Salazar was alive he'd always be a threat.

Sonny mumbled an unsteady hello and then paused. "Yeah, I know. They already found us," he said as if he'd been expecting the attack all along.

Tanya lowered her hands, opened her eyes, and tried to absorb the implications of Sonny's words; but his wincing and leaning against the Jeep stirred a concern that blotted out all other thoughts.

"Fine," he said and glanced toward Tanya. "She's fine. She's a fighter, that's all I've got to say." He threw in an assuring wink and patted her hand. Tanya latched onto his fingers.

"We need backup and an ambulance."

Salazar's eerie silence underscored Sonny's claim. "They're both hurt pretty bad—bleeding. Might be best to send a chopper pronto," he said before stating the instructions to their locale.

While Jack talked, Sonny rubbed his haggard face and finally answered with, "I'm going to be fine. I just took a few blows. " Another pause preceded his final comments, "Yeah. And thanks—for—for everything, all the work the last few weeks." He grimaced and sent a pain-filled glance toward Tanya before snapping the phone shut.

"Are you going to be okay?" she asked.

"Yes, it just got a little rough there at the end, but I'm fine." Sonny leaned close and brushed her forehead with his lips. "We need to sit tight until the ambulance and police arrive. After that, I'll get you outa here. Okay?" He squeezed her hand, and Tanya fleetingly realized she never got to see the ring . . . or say yes.

CHAPTER TWENTY-THREE

Tanya's eyes lulled open, and she grappled with the disturbing thoughts that had accompanied her journey out of sleep. After several seconds of straining to remember, she sat up and rubbed her puffy eyes. Shoving aside the comforter, Tanya covered a yawn and recalled the events of the day before.

After the FBI and paramedics arrived, they'd arranged for Drake's transport to the hospital and Salazar's transport to the morgue. Despite Salazar's continued threats, Sonny had regretted his death. He'd attempted a shot to incapacitate only and hadn't planned on the man having a massive heart attack. Tanya had been too numb to absorb the implications.

Sonny supported her through the questioning. Then, he expertly wrapped up the final details and escorted Tanya back to her cabin. She kept a tight reign on her emotions through the whole process; only when she and Sonny stopped in front of her cabin did she release the tears while Sonny held her. According to the FBI, they had enough on Drake to put him away for life.

After she'd composed herself, Tanya barely remembered Sonny slipping on the ring or the gentle kiss that secured their engagement.

Nevertheless, the diamond cluster now rested on her finger, and Tanya touched it. Even in the darkness, she imagined its sparkle. Sonny and she had agreed to set an official date next summer, so they'd have time to deepen their acquaintance. Tanya had gladly embraced his suggestion. They had much to learn and share before they said, "I do."

But the joys of being engaged were not what had awakened her. Grappling to recall those disturbing thoughts as she'd drifted out of sleep, Tanya slipped her feet into her house shoes and padded toward the cabin's bathroom. She flipped on the light and squinted against the brightness. Tanya checked her watch. Six A.M. swiftly approached. Sonny said he'd walk her to breakfast at seven.

The soft pelting of rain against the windowpane testified that the forecast had been correct. The rain began shortly after sundown and apparently continued through the night. She thought about the clothing she'd brought and decided her corduroys and hiking shoes were in order for chapel service, whether it was Sunday morning or not.

Yawning, she gazed at her engagement ring. The diamonds twinkling in the gauzy light spoke of Sonny's love, but her mind still strained for that dream. Something in it had been important . . . so important it jolted Tanya from her sleep.

She meandered to the window, raised the blinds, and gazed into the limbs of the bush in front of the pane. The nearby street lamp cast an eerie glow upon the rain-laden leaves, shedding droplets as swiftly as they fell. She stared at the leaves until they merged in a watery blur. As the image before her eyes grew less distinguishable, the memories from yesterday sharpened.

Finally, the battle replayed in Tanya's mind as vividly as when she'd lived it. Salazar and Drake had set a trap for them at the plateau, knowing Sonny would eventually bring Tanya there. Her palms grew sweaty as she relived Sonny's attempted proposal and

Salazar's crashing into their moment. The further she progressed into the memory, the more ragged her breathing grew. Some sub-conscious portent urged her to end the memory that had invaded her sleep, but Tanya couldn't stop the instant replay in her mind.

Finally, she arrived at the moment when Salazar yelled, *"Did you think I hired you to find my woman so you could romance her? Did you really think you'd get away with this?"*

The bush came into crisp focus. Tanya frowned. " 'Did you think I hired you to find my woman so you could romance her . . .' " she repeated and wrestled with the implications.

Did Salazar hire Sonny at some point? she questioned and balled her clammy palms. She remembered the day Sonny walked into her life. He'd asked if he could rent the apartment for his part-time photograph business, yet Tanya didn't remember seeing any equip-ment in the apartment the few times she'd been there. Of course, her asking him to stay as her bodyguard had changed the dynamics of their relationship. Nonetheless, if the photography was important enough for him to rent an apartment, she imagined he'd still utilize the space, even if she did let him stay there for free.

Her heart pounded as Tanya realized Sonny had arrived in her life right before the invaders cut her phone line. She'd accredited the timing to God's divine protection alone. Now she wasn't so sure.

"What if Salazar *did* hire Sonny to find me?" she whispered. "And what if Sonny realized after he found me he'd messed up? And what if he asked to rent the apartment for photography just as an excuse to be there when Salazar arrived?" She rubbed her eyes and tried to absorb the possibilities.

If that's what happened, she thought, *then he wasn't honest with me.*

"Why didn't he just tell me?" she whispered and then eyed the engagement ring. *Because he knew it would get him nowhere fast*, she deduced.

Her stomach knotted as another memory crashed through. When Sonny's phone rang, he'd readily taken the call and said, *"Yeah, I know. They already found us,"* as if he'd been expecting the attack all along. Then he'd added, *"And thanks—for—for everything, all the work the last few weeks."*

At the time, Tanya had been so dazed that the finer nuance of these statements had eluded her. Now she recognized another fact of Sonny's covering the truth: he'd known Salazar was a threat but hadn't told Tanya.

"How long did he know?" she whispered and imagined herself at risk for weeks without Sonny's telling her.

Tanya covered her face and tried to sort through the intricacies of the whole situation. She'd fallen in love with Sonny . . . or so she thought. And, he'd fallen in love with her . . . or so he said. But healthy relationships were based on honesty, and it appeared that Sonny had covered the truth. If Sonny could be dishonest with her and so expertly hide it before marriage, he could do the same after marriage— and perhaps with bigger issues, just like Ryan. She lowered her hands, sighed, and couldn't stop the dismay from mounting.

Finally, Tanya seized control of her emotions and made herself focus on the facts. The facts were that she was basing everything she'd assumed upon a memory of what Salazar and Sonny had said during a very heated exchange. Salazar was a murderous lecher, and Sonny had been rattled, to say the least. Before Tanya jumped to any conclusions, she'd talk to Sonny. Maybe there was a perfectly logical explanation for why he'd not informed Tanya that Salazar was at large, if he had indeed known that. And maybe Sonny really hadn't been hired by Salazar. Maybe Salazar had just been ranting.

Sonny sat across from Tanya in the cafeteria and wondered what was on her mind. She'd been unusually silent from the time he picked her up—not exactly what he'd expected for a newly engaged woman. Sonny had nearly asked her a dozen times what was bothering her, but had been bitten by cowardice every time. She'd barely nibbled a bagel and now sipped some coffee while staring out the window at the parting clouds. The rain had finally stopped, the sun was peaking out, and patches of blue promised a beautiful day.

"Wanta walk to the gazebo by the lake?" Sonny asked.

"Sure," she said after a long pause.

Trying to hide the ache in his gut, Sonny helped Tanya into her jacket. The paramedic said he thought Sonny's injuries were superficial and recommended Sonny make a trip to the ER. But Sonny had declined and promised he'd report to Tanya if he had any symptoms besides the soreness expected when someone has tried to kick you to Mexico.

When his abdomen inhibited his attempts to slip on his own coat, Tanya silently assisted. "Thanks," he said before they stepped into the cold morning together. Once outside, he took her hand, and the tension mounted with every step. By the time they arrived in the gazebo, Sonny sympathized with Jack's doghouse experience on a new level. Whatever he'd done, it must have been a whopper of a mistake.

Finally, he conjured all his courage and said, "Something's bothering you."

Tanya gazed at him through the morning light, her cheeks pale, her eyes full of questions.

Sonny couldn't take much of that expression, so he shifted his focus to the lake, as slick as a mirror, and wished the glossy surface could show him exactly what troubled her.

Finally, she said, "Yesterday, Salazar said, 'What's wrong with you, Mansfield? Did you think I hired you to find my woman so you could romance her?' What did he mean by that?"

Sonny's face stiffened. He vaguely recalled Maurice saying something to that effect, but he'd been distracted, to say the least.

"Did Maurice hire you to find me, Sonny?" Tanya pressed.

Sonny gazed at his boots and said the only thing that came to him, "Yeah."

"So when you came into my yard and asked to rent the apartment . . ."

"I had been watching you," he explained. "Salazar came to me as a man named Kelvin Stuart. He had a story about a wife who'd wrongfully divorced him and kidnapped their adopted son. After I found you and gave him your contact information, he had such an evil look on his face, I began to suspect I'd messed up. I second-guessed my willingness to find you. And the longer I watched you, the more sure I was that I wanted to hear your side of the story."

"My—my side of the story?" she squeaked. "Why didn't you ask that *before* you told him where I live?"

Sonny didn't bother to tell her he'd already posed that question to himself and hadn't liked the answer.

Her lips trembling, Tanya shook her head, and Sonny sensed this couldn't be a good sign. But now that the truth was out, he also couldn't stop with only half of it.

"Why didn't you tell me?" she asked.

"Would you have considered renting me the apartment if you'd known he hired me?" Sonny asked.

Tanya's only answer was a wide-eyed stare, and Sonny never remembered her looking so vulnerable. "Besides, after I got to know you, I really liked you a lot, and I didn't want anything to upset that applecart. But now that we're engaged . . ."

Tanya removed the ring, and Sonny's sore gut tensed. "I don't know about the engagement anymore."

"What?"

"I have to know I can trust you, Sonny, and you—you more or less lied to me and never corrected it, just like Ryan lied to Shelly."

"I never lied to you, Tanya," he protested and couldn't escape the parallels she was drawing between him and Ryan. The fear in her eyes said she dreaded Shelly's fate.

"You told me you wanted to rent the apartment for photography, and it had nothing to do with that. I don't even remember seeing any photography equipment up there. Are you even a photographer?"

"Yes, of course I am," Sonny said. "I can show you a list of my credits with clippings included!" He raised both hands. "I've just been so busy with my other jobs and with you and Coty, I—"

"How long did you know Salazar wasn't in jail before yesterday?" Tanya asked.

"Over a month," he admitted, and didn't even try to guess how she'd figured that one out. "I didn't tell you because he was supposed to be out of the country, and I didn't want you to be scared."

"So that's the reason you so readily agreed to stay when Coty came looking for you. It wasn't because—"

"Yes, it was because . . . !" Sonny hollered, and a trio of passing women looked straight at him. "Like I already said," he continued his voice low, "I just didn't want you to be scared. I didn't tell you because I cared about you."

The worry in her eyes diminished a fraction.

"I found out right before we went to the plateau yesterday that he was supposed to be back in the country. I *did* plan to tell you last night, but I didn't want to ruin the proposal with all that. Then, when everything happened the way it did—" He lifted his hands and was overtaken by the irritation that had been nibbling at his soul.

"You know, Tanya," he blurted. "I guess I really wasn't completely honest with you when we first met, but I did it to protect you. I laid my *life* on the line for you. I was going to use the money Salazar paid me to *pay you* to rent the apartment to protect you, and you're hung up over—"

"I know you did, Sonny," she replied, "and I appreciate it. I really do. But I'm so confused. I *hope* you wouldn't lie to me in our marriage about—about other things . . ."

"Are you implying that you think I'd be unfaithful just because Ryan was?"

"You seemed to be defending him," she countered. "And what he did was *so wrong*. How can you defend him?"

"I know what he did was wrong!" Sonny snapped. "I've messed up in that area, too, and I *know* it's wrong! But I can't help feeling his pain too."

"I guess all this has just made me start worrying that—" She stopped, bit her lips, and gazed toward the woods.

"What? That I'll mess up again?"

She didn't answer.

"So what's this *really* about, Tanya?" he asked, his voice as wobbly as his knees.

Tears brimming, she shook her head again and didn't answer.

"Is it that you don't want to marry a man with my past because you're afraid I'll repeat?" he rasped and wished he sounded less desperate.

"I—I never said that," she stammered.

But Sonny's sinking heart insisted that was exactly what she meant. "What's the deal with all this talk of grace, and how Christ is supposed to enable us to overcome and move forward? Don't you believe that?"

"I do!" She stood and balled her fists. "It's just that . . ." Tanya helplessly gazed at him as her eyes spoke a wealth of doubts that tore at his soul.

Stifling a groan, he opened his chilled palm and spoke the hardest words he'd ever said, "If you want to give me the ring back, that's fine. I don't want to push you into something you're not sure of."

A tear spilled onto her cheek. She sniffled, hesitated, and Sonny was tempted to fall to his knees and beg her to keep the ring. But finally, logic ruled his emotions. She had been honest about her doubts, and they were legitimate. Until she could come to terms with them, Sonny wouldn't pressure her.

She removed the ring again, and Sonny couldn't remember her putting it back on. Her fingers shaking, she laid it against his palm. The diamonds sparkled in the morning sun before Sonny curled his fist around them and snuffed out the spark.

CHAPTER TWENTY-FOUR

Two weeks later, Sonny drove his motorcycle as deep into Jack's woods as the narrow trail allowed. Then he turned off the engine, removed his helmet, lowered the kickstand, and got off. Laying his helmet on the seat, he gazed toward the sound of the river that raced through nature's habitat. He wasn't as much of an outdoorsman as Jack, but Sonny had frequented this sanctuary several times in the last couple of weeks.

After pulling up his jersey hood, he trudged through the briars and fallen limbs until he stepped onto the riverbank. The downed tree he'd chosen as his pew once again invited Sonny to sit and absorb the presence of the Creator. Sonny tucked his hands in his jersey pockets and claimed the smooth trunk. The nip in the air was just enough to need a jacket, and Sonny was thankful for the warm beam of sunshine that christened his corner of the woods.

Hunching forward, Sonny closed his eyes and breathed deeply of the smells of peat moss and fresh water. The river's murmur mingled with the murmuring of his disquieted soul and Sonny tried to focus on asking God to continue to help him get over Tanya; but today the effort was as wasted as a pebble attempting to halt the river's flow.

Sonny sighed and allowed himself to ponder the last couple of weeks. Tanya had chosen not to ride back with Sonny after the singles' retreat. She hitched a ride with some church friends and sent him a text message, explaining her plans. Sonny had packed and left the second he got her message. The trip home had been the most miserable of his life.

Except for work, he'd virtually hibernated the first week back, and wouldn't have merged into life if not for his ornery brothers not taking no for an answer. They'd dragged him to a Dallas Cowboy's game and made him cheer for every touchdown, whether he wanted to or not. Attending the game had at least brought Sonny back to the land of the living. Tonight, Ryan and Jack had insisted on taking Sonny camping and fishing at Lake Tyler.

Neither Jack nor Ryan had made a deal of talking about the breakup with Tanya; they'd just silently supported Sonny through some of the toughest weeks of his life. Sonny had been glad for their support . . . and their silence. Some things, a man needed to sort through on his own.

Sonny opened his eyes, peered into the swirling water. Since his church had been Tanya's, he hadn't attended services after the breakup. Even though Jack and Ryan had invited him to their church, Sonny had gravitated toward this isolated spot as his place of worship . . . for now anyway. He could thank Tanya for encouraging him to recommit his life to God—even if she couldn't stand by the commitment to him. In the last few weeks, that renewed relationship had given him the stability to keep his act together. The last time his life fell apart, he'd turned to alcohol. This time, Sonny didn't need alcohol. He had the Lord.

"Thanks for holding me up," Sonny whispered. "I don't know what hurt worst, you know? Losing Tanya or losing Coty. I seem to be on some sort of a self-destruct path when it comes to women and children. If You can get me over this one, I promise, I'll never repeat." Sonny shook his head and wondered exactly how many ways he would spell "fool" before he stopped the spelling.

The sound of someone trekking through the woods alerted Sonny that he was about to have a visitor. Expecting Jack, he was surprised to see Ryan step from behind a clump of trees.

"Hey, guy!" Sonny called and waved toward Ryan.

Dressed in a pair of hiking boots, jeans, and a heavy sweatshirt, Ryan strode toward Sonny's pew. "Jack said he thought you were out here."

"Yeah. This is my spot, I guess," Sonny explained and scooted over to make more room.

Ryan settled onto the log and scanned the river's bank. "We've started getting the camping gear together and are close to heading out."

Sonny checked his watch. "I didn't realize it was almost four," he admitted. "I guess I've been sitting here longer than I realized."

"Yeah . . . Jack's wanting to leave soon." He glanced up one end of the river, then the other. "Seen any deer?" he asked.

"I did a few days ago—a huge buck—but nothing today."

"Jack's got some corn feeders out."

"That's what he told me. He's determined to kill a trophy buck this year or bust."

"Maybe we should take up hunting," Ryan suggested. "It'd help get our minds off these women."

Sonny chuckled. "The women are going to kill us, you know that don't you?"

Ryan's smile held as much sadness as his eyes. "Looks that way," he admitted and his focus trailed past Sonny. "But hey . . . we'll persevere, right? We're Mansfields." He held up his fist, and Sonny bumped it with his.

"Yep, we're Mansfields . . . till death do us part."

Ryan winced. "Did you have to put it *that* way?"

Sonny snickered. "I had to get it in one way or another, doesn't look like I'll ever say it at the altar."

"Who knows?" Ryan said, lifting his brows. "Maybe God will perform a miracle after all."

"It's going to take one," Sonny grumbled.

"Maybe you should just do what I tried to do—go after your woman." He pushed at Sonny's shoulder.

"Oh, yeah, that really worked for you, didn't it?" Sonny teased.

"Has anybody smacked you lately?" Ryan asked. "I think you need it." His humorous tone belied any serious intent.

"Ha, ha, ha," Sonny drawled and whacked the top of his brother's knee. "Come on. Let's go see if Jack needs any help. I'm sure he needs me to tangle some fishing line or something."

"No deal," Ryan replied as they both stood. "I already took care of that."

"I don't know why the guy even lets me go with him. When it comes to camping he's like Davey Crockett, and I'm Larry, Curly, and Moe all rolled into one."

"Ah, you're not *that* bad," Ryan assured, his face impassive. "You're just Moe."

One month later, Tanya still regretted the way she and Sonny parted. She never intended for everything to spiral out of control. Ironically, on the way home, Tanya had been convinced all her doubts were in vain. Sonny Mansfield wouldn't repeat Ryan's mistake . . . and she didn't think he'd ever marginalize the truth with her again. But it was too late now.

She sighed, flopped onto the couch, picked up the remote, and flipped the TV station to CNN. She'd been following Drake in the national news all month. The story of his arrest and Salazar's death hit CNN within twenty-four hours. The corruption of the Ft.

Worth police accompanied information about Drake and Salazar several times a week.

Tanya suffered through a monologue on the economy before she was rewarded with Drake's image on the screen. Each new blurb revealed even more vile information, claiming he and Salazar were involved in all manner of crimes. Tanya shuddered when she thought of how close she'd come to being yet another of Salazar's victims. This time, the attractive anchorwoman announced that Drake's trial would begin shortly after the New Year. Drake's image sent a cold chill through her; and Tanya prayed that he never got out of prison and that his interest in her died with Salazar.

When a familiar rumble echoed up her driveway, Tanya held her breath and wondered if she were imagining the sound. She set the remote on the coffee table and stared at the front door until the slam of the vehicle's door sent her into a spastic stand. Tanya raced to her bedroom, peered past her blinds, and confirmed what she suspected. Sonny Mansfield trudged toward the garage apartment. Head bent, he held a set of keys and disappeared around the side of the garage.

Maybe he's come after his stuff, Tanya thought. Even though his clothing and suitcase had vanished one day when Tanya was at work, he'd not returned for the remaining furniture. And Tanya hadn't had the nerve to ask him to remove his stuff or return the key—despite Dolly's urging her to contact him.

She rested her hand along the wall and placed her forehead on it as a wave of nausea consumed her. Tanya's appetite had fluctuated between waning and nonexistent for a whole month, and she'd lost ten pounds. Just seeing Sonny would probably make her swear off eating for a week.

"Oh God," she breathed. "I don't know what to do. I've really messed things up, and I don't know if he'll ever forgive me."

Tanya raised her head and thought of Coty, now with her parents at the zoo. She was certainly glad they'd offered to take him. Tanya had done some much-needed housekeeping, and now Coty wasn't here to see Sonny's truck in the drive. She could only imagine the fit he'd throw if he didn't get to see Sonny. The first week without him in the apartment had been heartbreaking for Coty. He'd cried for Sonny every evening; and Tanya had cried for him every night when she went to bed.

"We love you," she whispered, and knew that her love was genuine. The real stuff was supposed to cover a multitude of sins, and it had. She no longer cared if Sonny marginalized the truth. He'd apologized. Tanya had also fully realized he'd done it to protect her. She'd have never let him stay if she'd known Salazar hired him. She'd have been afraid he was actually associated with Salazar somehow.

As for all that business about Ryan, that was between Shelly and Ryan. Tanya saw now she'd allowed her fear to get the best of her. If Sonny said he'd be faithful, then Tanya had to believe him. A solid marriage was based on that kind of trust, or it was no marriage at all.

"But that doesn't even matter now," she mumbled and cast another glance out the window. Seeing no signs of him, Tanya finally decided to busy herself in the kitchen until he retrieved all his belongings. Keeping a vigil by the window was insane and would increase her nervousness by the minute.

She'd walked halfway across her room when a car door slammed and Coty's voice exclaimed, "Sonny! Sonny here!"

Gasping, Tanya hustled back to the window to spot Coty running straight to the apartment. Ed and Shirley trotted close behind, but had as much luck catching him as they would an oiled cat.

*   *   *

Sonny entered the apartment only minutes before Coty and his grandparents arrived. He'd been raking leaves in his yard, across the street from Brookshire's parking lot, when he spotted Coty trotting across the lot at Ed and Shirley's side. Since Brookshire's was the only sizable grocery store in Bullard, Sonny had spent a full month watching the area in hopes of seeing Tanya and Coty. He'd brainstormed what might happen if he actually ran into them in that store, or any store around town. But he hadn't seen them once.

After days of prayer, Sonny had come to the conclusion that it was time to take Ryan's advice and go after Tanya. He'd finally decided that was his only avenue to sanity. She'd either tell him to get lost or they could work through their problems. Either way, Sonny would no longer feel as if he was hanging on the brink of despair. The fact that she'd put the ring back on before he asked for it now made him think that perhaps she'd been willing to work through their problems. But Sonny didn't know if Tanya was still in that frame of mind . . . or if she was so through, she despised the very sight of him. Whatever the case, he'd finally come to the realization that he loved her too much to leave things as they were.

So when he spotted Coty and his grandparents leaving Brookshire's, Sonny had dropped the rake, locked the house, and hustled to the apartment. He'd gambled that Coty would arrive soon and that once he spotted Sonny's pickup he'd come after him.

Now Sonny stood at the window, watching the little guy run toward the garage with Ed and Shirley close behind. Smiling, he waited for the inevitable. When Coty's voice echoed up the stairway, Sonny neared the door. The second Coty bellowed his name, Sonny could stand the suspense no longer.

He whipped open the apartment door and met Coty at the top of the stairs. The child wrapped himself around Sonny's legs and hollered, "Sonny! Sonny! You came ta see me!"

Sonny bent, pulled Coty into his arms, and hugged him tight. His eyes stung with the impact of such gigantic love from such a small heart. Coty smelled of peanut butter and crackers and Sonny had never been so glad to be exactly where he was.

"We're so sorry," Shirley O'Brien said from nearby.

Sonny opened his eyes to spot Tanya's parents, huffing their way up the stairs.

"We tried to stop him," she continued. "I'm sure you must be busy—packing—or, or, or . . ."

Ed continued the climb and extended his hand. Sonny offered a firm shake when Ed said, "It's good to see you," like he meant it.

"It's good to see you guys too," Sonny said and hadn't even thought about what he was wearing until this moment. While the old sweats had been perfect for a brisk day of yard work, he now wished he'd taken the time to at least upgrade to a pair of jeans. A nervous jitter hopped along his spine, and Sonny wondered how long it would take for Tanya to arrive, or *if* she'd arrive.

"Come on, Coty," Shirley admonished as she neared. "I'm sure Sonny's too busy to have you hanging on him like a monkey."

"No!" Coty protested. "I stay here with Sonny! He came ta see me."

Sonny tightened his hold on Coty in sequence with the child's increasing his grip on Sonny's neck. He closed his eyes and drank of the moment. "He's okay," he said, his voice thick as his heart swelled with a father's love. And in that second, Sonny didn't know *how* he and Tanya would work out their problems, he only knew they had to. Sonny simply could not spend another month like the last one. And he knew that permanently losing both Coty and Tanya simply was not an option. That old Michael Bolton number played in his mind. If he had to sleep in the rain or beg her back, he'd do whatever it took.

Opening his eyes, he realized Shirley and Ed were both focused on him holding their grandson. Shirley's heart was in her eyes, and both respect and hope cloaked Ed's features.

"We're *so glad* you're back," Shirley said.

Sonny smiled. "It feels good to be home," he simply said and wondered if Tanya would feel the same way.

Tanya paced her bedroom and debated exactly what she should do. Her parents and Coty had been with Sonny for nearly fifteen minutes. With every new minute that passed, her anxiety increased. Nevertheless, Tanya refused to allow the pressure of this situation to stop her from remaining coherent and acting logically, rather than on impulse. If she were to act on impulse, she would have already gone up to the apartment, feigning interest in Coty's safety. But that scheme would be as weak as it was easy to see through.

So Tanya continued to pace, only stopping to check her appearance. On a sigh, she turned from the mirror and didn't even try. She'd been cleaning house most of the day, and her makeup had faded, her ponytail had wilted. She covered her face with her unsteady hands and did the only thing that was left. Tanya prayed.

But "Dear God, help me" was all she could squeak out.

The words had barely left her mouth when the doorbell rang. Holding her breath, Tanya lowered her hands and stared at her reflection once more while her face gradually lost color.

The doorbell's second chime sent Tanya dashing from her bedroom, up the hallway. By the time she gripped the doorknob, she hoped Sonny stood on the other side and simultaneously dreaded the very sight of him. The dread came from not having a clue what she'd say; the hope, from wanting to reconcile more than she'd ever wanted anything in her life.

Coty's squeal accompanied her opening the door to see Sonny tickling a delighted little boy. Once he spotted Tanya, Sonny stopped. His questioning eyes mirrored the lonely uncertainty in his smile.

"Hello, Tanya," he said.

"Hi," she replied.

"Sonny came ta see me!" Coty exclaimed. "Let me in!" He squirmed out of Sonny's grasp and darted past Tanya. "C'mon, Sonny! You see my new horsey!"

"Do you mind?" Sonny questioned.

"N-no, of course not," Tanya said and stepped out of his way.

Sonny entered the house, and Tanya couldn't remember it feeling this much like home since the last time Sonny was here. Without a glance her way, Sonny sauntered toward the hallway and disappeared. Tanya rested her hand on her chest while a dozen possibilities whizzed through her mind. Maybe Sonny really had just come to see Coty. Perhaps he'd missed Coty as much as Coty missed him.

As Tanya neared Coty's room she could only hope the loneliness in his eyes meant he'd missed her as well. She stopped on the room's threshold to gaze upon a father helping his little boy onto the over-sized rocking horse.

"See!" Coty exclaimed. "It goes back and forth!" He pulled on the handles and then leaned back and forth repeatedly until he'd revved the horse into a rocking frenzy.

"Ride 'em cowboy!" Sonny cheered and then spotted Tanya.

She crossed her arms, leaned against the doorframe, and feigned a calm persona. "Dad found that at a secondhand store. Coty hasn't stopped riding it since."

"He dragged me over here to see it, actually," Sonny explained. Even though his eyes were now guarded, a wealth of unspoken communication hung between them.

One second Tanya thought Sonny had come to see her . . . to tell her he loved her . . . and the next, she feared his story about

Coty dragging him here was the only reason he'd arrived. Confused, Tanya broke eye contact and focused on her son.

"He really enjoys seeing you," she said and pressed her lips together to stop the trembling.

"Yeah," he said and tousled Coty's hair.

As the trembling moved to her knees, Tanya decided to get to the bottom of his sudden appearance and once and for all put herself out of her misery. "So . . . I guess you came to load up your furniture?" she questioned and shifted her attention back to him.

Still focused on Coty, Sonny didn't answer. Tanya was on the verge of repeating the question when he finally lifted his gaze and said, "No, I didn't, actually."

"Oh."

He didn't look away, and neither did she. "I, uh, actually wondered . . ." He hesitated, gazed at the floor.

"Yes?" Tanya breathed while Sonny's features softened.

"Kiss!" Coty exclaimed. "Sonny kiss mamma again!"

Tanya's eyes widened. Her mouth fell open. She gazed at her son while her face heated. Coty had slowed the rocking and now gazed back at Tanya like he had the answers to all her relationship problems.

The silence that followed increased Tanya's embarrassment tenfold. She dared not look at Sonny, but couldn't stop herself.

And Sonny's words shocked her as much as Coty's. Lifting a suggestive brow, he focused on her lips, and said, "Maybe that's not such a bad idea." His attention trailed back to her eyes, and Tanya lost all ability to breathe.

"Sonny . . ." she began.

"Have you missed me, Tanya?" he asked as he neared. "Because I sure have missed you. It's been the worst weeks of my life. I don't know how everything went south so fast, but I'm willing to crawl across the desert if you'll just—"

He stopped within centimeters, and Tanya could no longer pretend composure with her pulse hammering her temples. She wasn't certain who reached first and didn't care. The end result was the same. Sonny pulled her into his arms and held her close while his warmth seeped into her soul.

"I'm so sorry about how everything happened," he breathed. "I really didn't mean to lie to you. I was just trying to protect you."

"I know . . . I know," she responded.

"And you've got to believe me, Tanya . . ." He pulled away, cupped her face in his hands, and continued, "I've seen what Ryan's gone through. And I've already lost one family. Don't think I'll ever do anything to jeopardize this one."

"I know," she repeated. "I believe you. I'm so sorry I doubted you."

"You had every right to question," he admitted. His gaze trailed to her lips once more, but he cut a glance toward their captive audience. Coty sat on his horse, gaping at them as if entranced by the big screen.

Chuckling, Sonny scooped Coty into the crook of his arm while slipping his other arm around Tanya. "Sonny loves Coty," he said and brushed his lips against Coty's cheek. "And Sonny loves Tanya." He bestowed a gentle kiss upon Tanya's lips that left her aching for more.

"Tanya loves Sonny too," she responded and leaned closer for a family hug.

Dear Friend,

Often, people ask me, "Who are your favorite characters in your novels?" Over the years, several characters have stood out as all-time favorites, and Sonny Mansfield falls near the top of the list. The reason I enjoyed writing Sonny so much is because he's a long way from having it all together, but he's got a good heart and has *so much* potential.

I think of the woman caught in the act of adultery in John 8:1-11. The religious leaders brought her before Jesus with condemnation in their hearts. But Jesus didn't condemn her. Instead, he challenged the religious leaders by saying, "If any one of you is without sin, let him be the first to throw a stone at her" (v. 7).

Many times, we use this verse to teach that we shouldn't condemn people like the adulterous woman . . . or people like Sonny. But what we miss is that we all *are* this woman . . . and we all are Sonny. Maybe their sins aren't the same as ours, but we're all in need of a Savior. At some point, we've all be guilty of idolatry—putting ourselves on the throne of our hearts, rather than placing Christ there.

The religious leaders were as guilty as the woman they thrust before Jesus. Likewise, Tanya O'Brien is as much in need of a Savior as Sonny—even though she's lived a morally pure life. When she tells Sonny, "We're all on the same plain. I need a Savior as much as anyone. Without Christ,

I'm bad news, Sonny. No telling what I'd do or where I'd be," Tanya is speaking the eternal truth Jesus was trying to drive home with the religious leaders.

Any time I've asked the Lord to show me where I'd be without Him, it's a very humbling experience. I'm reminded of a line from an old song, "Show me where you've brought me from and where I could have been." Without the Lord we all could have been as shipwrecked as Sonny Mansfield. Realizing this makes me ever more thankful for God's guidance and presence in my life...and ever more determined to stay in the center of His will. Like Tanya, I'm no good without Him.

In His Service,
Debra White Smith

DISCUSSION QUESTIONS

1. Sonny Mansfield is a man who has made wrong choices in life. Romans 8:28 states, "And we know that in all things God works for the good of those who love him, who have been called according to his purpose." Discuss how God uses Sonny's wrong choices to bring an answer to Tanya O'Brien's prayers.

2. The tattoo on Sonny's arm represents his love and respect for his uncle Abe. Reflect on the songs "Faith of Our Fathers" and "Find Us Faithful" and discuss how Uncle Abe is an example of the powerful themes of these songs

3. Even though Tanya followed the will of God in adopting Coty, she encountered a stalker on the journey home. In Matthew, Jesus told His disciples to follow Him. As a result of obeying the Lord, they were flung into a storm (8:22-27). Discuss how sometimes obedience to God can lead us into a storm.

4. If God allows such storms in our lives, how does He use these storms to shape us into His image?

5. How did God use the trauma of Tanya's being stalked to change her for the better?

6. Discuss Tanya's high expectations for the man she would marry. While we should set high standards for our mates-to-be, at what level can expectations become unrealistic?

7. How do unrealistic expectations affect married couples?

8. When Sonny learned that his son was placed for adoption, he turned to alcohol, instead of God, to deal with his pain. But often, good Christian people turn to "church approved" behavior, instead of God himself, to cover pain. Discuss such behavior and draw an analogy between Sonny's blatant use of alcohol and covering pain in "more respectable" ways.

9. Throughout the story, there are several references to Sonny's brother, Jack, praying for his spiritual awakening. How does Sonny knowing Jack is praying for him influence his decisions?

10. Sonny eventually dedicates His life to Christ and sings the song, "He is Lord." Discuss the difference in knowing Christ as Savior and making Him Lord of our lives.

Don't Miss the Next Book in the

LONE STAR ★ INTRIGUE
SERIES

Coming Soon From

AVON
INSPIRE

Ryan Mansfield's boots crunched against the loose gravel scattered along Highway 69's wide shoulder. He approached the stopped SUV with as much caution as determination. Last year, he'd been sucked into a shootout when an angry driver didn't think he deserved a ticket . . . let alone a citation for driving while intoxicated. The night had a way of bringing that memory into haunting focus.

His flashlight's beam snaked across the pavement as he glanced toward the horizon. Dusk was disappearing, and a creamy gibbous moon hung from the sky like a ballroom chandelier. The November cool sucked all the haze from the air, leaving room for stars to dazzle. Ryan stopped a shiver and wondered if Shelly would ever believe just how lonely he was without her . . . and how much the long, autumn nights sharpened his loneliness.

Forcing himself to focus on the task at hand, he paused near the driver's side as the tinted window slid down.

The worried eyes that peered up at him didn't belong to a threatening stranger but to the woman he knew better than any other. "Shelly! Good grief! I was just—" Ryan blurted and stopped himself from admitting he'd been thinking of her.

The dashboard's glow heightened her petite features, and Ryan wished he could tell her how pretty she was.

"Ryan!" she gasped.

"Daddy! Daddy!" Sean's face appeared near Shelly and then the back door popped open. "Daddy!"

"Sean! No!" Shelly ordered.

"It's okay. I've got him," Ryan said and scooped his son into his arms. Sean's damp hair smelled of shampoo, and Ryan tousled it.

"How's my champ?" he asked, hugging his son tight.

"I'm going home with you!" Sean declared.

"No . . . we're going to Granna's to spend the night, remember?" Shelly said. "It's Granna's birthday tomorrow, and she's taking you to the fair." Her focus shifted to Ryan. "That's what Mom's 'getting from Sean' for her birthday." Shelly drew invisible quotes in the air.

Ryan smiled and patted his son's back. "Sounds like the best gift in the world to me."

Sean laid his head on Ryan's shoulder. "Please, Daddy!" he begged, his hold on Ryan's neck increasing. "I still wanta go home with you."

"You're going to Daddy's *next* weekend," Shelly insisted.

Ryan sized up her determined expression and knew this was one weekend she couldn't relent. They'd amazingly managed to juggle parenting duties for years now with a cooperation that had escaped every other element of their marriage. Somehow, they'd set aside their own preferences for what was best for Sean. As a result, Shelly gave Ryan more than his share of the dad-time the courts had outlined.

They'd adopted Sean as a newborn when Shelly's schizophrenic sister gave birth out of wedlock. The stress of a baby hadn't helped their selfish relationship; but the tumultuous marriage hadn't stopped the fierce love they both felt for Sean. Ryan never had a biological child, but he couldn't imagine loving one more than he loved his son . . . and he knew Shelly felt the same.

A lump in his throat, Ryan chuckled and tried to make light of the awkward situation. "Just wait until next weekend, okay? And then the week after that it's Thanksgiving, and we'll be together all week. We're going fishing at Uncle Jack's and horseback riding . . . and maybe even camping."

Sean lifted his head. The patrol car's flashing lights illuminated the expectation in his widened eyes. "Camping?" he exclaimed. "You promise?"

"You bet," Ryan said, "but you've got to cooperate with your mom now. I think she's in a hurry," he added on a dry note and eyed his ex-wife.

"Uh . . ." Shelly glanced down and then lifted her gaze. "I was supposed to be at Mom's an hour ago. You aren't going to give me a ticket, are you, Ryan?" Her question held an incredulous note, and her big brown eyes begged him to let her off.

He hesitated . . . only because he didn't want her to know just how much her request affected him. Truth was, all chances for a ticket had vanished the second he saw her.

"What's the deal with this SUV anyway?" Ryan asked. "I thought you were still driving the minivan."

"This is Tim's. He's letting me borrow it while the minivan is in the shop. Something with the transmission. It's been a wild week. My alarm system on the house malfunctioned, and a family of squirrels has been in the attic. I think they've done something to the wiring on the alarm system. Then the dog next door got out and chewed up Sean's shoes." Shelly waved aside the problems, and her sizable engagement ring flickered blue in the flash of the patrol car's blinking lights. "And that's just the first three days. All I know is Dad's taking care of the alarm and Tim's taking care of the car."

"Oh," Ryan said, his voice flat. *Daddy always did take care of everything*, he thought and didn't even want to consider Tim. Over the past few months he'd come to despise the name Tim. Last week, he'd even snapped at some poor guy bagging his groceries, just because the name displayed on his badge was *Tim*.

"I'd really like you to get the alarm system fixed ASAP," Ryan encouraged. "I don't mind taking care of it. Your dad lives an hour away."

"I know. I just hated to, well, bother you." She looked away.

Or didn't want me involved, Ryan thought and tried not to wince.

"Dr. Tim gave me a new ball glove." Sean wiggled toward the ground. "Here—I'll show it to you!" he offered and reached for the door handle.

Ryan stopped short of refusing his son's offer, simply because he sensed how proud Sean was of his new gift. Once Sean settled onto the backseat, he lifted the glove for his father's inspection. "See?"

"Very nice," Ryan said, running his fingertips across the high-grade leather. *The thing must have cost the price of a root canal*, he thought and wondered if there was no end to the dentist's money. The best Ryan could have ever done on his salary was a Wal-Mart special.

He clicked his son's seat belt in place and kissed his forehead. "Listen, you be good for your mom, okay?" he said, his voice thick. "And I'll see you next weekend."

"And then camping the next?"

"Right-o, champ." He doubled his fist, and Sean bumped the top with his own fist.

After slamming the door, he shifted back to Shelly's window and attempted to soften the admonishment he couldn't hold at bay. "Try to keep the speed down, you hear? Your mom can wait. She's waited before. Besides, I kinda like that little guy in the back."

"You only clocked me ten miles over the speed limit," she groused.

"Lots of people in the grave have said the same thing."

"That's the speed limit not far up the road anyway."

"Yeah, but the road here has a lot more twists and turns."

Shelly cut him an upward glance and then studied the steering wheel.

Ryan considered another remark, but decided to stop the tense exchange before it got out of hand. The pause stretched to awkward, and he said, "Well, I guess I'll e-mail you next week, and we can set up a time for me to get Sean."

"Oh, sure," she said before Ryan walked away from the vehicle.

"And, thanks . . ." The offer of gratitude was so faint, Ryan wondered if he'd imagined it. He glanced back. Her faint smile held a hint of the appreciation in her voice.

He lifted his brows to prompt an explanation.

"You know," she continued, "for not writing a ticket."

"Sure," he replied. Trudging back to his car, he thought it odd that she would believe he'd actually issue her a ticket. After all, Shelly was his wife . . . or at least, she used to be. But in his heart, she was as much his wife as she was the day they each said, *I do.*

The vehicle's flashing lights pierced his vision like the memory of their shattered relationship slashed his soul. He paused by the door, waited until an approaching vehicle whizzed past, and watched her pull away. Sean's face appeared in the back window. He waved, then rested his hand against the window.

He's gotten out of his seat belt! Ryan thought and prepared to call Shelly on her cell phone if she didn't immediately re-fasten it.

Ryan returned the wave. "Fasten your seat belt, buddy," he mouthed, hoping Sean could read his lips.

The vehicle slowed and pulled back to the curb before stopping. Sean's face disappeared, and Ryan knew Shelly was enforcing the seat-belt rule. Even though she pushed the speed limit here and there, she was a radical about wearing seat belts.

"At least I can count on that much," he sighed. Ryan whipped open the door, dropped behind the wheel, and turned off the flashing lights. Another long night on the highway awaited him. He'd asked for a change to night shift last year when he realized working nights stopped him from sitting in an empty house once the sun went down.

"Oh God," he prayed, "I know I'm the one who blew it but, please, somehow, bring her back to me." With Shelly pulling back onto the highway, Ryan rested his forehead against the steering wheel and groaned over the next words, *"Please, please* stop her marriage to Tim Aldridge. Oh Lord, I need a miracle."

Shelly Mansfield rolled over and opened one eye. According to the digital alarm's glaring red numbers she had only five minutes left to sleep. Groaning, she pulled the comforter up to her nose and wished for another hour. While she enjoyed serving on the church praise team, it robbed her of the extra sleep she'd normally get. The team met for practice an hour before Sunday school.

Of course, that also meant she and Tim had another hour together on Sundays, since he also sang on the team. Occasionally, they were assigned a duet, and everyone said they sounded professional. Shelly shivered and smiled. She enjoyed mingling her voice with Tim's and could hardly wait until they would fully mingle their lives as one in just three short months.

Ryan's disapproving expression floated across her mind, and Shelly tried to purge him from her thoughts. When she rolled down her window Friday night, Shelly hadn't expected Ryan. She also hadn't expected to be taken aback by just how good he looked, standing in the shadows in his uniform like some lonely cover boy who only had eyes for her. But then, Ryan Mansfield always had been a good-looking man—one that turned female heads in any crowd. She squeezed her eyes tight and reminded herself that that had been the problem in their marriage. Ryan had turned one too many heads and finally gave in.

Shelly had just been getting over the devastation when he claimed that he'd found the Lord and wanted to reconcile. But by then, she and Tim had already begun a relationship. On top of that, Shelly doubted she could ever trust him again. He was one of those men who maturity enhanced; the older he got, the more attractive he became. The more attractive he became, the more women noticed. The more women noticed . . .

The old emotions stirred out of nowhere . . . betrayal, devastation, confusion . . . and Shelly sat straight up. "I refuse to go there," she muttered and shoved aside the covers. She'd spent a whole year with a counselor, sorting out her wounds and trying to heal. Shelly Mansfield had finished wallowing in the pain a long time ago.

The alarm's squawk accompanied her feet touching the carpet. As she turned off the alarm, her gaze slid to the other side of the bed to find it empty. Despite her admonishments that Sean should sleep in his own room, he often crawled into her bed in the wee hours. Most of the time he claimed he didn't remember moving to her bed. A time or two in the last few months, she'd found him curled up on the floor in his room . . . or on the sofa. The pediatrician chalked it up to sleepwalking. Shelly immediately installed some childproof locks on the doors leading outside.

"He was probably too tired from yesterday to even sleepwalk," she mumbled while thrusting her feet into satin slippers and donning the matching robe. The fair had certainly exhausted Shelly. If not for her dedication to the praise team, she'd have spent another night with her parents and slept in this morning.

The smell of freshly brewing coffee lured her down the hallway. Even in her exhausted stupor last night, she'd remembered to set the coffeepot's timer and prepare the unit for a fresh brew.

Nearing Sean's room, Shelly detoured long enough to make certain he was still in his bed. But only a few steps into the chilled room revealed the bed was empty. Shelly stepped to the light switch, flipped it up, and scanned the floor. Still, no Sean. Assuming he must have landed on the couch this time, Shelly swiveled toward the hallway, but stopped. Something was wrong. As her disoriented mind grappled for logic, her nose grew colder by the second.

Shelly touched her cheeks. For some reason, the room was cooler than the hallway. She twisted back around. Her gaze darted to the window. The curtains printed with toy trains shifted with the sound of autumn's breeze dancing among the backyard oaks.

She rushed to the curtains, shoved them aside, and stared at the opened window. "Oh no," she gasped. "No, no, no!" Her desperate mind insisted Sean must have somehow crawled out the window in his sleep. As she looked up she spotted a precise square cut out of the pane. The resulting hole was just large enough for someone to reach through and unlatch the lock.

Debra White Smith

DEBRA WHITE SMITH is a seasoned Christian author, speaker, and media personality who has been regularly publishing books for a decade. She has written over fifty books with over one million books in print. Her titles include such life-changing books as *Romancing Your Husband, Romancing Your Wife, It's a Jungle at Home; Survival Strategies for Overwhelmed Moms*, the Sister Suspense fiction series, and the Jane Austen fiction series.

Along with Debra's being voted a fiction-reader favorite several times, her book *Romancing Your Husband* was a finalist in the 2003 Gold Medallion Awards. And her Austen series novel *First Impressions* was a finalist in the 2005 Retailers Choice Awards.

Debra has been a popular media guest across the nation, including Fox TV, The 700 Club, ABC Radio, USA Radio Network, and Moody Broadcasting. Her favorite hobbies include fishing, bargain-hunting, and swimming with her family. Debra also vows she would walk fifty miles for a scoop of German chocolate ice cream.

ALSO BY
DEBRA WHITE SMITH

TEXAS HEAT
The First in the
Lone Star Intrigue Series
ISBN 978-0-06-149316-4 (paperback)

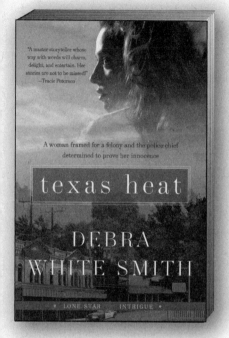

"A master storyteller whose way with words will charm, delights, and entertain. Her stories are not to be missed!"
—Tracie Peterson

A woman framed for a felony and the police chief determined to prove her innocence

texas heat

DEBRA WHITE SMITH

LONE STAR INTRIGUE

The last thing Jack Mansfield ever wanted was to arrest his former sweetheart—but he's the police chief of Bullard, Texas, and records indicate Charli has embezzled more than $100,000 from the bank where she works. Now she sits in a jail cell, accused of a crime she did not commit, with a little girl waiting on the outside. Jack's unrequited love for Charli drives him and his private-eye brother, Sonny, to prove her innocence and find the perpetrator. But Jack and Charli will never have their happy ending if she goes to prison . . . or is murdered by the person who framed her. Will they find the true culprit in time to save Charli's life and finally give their love a chance?

"Debra White Smith is a master storyteller whose way with words will charm, delight, and entertain. Her stories are not to be missed!"
—Tracie Peterson, Bestselling Author of the *Alaskan Quest* Series

"A suspense-filled tale of deceit, embezzlement and murder that will keep readers on the edge of their seats. . . . This series should prove to be a favorite among readers."
—*Times Record News* (Wichita Falls, Texas)